W9-AXK-933
3 3144 00414 5618

ALSO BY FRANK HUYLER

The Blood of Strangers

THE LAWS OF INVISIBLE THINGS

THE LAWS OF INVISIBLE THINGS

FRANK HUYLER

HENRY HOLT AND COMPANY • NEW YORK

HUYLER

Henry Holt and Company, LLC
Publishers since 1866
115 West 18th Street
New York, New York 10011

Henry Holt® is a registered trademark of
Henry Holt and Company, LLC.

Distributed in Canada by H. B. Fenn and Company Ltd.

Library of Congress Cataloging-in-Publication Data

Huyler, Frank, [date]
The laws of invisible things / Frank Huyler.—1st ed.
p. cm.
ISBN 0-8050-7330-2
1. Physician and patient—Fiction. 2. Physicians—Fiction. 3. Diseases—Fiction.
I. Title.

PS3608.U98L39 2004
813'.6—dc21 2003051116

Henry Holt books are available for special promotions and premiums. For details contact: Director, Special Markets.

First Edition 2004

Designed by Kelly S. Too

Printed in the United States of America

1 3 5 7 9 10 8 6 4 2

For Helena

He that hath an ear, let him hear what the Spirit
saith unto the churches; To him that overcometh will I give to eat
of the hidden manna, and will give him a white stone, and in the stone a new name
written, which no man knoweth saving he that receiveth it.

THE REVELATION OF ST. JOHN THE DIVINE

THE LAWS OF INVISIBLE THINGS

He was of medium height. His shoulders had a faint but noticeable roundness to them. His belly was flat still, but wrinkles were beginning around his eyes, and his black hair held its first sparkle of gray. For the first time, in the mirror, he could see age in his face. He was thirty-five years old.

For the most part he dressed carefully: crisp blue shirts, red ties, oak-colored shoes for the office. Nonetheless, he knew he was an average-looking man, lost in the crowd, with nothing about him—not his face, not the faint ungainliness of his gestures, nor the mildness of his voice—to give him away. He might have been anyone, passing through the middle ground, going anywhere.

It was Thursday, and the streets seemed pristine and lovely in the early morning, the neighborhoods full of stillness. As he drove to work, the leaves of the trees stood out with startling clarity, and looking at the grains of the light gray asphalt, and the blades of the clipped grass, he felt as if he had put on a new pair of glasses. He had experienced this sensation before. In the past it had been linked with events in his life: the exhilaration he had felt the day after he'd won a science prize in high school, or when he'd first slept with a woman—really a girl—his freshman year in college. The world had seemed transformed, and he had felt at the edge of something. But as he'd grown older, moments like this distanced themselves from the events of his life. It was another day, the middle of another week. His hair, wet from the shower, darkened the collar of his suede jacket, and the bones of his chest felt somehow dry and brittle as he sat in the warmth of his car and headed down the street.

His office was in a two-story brownstone on a tree-lined street not far from downtown. He parked, got out, and crossed the street toward a green door recessed in the brick with a new plaque: MICHAEL GRANT, MD. INTERNAL MEDICINE AND INFECTIOUS DISEASE. Already his name on the yellow brass seemed like a permanent fact.

It was cool outside, just cold enough that the sound of grit—shoes on gravel, keys inserted into locks—carried in the air. He could tell from the parking lot behind the building that his morning would be a full one. In the past he had known whom to expect, he had checked his appointment book, but recently he had stopped doing this. The pile of charts would be waiting as usual on his desk, the pot of coffee would be brewing when he entered, and Susan, their nurse and receptionist—a plain heavy woman in her fifties, who wore her kindness for everyone to see—would look up and smile and say good morning in exactly the same way she had greeted him ever since he joined them fresh out of training. He'd been here only seven months, but when the year was up he had every expectation that Ronald Gass, the owner of the practice, would honor his promise of partnership. And so this would be his life, here in this North Carolina city, with these two hundred thousand strangers.

But this morning, three weeks after he had seen the child, he had absolutely no interest in talking to or consoling or interacting in any way with any of the two dozen or so patients he would see over the next ten hours. He sat at his desk and they came in and sat down also, one after another. They spoke, they wanted things. He drank his coffee and felt the silence of the office settle inside him, even as he listened and replied and looked into their eyes, aware that he might not recognize them if he met them on the street. He should be through it, he should recognize it for what it was—but the child was there all the same, and he struggled to turn his attention yet again to the man before him.

"How have you been doing?"

"Pretty well."

"I've got good news for you. The viral titers are undetectable, just as we hoped."

And without warning the last patient of the morning, whose chart sat open before him, started to cry. He didn't cry with silence or restraint, which is how, Michael thought, tears should be shed; rather, his face turned red and folded up, and he started to sob in the close confines of the office. He sobbed, and he thanked Dr. Grant.

Michael sighed. This happened perhaps once a month, and almost always for good news. Nonetheless, there was something in the man's tone, in the intensity of his tears and his thanks, that caused Michael to shift in his chair. This man wanted to live so deeply—or at least at this moment he did—and the promise of life flooded through him like something large and boundless and merciful. Who knew what the evening would hold, what hollow full of cigarettes and wine and teary drunken talk, but for now the man knew what he wanted, and it was life; it was the recession of the dark; it was to weep with joy.

"We'll leave you at the same dose for now, Mr. Winslow," he said. "We'll check the titers again in three months."

Lunchtime. There was a park a short distance from his office, and he sat in the sun with his tie loose and the coolness of air enveloping him. The awnings in the doorways of the brownstones overlooking the park fluttered and settled. There was a black center fountain, some iron benches, a few people feeding the birds. He could imagine spending a lot of time like this. Someone might come up and talk to him, he might strike up a conversation with the old man who walked here every day, but this, while not impossible, was unlikely. The problem, it occurred to him, was that we think of life in circular terms but instead we get an uneven line, and this park bench is just one point on the line, one point only, and nothing ever circles back and becomes whole as we know it should.

The facades on the brownstones were inscribed with gray stone flowers below the windows, stone flowers that somehow struck him as ironic as he sat on his bench. Then he looked at his watch and got up to go.

He had not eaten breakfast. But he didn't feel his hunger; he noticed it. It was there with him, and he felt its cleansing power, the way it made his mind go clear and still.

Which explained the sandwich waiting on his desk when he returned, with a note from Susan, the receptionist, saying simply, *Eat this now*. He chewed methodically, looking at the empty chair that faced him and would soon be full again. He used this room for follow-ups and histories, to speak with his patients. The examination room was down the hall. For the most part he found that his patients were more likely to talk when they knew they would not be touched.

And talk they did, as he nodded and made marks with his pen. At first, those who think they are dying are nearly silent. Their questions are the kind that require internal momentum to ask, questions like "How much longer do I have?" and "What should I tell my friend?" But then, as weeks and months and years pass, and new drugs emerge, and there is hope, they begin to try to talk their way out. They are full of talk, full of everyday details, all laughter and greeting.

"You have a message, Michael," Susan said, peering in his door. "I'm leaving early today, but it's on my desk. It sounded urgent."

He did not thank her for the sandwich at first, and this small discourtesy hung for an instant between them. But then he remembered, and said what he needed to say, satisfied that another day had passed undamaged through his hands. And so it would have done, had he not gone to her desk for the note pad that lay next to the telephone.

The cemetery just outside of town did not allow headstones. Only markers were permitted, flat on the ground. From a distance, the cemetery looked like a field of mown grass, with bouquets of flowers. Usually, there was an awning somewhere on the wide expanse, covering an open grave. The city was growing, more people moved in each year, and there were services here nearly every day of the week. A quiet black fence with gold trim surrounded the open acres, and at one end of the field, at the edge of the pine woods, stood a small brick chapel already. Several of the graves in the cemetery belonged to former patients. Somewhere, John and Christopher lay together—this he remembered—and somewhere else Roger lay alone.

He stretched, glanced at his watch, and wandered back to his place under the tree. It was shortly before six in the evening. He was trembling.

He stared at the earth at his feet and the black, coiled roots of the pine. He had planned his first words carefully but he had no idea what would follow, how difficult it might become. He tried to let his mind empty out onto the grass. He'd brought flowers and held them carefully, so as not to wrinkle the paper they were wrapped in. A tracery of fine ants, as small as the tips of pins, flowed from a hole by the root, and he watched them. The grave was a few feet away.

They were precisely on time. She walked without grace across the grass, a wide black woman in her middle twenties, wearing a red dress and a blue ribbon in her hair, as if she were going to church. He assumed she was the child's mother.

The dress and the ribbon reminded him of the mobile that had hung above the crib in the ward—red and blue, bright in the light from the window. It had spun, slowly, as the child slept on, tucked beneath the sheet. The darkness of her face, her small hands near her mouth, her braided hair, with white and blue beads at the end of each strand, the labor of hours, the sound of her breath, steady, as soft as cotton—all this came back to him again. They were nearly upon him.

The Reverend Thomas Williams was a black man who looked to be in his early sixties. He was tall, large-framed, with thick shoulders and the beginnings of a belly, and his skin was a light, flecked brown, like a trout. His eyes were many shades darker, calm and steady, below a finely wrinkled forehead. Were it not for the many coils of gray in his hair it would be hard to guess his age. He wore a red tie, which matched the woman's dress, and a dark suit with a tiny white rose pinned to the lapel. He was the child's grandfather, and they had met only once, six hours before the child had died, when Michael had reassured him.

Michael took a breath, stood up, and came out of the shade to meet them. The woman breathed loudly, and the Reverend's face was damp from the sun that fell heavily on the field.

"Thank you for coming, doctor," Reverend Williams said, as they approached.

"Let me say," Michael said, on cue, shaking the extended hand, "how sorry I am for your loss."

"So you were my girl's doctor," the woman said, looking at him.

"One of them," he answered. "I'm sorry."

She made no reply.

For a moment it occurred to him this was revenge, that she was going to shout and cry and accuse him. That he would have to stand and receive.

"I hope you understand," he said carefully, "how shocked all of us were by this."

She looked at him with flat black eyes, in silence.

"I brought you this," he said, and held out the bouquet of flowers. After a moment she nodded and took them from him.

"I asked you to come," the Reverend said, quietly, "to say a prayer with us. That's all."

Michael felt deeply unsettled. With an effort, he nodded.

The Reverend stepped forward to the grave, gesturing for Michael to join him. Michael did so, and then, without warning, the Reverend reached out and took Michael's hand in his. The man's palm was warm and firm, intimate. Michael resisted the urge to break free with an act of will. He felt somehow reduced; he held his breath like a small boy and stood over the grave. The Reverend, he realized, had done the same to the child's mother.

"Let us pray," Reverend Williams said, bowing his head, quiet for a moment before continuing. What followed came easily, as if it had been rehearsed. He spoke in a strong, clear voice, head down, eyes closed.

"This poor widow hath cast more in than all they which have cast into the treasury, for they did cast in of their abundance, but she of her want did cast in all that she had, even all her living.

"But God is our refuge and strength, our help in trouble; therefore we will not fear, though the earth be removed, and though the mountains be carried into the midst of the sea, though the waters roar and be troubled, though the mountains shake with the swelling, there is a river whose streams shall make glad the city of God, the holy place of the tabernacles of the most High. God is in the midst of her; she shall not be moved, and God shall help her."

"Amen," the woman said. She was crying as she hiked her dress and bent her fat legs to the grass, then touched the stone with her finger, gently, as someone might brush a strand of hair from a forehead. She placed the flowers beside the grave, cried for a while longer, then rose and wiped her face with her sleeve.

"I won't bother you, Dr. Grant," she said, standing with them again. "I'm leaving it in God's hands."

She looked at the Reverend, who put his hand tenderly on her shoulder as he spoke.

"Why don't you go on ahead."

She nodded and leaned against him briefly before leaving them, trudging across the field at the steady, determined pace of one who might walk for miles.

"She's leaving town," Reverend Williams said. "She's going back to be with her family."

"I thought she was your daughter."

The Reverend shook his head. "No," he said. "My son was the father."

"I'm sorry," Michael said again.

"Doctor," the Reverend continued, "I want to ask you something."

"Yes?"

"If you had given my granddaughter antibiotics that morning instead of waiting, would she still be alive?"

It was the question Michael had feared most. He felt as if he had heard a cough downstairs and knew the house to be empty.

"I don't know," he replied, carefully. "It was an overwhelming infection, and it was probably too late even then. But it's possible."

Reverend Williams was silent.

"I want you to understand," Michael continued, "that we did everything by the book. Antibiotics are not recommended until you know there is a bacterial infection. Giving antibiotics too often is why there is so much antibiotic resistance. Cases like this are very rare."

"Well," Reverend Williams said finally. "You're an honest man, Dr. Grant. It was the answer I was hoping to hear."

"What do you mean?"

"I made some inquiries. I know that what you said is true in such cases. But had you not come here today, or had you lied to me just now, I don't know what I would have done."

Michael was silent. They were walking now, back toward the cars.

"The terrors of this world," the Reverend said, "answer to no one."

Michael felt as if he had to be very calm. "Thank you," he said, wondering if he should have spoken at all.

"But I may need to reach you again," Reverend Williams said. "Do you have a card?"

"Of course," Michael replied quickly. "I'll give you my home number. Please call any time. Let me know if there's anything I can do."

"Thank you, doctor," the Reverend said, studying him carefully. "Let me give you my card as well."

Dr. Ronald Gass was tall and stooped, with large pale ears and a thin salt-and-pepper mustache. He was balding and quiet, a private man, distinguished primarily by a sense of studied and distant intelligence that seemed to drift out of him. For the moment, until the details of their partnership were ironed out, Michael was Ronald Gass's employee.

A few months before, just after Michael had joined the practice, Dr. Gass's wife of some forty years had finally died. Her death, from colon cancer, had been a painful one. Dr. Gass had nursed her at home. He came to the office, saw patients all day, then went home and took care of his dying wife, feeding her soup, carrying her to the bathroom to urinate, changing the gauze dressing on her weeping red abdomen as the tumor followed the surgical scar out through the muscle and into the light of day.

Even at the end, Gass had revealed nothing. He did not lose weight. He did not look drawn. He still came to work with the same brown paper bag of lunch his wife had always prepared for him, and he had welcomed Michael into the practice with what seemed, at first, like quiet and collegial respect.

In the months of their cordial, well-mannered professional association, they had never yet had dinner together. The explanation had been unspoken but clear enough—Gass's wife, his private suffering. But now, as if to make amends, Dr. Gass was inviting him into his home.

"Thank you, Ronald," Michael said, because he knew he had to. "I'd like that."

He was sitting at his desk. Dr. Gass's head and most of his long neck protruded through the doorway of the office.

"I know it's short notice," Dr. Gass said, "but if you don't have plans. About seven?"

"Is there anything I can bring?"

"No, no. Nothing to bring. Come around seven. I'll see you then."

Michael sat back, and struggled to return his attention to the journal article he was reading. It was a review of the latest treatments of elephantiasis, which Michael had never once in all his training been confronted with.

There was the obligatory photograph: a young woman, sitting in the shade, wearing a sari, her leg monstrous and irregular, swollen nearly to the size of her body. She had unwrapped it for the camera. Such photographs invariably appeared in articles on the disease. It seemed to him to have been chosen with zest, that subtle and particular enthusiasm for suffering that characterizes the medical literature. To look coldly in the face of all that nature gives us. To not turn aside.

The parasite enters the lymphatics and occludes them. Deformity occurs late in the course of the disease. The limbs swell to the point of immobility.

In the past, such articles had been a source of fascination for him, an invisible world, intricate and mysterious: the life cycles of alien things, some of which were not even formally alive at all. Viruses, dead strings of genes, or spores that might sleep for millennia in unearthed tombs. The way they offered themselves, in brief glimpses. The way they rose and sometimes fell away, after only a cluster of cases, and at other times swept across whole populations like the light of the sun.

The parasite is mosquito-borne. *Wuchereria bancrofti*, named for its discoverer. It shows a nocturnal periodicity, swimming into the cutaneous blood vessels at night, then migrating back to the internal organs, especially the lungs, during the day. Years pass, the limbs begin to swell. The owners of the limbs live on.

RONALD GASS LIVED IN THE SUBURBS, AND HIS DIRECTIONS WERE CLEAR and precise. His house, to Michael's eye, was exactly the same as the two houses directly across the leafy street and similar to the rest. Two stories, white clapboard. A yard with an apple tree.

It was the kind of neighborhood that people both aspired to and settled for. Large houses, with half-acre lots, but not mansions. Tall trees, sunlight pouring through the greenery and falling in different shades of yellow on the street. It was, in fact, exactly the kind of neighborhood he expected. A quiet place, mostly too expensive for couples with small children. Children, he thought, tended to visit places like this rather than live in them.

Standing in front of the door with a bottle of wine under his arm, he wondered why Gass was still in this house, which was clearly too big for one person. He wondered what Gass did during the empty hours.

He rang the bell. Gass opened the door immediately, as if he had been waiting on the other side with his hand on the knob.

"Michael," he said. "It's good of you to come. Can I take your coat?"

The man seemed slightly ill at ease, and in that moment Michael wondered how he would possibly get through the next several hours. He handed Gass his windbreaker and the wine and thanked him.

The house was full of Gass's dead wife. The hall closet still held her clothes; Michael clearly saw a woman's coat as Gass opened the door and carefully placed the windbreaker on a hanger. A large photograph hung in the hallway—Gass and a woman with prematurely white hair. Though they stood next to each other and she grasped his arm, there was somehow a sense of space between them. Gass noticed his look.

"Clara died six months ago," he said.

"Yes, I know. I'm sorry, Ronald. It must be difficult."

The service, Michael recalled, had been private. In any case, he had never met the woman.

"It is the way of the world," Gass said. "Can I get you a drink?"

"Absolutely," Michael said. "Whatever you've got."

"I have some whiskey."

"That would be great."

They were in the living room now. Overstuffed chairs, a couch. A good Persian carpet. A few prints on the walls, well framed. A room like a thousand others. Prosperous, groomed. Gray and blue. It was so anonymous as to be liberating. Through the windows, the lawn opened. A squirrel paused by a feeder, its jaws working. Dr. Gass came back with two glasses of whiskey in his hand.

"Nice place you've got here," Michael said, as Gass handed him the glass of whiskey.

"Thank you," he said.

Michael did not know what to say next. He took a sip of whiskey.

"It was Clara's," Gass continued impassively. "There is little left for me here now that she's gone."

Michael stood still and held the cold glass of liquor. "You do have your work," he managed. "That's important."

Gass considered this for a moment. "Yes," he said. "We both have our work, don't we?"

Michael felt stiff, uneasy. The conventions of small talk suddenly seemed to have been suspended.

"I'm sorry about your wife."

"And I am sorry about the unpleasantness with the child."

They looked at each other. Gass appeared calm.

"It's not the same," Grant said.

"No. I'm sorry I didn't have you over sooner. But with Clara. . . ."

"I understand completely. There's no need to explain."

Gass nodded. "Just remember, Michael, that culpability is not as important as people think."

"It's not?"

"In the end," Gass said, "it matters very little."

"Why is that?"

"The result is the same. Clara might have been murdered, or killed by a drunken driver, but she wasn't. Instead, she just ignored blood in her stool for a year."

Gass appeared utterly unmoved, as if he were talking about anything in the world, anything at all. They were still standing.

"Do you mean it was her fault?"

Gass considered. "No," he said. "I didn't want you to think that I was judging you, that's all. All of us make mistakes from time to time. Some of them are costly."

Michael nodded, but the point, if there was one, was lost to him.

"It's been difficult," he said quietly. Gass nodded. "Sometimes it's important to talk about these things." Gass gestured to the sofa. "Why don't you tell me more about what happened. Would you like some more whiskey?"

"No, thanks."

Gass smiled and sat down in the chair immediately below the white muslin drapes by the window.

Michael looked down at his drink. It was useful to have props, he thought: to have something to do with his mouth and his hands.

"The child looked fine," he said, as he sat down on the couch. "I went to see her before I came to the office. The family had asked the pediatrician for a second opinion. She'd been sick for several weeks, and the pediatrician finally hospitalized her. She had a fever and was dehydrated, but that was it."

"Did you examine her?"

"I looked at her, but no, I didn't. Not carefully. She'd just gone to sleep and the nurse didn't want me to wake her up."

Gass shook his head slightly.

"They can lead you astray," he said. "You have to watch them."

"I know. I should have done a good exam. But I don't think it would have changed anything. Her vitals were fine. She was taking her bottle. So I held off on the antibiotics."

Gass nodded. "Antibiotics would probably not have made a difference. You know that, Michael."

"Her blood work the evening before was normal. Her urine was clean. Her chest X ray was negative."

"What about that morning?"

Michael hesitated. For an instant he almost didn't tell him, but then it was out, too late to be taken back.

"That's the problem," he said. "The morning labs were drawn late, and I didn't see them."

"How did that happen?"

"She'd been awake all night and finally went to sleep. The nurse asked the lab tech to come back later. They hadn't drawn her blood when I saw her."

"So you never saw the results?"

"Not until after she was dead. The lab never called me or anyone else. They just stuck the results in the chart and forgot about them."

Gass sighed. "And you forgot to go back and check them."

Michael tightened his grip on his glass. "Yes," he said. "I forgot to check."

Gass was silent for a moment. "How abnormal were they?" he asked finally.

"She had a white count of one point two. The differential was ninety percent bands."

"Sepsis."

"Yes. Overwhelming sepsis. She was dead by the afternoon." He shook his head.

Michael realized, and it astonished him to realize, that his eyes were full of tears, that his hands were trembling. He felt ashamed. Ronald Gass had struggled in silence, betraying nothing to the outside world. It was clear now that Michael wore every thought on his face.

"What did the autopsy show?" Gass asked.

"The mother wouldn't let them do one. She was distraught."

Gass nodded. "I suppose that is understandable," he said.

Michael did not reply. He took a swallow of whiskey and looked down at his feet. But Gass continued.

"Does the family know you never saw the blood work from that morning?"

Michael shook his head. "I don't think so."

"Then hope they don't find out. You didn't tell them, did you?"

"No. I didn't tell them."

"Good. Then there's a chance it will blow over. In the meantime, my advice to you is to be as nice as possible to them. Tell them how sorry you are. Explain what happened. But don't appear as if you have something to hide."

Michael nodded.

"They're less likely to sue you if you pay attention to them. Remember that. This could be a large judgment."

"I know," Michael said. "I've met with them."

"Good," Gass said.

They were silent for a moment. Gass sipped his drink.

"Have you ever been sued, Ronald?"

"Never. I've been fortunate."

Michael had somehow expected that answer.

"But I've made mistakes, Michael. All of us have. It is important to put them behind you, particularly when you're just starting out."

"I wouldn't want this to reflect badly on the practice," Michael said carefully.

Gass did not respond directly. "Enough talk about business," he said, rising from his chair. "Dinner is almost ready. Let me introduce you to Nora. We'll discuss this another time."

"Nora?"

"My daughter. She's in the kitchen."

The house was quiet, but periodically the dim sound of flowing air rose out of the background. Through the window, the smooth black trunk of the apple tree rose above the street, its branches hanging over the lawn.

Michael stood and allowed himself to be led through the hall to the dining room.

The large table was set for three: white napkins, a blue tablecloth, a bowl of apples as the centerpiece. There was a small salad of red cabbage next to each place.

A woman stood next to the table, arranging flowers in a vase. She looked up.

"Nora," Gass said formally, "this is my colleague, Michael Grant."

Nora Gass looked to be in her mid-thirties. She was dressed casually, in jeans, a red cotton blouse, and a gray wool cardigan. Dark hair nearly to her shoulders, a few clear streaks of gray. A fine-boned and angular face. She wore a pendant, a small deep blue stone. His immediate impression was that of restraint and elegance and, if not beauty, then something near it.

"It's nice to meet you," he said automatically.

She smiled and walked around the end of the table. "I'm Nora," she said, and extended her hand.

"Michael," he replied, trying to smile back. Her handshake was firm and quick, though not unfriendly.

"I hope you're hungry," she said.

"I am," he replied. "And this looks great."

Just then Gass's beeper sounded on his hip. Gass sighed. "Excuse me for a moment," he said, and left the room.

Michael stood stiffly. "You're joining us for dinner?" he asked, finally.

"I was planning to," she said. "I hope that's OK."

"Of course." He felt himself flushing.

"We don't have company often," she said. "Usually it's just the two of us."

"Do you live here? Or are you visiting?"

"I came back a few weeks ago to help pack up my mother's things. I'm not sure how long I'll stay."

He nodded and took a sip of his drink. "I didn't know that."

She smiled. "He can be pretty close-mouthed," she replied. "But I think it's been good for both of us. Did he tell you I'm going to help out at the office?"

"No, he didn't."

"Just a couple of days a week. Some of the bookkeeping needs attention."

He had the sudden image of Susan, with a perplexed look on her face, holding a pencil to her pursed lips and peering down at the pile of papers on her desk.

"I guess Susan's not much of a record keeper," he said. "But I know she tries."

"I love Susan," Nora said. "I've known her for years. She suggested it. It'll give me something to do."

"Oh," he said. "Is that what you were doing before?"

"Sort of. I owned a small business."

"What kind of business?"

"A bookstore."

"You must like to read," he said.

She almost laughed. "Yes," she said. "I do."

She seemed very composed as she stood there, calm, faintly amused, studying him. He felt foolish and uneasy.

"Do you like working with my father?" she asked suddenly.

"So far it's been a good arrangement," he said. "For us both, I hope."

"He works hard," she said. "He needs someone who will be able to take over for him someday."

"Well," he said, "that's the idea, but who knows what will happen."

She smiled, and there was a brief silence.

"I'm sorry about your mother," he said. "My father died a few years ago and I know what it's like."

"I think it's different for different people," she replied. "But thank you."

She looked as if she were going to continue, but just then Gass's voice rose out of the kitchen.

"He is to have no more refills. If he ran out, there is nothing I can do. Tell him that. And tell him to keep his appointment."

Nora listened intently. A few moments passed, and then Gass returned, shaking his head.

"I'm sorry," he said. "Telling the pharmacy not to page me after hours is like talking to a stone."

"What was it?" Nora asked.

Gass looked at her. "A patient," he said, "tried to refill a prescription for narcotics when there were no refills to be had."

"Narcotics? For pain?"

"More likely for pleasure."

"Why is he in pain?"

"He has AIDS," Gass said, looking hard at her. "He has a neuropathy that causes pain in his feet. But he is also a drug addict, and that is why he has AIDS. He is trying to use me as his personal supplier."

There was an awkward silence. The three of them stood there.

"What difference does it make?" Nora said. "He's dying. Does it matter?"

"It matters."

She shrugged, then looked at Michael. "Never mind," she said.

"Ronald," Michael said quickly, into the brief tension that followed, "Nora tells me she's going to be working in the office a few days a week."

Gass nodded. "Didn't I mention it to you?"

Michael shook his head.

"Oh," Gass said. "I'm sorry, I thought I did. Susan has many talents, but bookkeeping isn't one of them. We need someone. Nora offered to help in the meantime."

"It will be a new experience," she said, smiling. "A business that actually makes money."

Gass smiled also and slapped Michael lightly and awkwardly on the shoulder.

"Come on," he said. "Let's have dinner."

Jonas Williams was the fifth passenger on the bus. He wore an army coat and a baseball hat and he moved with care, lifting his canvas bag up into the bin over the seats before sitting down by the window. He was in his late twenties, with light brown skin and hazel eyes and a quiet, milky face. His eyes were unusually bright. He did not shift in his seat but sat calmly, his head slightly angled toward the window and the view of the bus station. The interior of the bus smelled strongly of diesel exhaust and faintly of industrial cleaner.

The bus was mostly empty; each passenger had their own row of contoured brown vinyl seats. The driver swung up from the street—a heavy white man going bald, with a circle of gray hair ringing the pink flesh of his scalp—turned to look down the aisle with a quick dispassionate glance, then pressed the button that closed the door, and started the engine.

If Jonas Williams noticed any of this he gave no sign. His eyes were closed now, his head back against the headrest, his lips slightly parted, a glint of gold in his mouth, a tiny sparkle of saliva. The bus pulled out onto the street, and the town flowed slowly past the windows, giving way to the open country of the highway. The distance was all blue sky, and farmhouses, and tobacco barns on the edges of green fields.

The bus settled into its rhythm, the driver in sunglasses holding the large flat wheel like a plate in his lap, sitting up high, looking in mirrors, glancing left and then right, the bus all the while solid and straight.

Jonas sat in the half sleep of long journeys, nearly awake, nearly aware, but a deep part of him gone somewhere else. The effort of resistance was beyond him. His left eye showed him a shower of sparks whenever he looked into a light, and he was full of lassitude, of absence, and the need for quiet.

He did not intend to get off the bus. He intended to continue without speaking to anyone. He was a blank man on a bus; he was passing through; the fields were opening for miles on either side; and, looking out the window, there seemed more than enough time, and more than enough distance, to get lost. Light fell through the corn rows, his left eye flashed like a metronome, the face of the driver was all over the mirrors, and he sat as still and empty as glass.

The telephone rang later that evening. Michael was in the kitchen, washing a few dishes. He rarely received personal calls, and his first thought was of his mother: another fall, perhaps, in the nursing home. But it was Reverend Williams.

"I'm sorry to call so late," the Reverend said. "I hope I'm not inconveniencing you."

"Not at all," Michael replied, as his heart began to pound. He held the telephone tightly.

"I have a favor to ask, Dr. Grant."

"Of course. Whatever I can do."

"I would like you to evaluate my son. As a patient. He's back in town."

"Your son?"

"He's not well. He wants to see a doctor."

"What's wrong with him?"

"I don't know. But he's not himself. He can tell you."

Michael was silent for a long moment. "Of course," he said. "Have him call my office. I'll fit him in."

"Thank you," the Reverend said.

Michael hung up the phone and wandered out of the kitchen into the living room. He suspects nothing, Michael thought, so I have to go along. But the whole of it seemed unreal, strange and troubling, and as he sat down on the couch he wondered if he should confide in Gass again.

The living room was brightly lit with polished oak floors and white plaster and moldings from the twenties. He had furnished the house alone, conscientiously, but without a great deal of care. A black leather chair by the television, plates and bowls, a few reproductions on the walls framed in glass. A scattering of photographs, two Persian rugs, a thick translucent coffee table ordered from a catalog. The house was small but it was clear and exact, and it had an order he thought suited him. It also had a past, which he'd found while refinishing the doorway, sanding down through the layers of paint. Lines, in pencil: the heights of a family. MARY, APRIL 1931. STEVEN, SEPTEMBER, 1930. A faint tracery. Children, then. A father and mother, long gone. The absence below the lines, flowing to the floor. Tender ghosts. Steven, he thought, and Mary, giggling, standing up straight to the ruler, wanting to be measured and to be tall. Others had been here before him.

The cleaning lady came once each week, and sometimes she left flowers in the vase on the kitchen countertop where he left her money.

The house was not so different from those of his childhood: each one alike, every two or three years, even as they grew slightly larger. The sound of jet aircraft overhead endlessly, both night and day—the vast flat spaces of the Dakotas, the Iowa cornfields, and then, finally, the more settled green of Germany, where he had gone to the American school. But the houses on all the bases were constant—streets of majors, streets of colonels—and thinking about them reminded him of his father, toward the end, on one of the last visits, the thread of oxygen shining on his face, upright all night in the chair—Where are you going, Mike, to the library?—or earlier, erect and clean, in his officer's uniform, his black brush-cut hair, drinking his coffee in silence in the kitchen.

But it didn't matter now, not even a little, and in any case these events, even Ann, had been nothing to speak of on any larger scale. They were the kind of thing nearly everyone undergoes at some point in their lives, but they had emptied him nonetheless. His father. His marriage. The rigor of his studies. A grinding past, uninteresting—which, he supposed, explained him as well as anything else and had somehow led him here, to this house, the first he had ever owned. I might move away, he thought suddenly. There is nothing to keep me. It would take just a moment. A dozen telephone calls, a handful of checks, my signature. Nothing more.

On the surface it seemed as if the dinner had simply been an act of kindness on Gass's part, as if Gass had recognized him as a kindred spirit in some difficulty. But there was also something else about the meal—the settings, the difficult small talk, the tension between Gass and his daughter—that troubled and unsettled him. It wasn't just kindness; it was the *performance* of kindness. It had the elaborate feel of ritual—first, confessions; then repast; then Gass's hand on his shoulder as he stood in the doorway, putting on his coat.

"Thank you for coming, Michael. I'm sorry we didn't do this earlier."

He might have reassured me, he thought, but he didn't. He might have said it would be all right.

It was after ten, his usual bedtime, but he felt restless and once again far from sleep.

The child, these weeks in the ground—a seed cast into the earth, a little fist in a dry socket. How quiet she had been, sleeping in the crib on the ward as he stood above her, watching her easy breath, the nurse waiting impatiently in the doorway.

"She looks good," he'd said—he remembered the words exactly—and the nurse had nodded and thanked him for not waking her.

He stood up suddenly from the couch. He stretched, glanced at his watch. Then he went upstairs, changed into his running clothes, and came back down. He took a single key from the drawer to place in his pocket, turned off the lights, stepped out into the night air, and locked the door behind him.

He began to run easily through the deserted streets, through the pools of the streetlights and the close houses, some with lights, others cloaked in sleep. He felt the air brush against his body; he felt it on his throat and hands and between his thighs, as his breath grew heavy. He concentrated on the pace, on the asphalt; he felt his speed rising; and he felt his mind begin to recede into the insistence of his body. He was careful not to let himself rest. He ran fast enough to pin his thoughts still. He ran for five miles, knowing the distance exactly, and arrived back at his own door gasping and shaking.

He took a shower. He looked at himself for a long moment in the shaving mirror—black hair, brown eyes, the spidery beginnings of age again, the slightly yellow tint of his teeth from the coffee. He looked drawn and worn. But there were three days off now, a long weekend. He thought he might go away. He needed to get out of town.

Michael chose the seaside. It was only a few hours away, but it was the first time since his arrival that he'd gone anywhere at all. It was a relief to drive through the flat fields, slowing for tractors on the two-lane road, stopping for gas and sweet tea and the slow measured voices of the South. The South was new to him—as everywhere, more or less, was new to him.

The seaside was dark when he arrived. After checking into his room and leaving his suitcase on the wide bed, he opened the curtains on the doors that faced the Atlantic across thirty yards of beach. High tide, the moon a whisper of itself, the overcast sky sparse with stars.

His room came with a small patio. He shed his shoes, stepped out onto the concrete, and sat down on the iron chair by the iron table. Ocean air flooded the room. The sea was close, at the high-tide mark, and indistinct in the heavy darkness, like an animal breathing in the undergrowth. Only the flashing white line of surf was visible, and then the sheets of foam crackling up into the light cast from the windows of the hotel. He felt the edge of the water strongly, and the warm wind from the south in his face. He was glad to be alone.

Loneliness was something one grew accustomed to, he thought, and it passed like everything else. Even when it was sought, it passed.

He got up and went inside and closed the window and turned on the sleek black television that sat on the bureau and then lay down on the tight, wide bed with the remote in his hand. The ducts of central air-conditioning rumbled on and off. He heard nothing through the walls; the occupants of the adjacent rooms were either absent or, like him, silent. After a few minutes he turned off the television, opened the windows, and lay back again on the hard mattress. In the distance, he could hear the sound of a plane.

A memory—a childhood vacation with his family, when he'd tried to swim to a float just past the breakers off the beach. How old had he been, ten? Twelve?

It hadn't looked far, and yet, just when he was through the breakers, he'd found himself in a strong sideways current. No matter how he struggled, neither the float ahead nor the beach behind grew nearer. He remembered that moment so clearly, the sudden recognition that he might not reach either the float or the shore. He was alone in the water, and time had passed anyway. His hands and feet had kept waving, his mouth opening and closing, but he was somewhere else, and when finally the green, barnacle-covered wood of the float had risen up against him he had felt as if he were another person entirely—a person to whom wishes were granted. It was not fear, exactly; it was more like knowledge. All these years later, he could still feel the hot bleached planks beneath the palm of his right hand. He had waited for a long time, clinging to the the float, letting its rough underside scrape his belly and thighs, before he had the strength to pull himself up into the bright unsteady sun. Only then was he afraid—shaking, his legs trailing in the water.

His father had let him sit on the float for an hour before coming to get him. They'd watched each other, his father under the wide umbrella, smoking his endless cigarettes, reading, pausing every so often to glance at his watch. Teaching a lesson.

His father had been an air force navigator, and many times it had occurred to Michael that his father's entire working life had been spent both hoping something would happen and hoping it wouldn't. A disciplined patience, guiding heavy bombers across continents, point A to point B and back again. Bomber missions were long, sometimes lasting an entire day or night. He would often leave early in the morning, before sunrise, and come back late, and sometimes he had crossed half the world. Point A was officers' housing in the Midwest, their home, and point B might have been anywhere: Diego Garcia, the Aleutians, or somewhere picked at random over the ocean, where they would refuel in midair. The tedium must have been vast, high up, in sun and blue sky, hour after hour, cigarette after cigarette, as the earth, so lovely and frail, passed in silence below. Green jumpsuits, white helmets, wires for the microphone, the car starting in the driveway—doing it again and again, doing it in his sleep, until enough years passed for him to retire and take a job with an air freight company. The pay was better, and that—in addition to his father's military pension—had made them suddenly well-off, prosperous enough that Michael's schooling, though expensive, did not strain them. The air freight company, like the air force, moved them often, and most of the crews were ex-military, so apart from increased prosperity their lives had changed little. But the cargoes did change—suddenly it was fresh flowers and mail instead of nuclear bombs—and once, when Michael had asked his father if he felt any relief about this, by which he meant a lessening of burdens, his father had only shrugged and said it was pretty much the same when you were sitting up front.

Even now, or perhaps especially now, the sound of jet aircraft was the sound of something else, and it was difficult not to think of his father, a tight thin man, with his crew cut and sunglasses and his easy smile, heading out toward the edge of the world and talking about none of it.

His mother was something else entirely. She was gentle, with few formally voiced opinions, and rarely spoke ill of anyone. It was as if she had made a conscious decision, somewhere in her youth, to pursue the quiet path, and Michael realized only as an adult that this required a discipline of its own, a refusal to acknowledge anything but the best in others. It was also, Michael thought, a kind of maddening blindness, which comforted him even as it puzzled him. On the telephone with other wives, at barbecues, waiting—this made up the bulk of her days when Michael was a child. But it was she who insisted on taking him, each Sunday, to the Methodist churches on the bases, where the defense of freedom and the work of God were woven together again, and the chaplain led them all in pale affirming hymns. His father went rarely, and though he did not complain there was always a reticence in him, a hint of unasked questions. Michael's mother was not the kind of woman to wear her faith on her sleeve, but nonetheless Michael had always known it was not a formality for her; it was real and precious, and there were moments when he had seen her, on those tedious mornings, whispering along from memory. She would raise her head and smile, and even then Michael would wonder what it was that she could hear and he could not.

Often, on Sunday afternoons when Michael and his mother returned from church, his father would put down the paper and take him into the back yard. Depending on the season, they might throw a baseball or a football, but either way the quick elegance of his father's throw, and the ease of his catch, contrasted clearly with Michael's own clumsy efforts. Michael's father, though not a large man, had been quick and strong, a good athlete, and Michael had always sensed that his own ungainliness had been a source of disappointment. His father had smiled and shaken his head and called him his mother's son and ruffled his hair, and both were relieved when Michael grew old enough to spare his father of the responsibility. Nonetheless, Michael remembered it so clearly—the easy arc of the ball, back and forth, and his father's blue eyes and white teeth, and the distant contrails in the sky, until his mother called them in to dinner. She would say grace and smile at her husband and son as she filled their plates, and sometimes, if he felt like it, his father would ask about school. Michael had always been a good student, even at an early age, which generated great pride in his mother and dubious approval from his father. But they were familiar strangers, he and his father, in formal orbit around each other, and nothing, not even his father's illness, had quite managed to change the mystery of that fact.

THE NEXT MORNING THE SEA WAS SO BEAUTIFUL AND ALIVE IT ALMOST made him happy. It was early, the sun shone on the whitecaps and the gray-green grass on the surface of the dunes, and gulls hung like flags a few feet above the water. He ran down low, near the surf, where the sand was firm beneath his feet. Fisherman were out already, with lawn chairs and baseball caps, and he had to duck beneath their faint, translucent lines as he ran. He kept going down the beach, one mile, then two, then three, past the growing numbers of walkers. The sun grew brighter.

Around a bend, he saw a cluster of human figures at the water's edge. Even from a distance he could sense their urgency. Each had a fishing pole, and each cast again and again into the waters just past the breaking surf. They were shouting. From farther down the beach he could see other fishermen, carrying rods and coolers and folding chairs, converging at a low trot.

For a hundred yards, the surface of the water shook and glittered like broken glass. Thousands of fish were feeding on the surface, and the fishermen around him cast again and again, reeling in full hooks, their rods bent double.

"What are they?" he asked, and a woman answered.

"The blues are running," she said. "Bluefish. You don't even need bait."

It was true. Many of the fishermen cast empty hooks and caught fins, eyes, tails, tearing them off into the coolers before casting again. Something like this happened, Michael learned later, only once or twice a year.

It went on for five minutes, then ten, then twenty, until finally the frenzy began to lessen and the surface of the water settled once again to its former color. The school was leaving, turning back for the open sea. In a few moments there was nothing left at all, just empty water, folding and unfolding on the flat body of the sand, and the fishermen gathering the remnants from the beach like so many blue and trembling leaves.

Ronald Gass sipped his tea and watched his empty garden through the back windows of his house. He was not a superstitious man, but it was easy for him to imagine his wife there, on her knees, working the trowel in and out. It was the last thing she had given up. A rabbit sat feeding by the fence, growing still every so often, and he watched it.

Clara had gone gray early in life and thus for many years had looked much older than she was. She had had light blue eyes and pale wrinkled skin and a prominent Adam's apple for a woman. Her garden had grown over the years, and the rabbits had always played havoc with it. The new shoots were rooted out and eaten, and even the flowers at times seemed wilted and uneven from their efforts.

When she was well, Clara had never minded the rabbits, even on those summer mornings when all the radishes were clipped right out of the earth and a month of weeding went for nothing.

But after her diagnosis, she had changed her mind. Each evening she would fill Havahart traps with diced carrots and celery and set them out in the grass. At first, as the rabbits began to appear, motionless in the cages, he had helped her drive a few miles and release them. She had watched them bound off through the meadow in silence.

But as her disease progressed, and he saw the weakness gathering her in its arms, the trips to the meadow were too much.

He had once come home unexpectedly, in midmorning, from the office. She had been out back, and he'd watched through the windows as she took the steel cage and placed it down at the rear of her car, and started the engine, and let the gray exhaust wash through the bars where the rabbit trembled and gasped. Afterward, she'd pitched the small body deep into the compost and covered it carefully.

He had said nothing. She had seemed tranquil to everyone, with her bright receding eyes and the magical aura that always attends the dying. But he knew better.

The day she died, after her cremation, Gass had taken her ashes directly from the funeral home to the cemetery. The cremation itself had lasted most of the afternoon. Despite his years practicing medicine, and the many deaths he had witnessed over this time, he had never learned that cremations take hours. He had always imagined a white-hot all-consuming fire, where coffin and hair and cloth went up together in a few short minutes. But Clara had taught him that cremations are a slow reduction to powder. The heat is given time to work. The result is a bag that weighs perhaps ten pounds, a fine gray silt: all, he'd thought, that we irreducibly are.

He had taken her in the back of a cab, because he did not want to drive, in an elegant green cardboard box with the gold emblem of the funeral home on the lid. She was warm still, and as he sat there in the back he had felt her gradually cool on his thighs. It felt so intimate, so strange. He knew immediately that he would never forget this sensation, that for the rest of his life he would remember her cooling on his thighs in the back of a yellow cab as they drove to the cemetery and were finally done. He had poured her into a pine box and put her in the grave, and then the cab had taken him home.

Once again Gass felt the absence of his own life, or the distance of it, and just then, as he sipped his drink and looked out at the garden, thinking of Clara, he felt himself beginning to smile, for no reason on earth that he could think of. So he smiled, for a few short seconds, until his features composed themselves once more, and he was stern again, a stern thin man, looking out the window at the green shadows cast by the maple trees in the back yard.

The most time-consuming and serious of the Reverend Thomas Williams's many tasks was the preparation of his weekly sermon. He began work on Monday night and by Thursday or Friday usually had a serviceable draft, and then he would go down into the basement of the church and refine it. He went down to the basement to find the sermon's center, the place where he became a vessel and the sermon began to speak on its own.

And though he never knew exactly how close to the final version he was, even on Sunday mornings, the basement sessions helped clarify him and eased his restlessness and sometimes gave him the gift of themselves, when he felt like an arrow, a rigid finger, or an iron bar, pointing in one exact direction, and the ache of such moments made all his effort worthwhile. Other times he was uncertain, and he had promised himself many years ago that he would privately acknowledge this uncertainty, though he had also learned that his flock was frequently incapable of such distinctions. Thus his sermons had an inner life as well, and were not made simply to be heard.

The basement was carpeted and quiet. There was a lectern in the center of the room. The walls on all four sides were lined with full-length mirrors—for years, the room had also been used as a dance studio. When Reverend Williams first went down into the basement he had found the mirrors distracting, and he had considered a place of dancing questionably housed in his church; but time had passed, and the sleekness of the young women in their leotards had grown less striking in his eyes. In any case, he felt his use of the room—the holy use—more than outweighed whatever sins were in the hearts of the dancers, and in his lighter moments he had come to wonder if the true sin were not in the minds of those who would question innocence rather than assume it. By this he meant himself.

Reverend Williams had a clear code of conduct in the basement. First he would take off his suit jacket and hang it on one of the many hooks by the door. He would ensure that the door was firmly closed, so that no sounds could carry up the stairs into the empty church hall. Then he would turn down the lights, not to darkness but to a kind of twilight, so that the mirrors gave him the illusion of space and distance. Finally, he would lay out the manuscript before him on the lectern and turn on the small reading light.

As he stood there in the center of the room, he willed himself to be still and let the silence and the distance of gray light fill him. He looked down at the well-lit pages and began, his eyes on the center, becoming nothing but a wick, as he thought of it, nothing but the filament in a bulb, his voice moving out into the flat glass like wind into a field, and let us bow down, and let us feel the responsibility upon us, which begins with the Word, and ends with the Word, and let it relieve us of our debts, let it flourish in the crowd of eyes and in the chorus of tongues, and let it ask this of us: Do we forgive or do we exact repentance? Do we exact repentance? The iron bar exacts, the lash exacts, the work of lawyers and moneylenders exacts, and do we then exact, though we are righteous, though we are merciful and strong, that which the Lord asks of us?

He was shaking. The room was quiet, and he knew—though he had not finished, in fact had hardly even begun—that the sermon was complete enough and he would do well to leave it alone for the days that remained. He felt relief because though this sermon was one of many, there were times when he had not felt strong, had not felt the confidence expected of him. He had felt tired—he had felt his age, which was past sixty—but this week the sermon had come to him like a gift. His mind was free for other more pressing matters.

He thought rarely of the past because it had been a source of pain for him, but now he did so. Even now, though many years had passed, Reverend Williams could sometimes feel his son's presence behind him, his quiet boy, waiting patiently for the ice cream that would follow on the way home.

He shook his head, gathering his papers, feeling suddenly weary and alone and not at all certain. He turned on the light, collected his coat from the hook on the door, and made his way up the stairs into the empty hall of the church. The stained-glass window, the result of two years of continual fund-raising, was luminous and silent, and he stared at it for a while before carefully locking the side door and entering the heat of the late afternoon. He felt light-headed, and for an instant, before his eyes adjusted to the brightness of the day, he felt as if he might fall.

For no reason that he could point to, Ronald Gass began to trouble Michael in sleep. He kept hearing the older man's voice. He expected more of his dreams than the likes of Ronald Gass; nonetheless, it went on for several nights, even though the dreams themselves were nothing to speak of, no more interesting than buying shoes or gathering old newspapers.

Michael had taken this job, consciously, as a place to start again. He'd seen the advertisement in a medical journal and called on a whim. A prosperous practice, a good location, but what attracted him most was that it was both quiet and far away.

But now here he was, at that faraway address, and suddenly the tumblers of his life seemed to have clicked into place. Instead of starting again, the world was becoming fixed and hard around him, and his profession, the one he had so arduously chosen for himself, was cooling into iron. The promise of youth, he thought to himself, was really the possibility of change. Now those once-casual choices were made with greater effort, with decades invested, and his work had bound itself to him like the color of his hair or his name. He was Dr. Grant, even to himself; he could not in truth conceive of himself in other terms. It could be this, he thought—these patients, this office—these next thirty years of life.

He also knew, dimly, that such thoughts offered no solutions. He felt the weight of profundity without its content. He offered himself clichés. He drank his coffee and brushed his teeth and drove to and from the office and collected his money and continued. Even the great struggles of his patients, the men and women whose lot he watched, felt distant, their real sufferings and deep fears and occasional pure bolts of joy as detached as a kaleidoscope or a freak show at a country fair. They would keep coming, whether he lay awake or not, and he would have to smile and shake their hands and let them trust him.

He had met Ann, his former wife, when they were both medical students. They had chosen the same specialty, internal medicine, though he had gone on to infectious disease and she was now finishing her cardiology fellowship on the other side of the country. She had been a relentlessly superior student, far better than he was, graduating very near the top of their class, and looking back he knew that some part of his attraction to her lay in the keenness of her mind. Several of her professors had formally called her brilliant, and though for his part he had done well enough, he had simply been one more intelligent person in a class of hundreds.

Ann's father was a Lutheran minister, and he had always attributed her discipline to this, although as time passed he'd wondered if anything could explain discipline like hers so easily. It had taken him a good while to see it. She had simply seemed restrained and quietly serious, and he had pursued her with a fervor that now, in retrospect, astonished him.

She had been sitting alone, in the back of the auditorium, intent on the slides projected on the screen. Most of the students sitting that high up dozed in their chairs or whispered to one another, and normally he himself sat farther down, closer to the speaker. But that day he'd been late and entered through the back, and there she had been. He'd sat down next to her, trying to keep his attention on the lecturer, but all the while unexpectedly aware of her body beside him, her long brown legs, her shorts and running shoes, her small firm hand on her page of notes. And when the lights went up at the end of the lecture, he had turned to her and introduced himself.

She was a runner, and for a time it was something they shared.

They went together, before the lectures began, when the campus was quiet, and even now it was a happy memory for him, running easily through the early morning, their breath coming in gasps as they sprinted the last few hundred yards to the gym. How intense his desire for her had been.

Ann was the kind of young woman who had never been pursued. Her college days had been spent, for the most part, in the library and the chemistry lab. Nonetheless, she was attractive in a distant, discrete kind of way, gray-eyed and clear, so he had known from the start that she was not one of those women who had been driven to their studies by social awkwardness. Rather, she had chosen them.

He had never been a pursuer, and why he had suddenly become one was a source of puzzlement for him. But he had, and she'd filled his thoughts, and there were times when he thought he would never tire of the sight of her, with her wavy light brown hair cut short, blond at the nape of her neck, and her small perfect teeth, and her calm eyes. She was awkward and delicate, with a tiny white triangle of a scar at the left corner of her upper lip that folded and rose when she smiled.

Once, casually, she had mentioned that when she was a very young child her parents had briefly considered the possibility that she was autistic. She hadn't talked until the age of three, and only then, listening to her sudden full sentences, did they relax and stop worrying. She'd smiled when she said it, but the remark had stayed with him. He could see it in her—a faint otherworldliness, a lovely alien whisper—and ultimately he decided that it was this, more than anything else, that had drawn him to her.

She had accepted him calmly, for reasons that even now, or perhaps especially now, he didn't understand. They had married, they had gone on to residency together. All the long nights of call, week after week, and the odd rhythm of sleeplessness, the vast white lights of the wards—so many notes; so many nursing stations, lectures, presentations; so many fevers and so much flesh, in light and dark, back and forth and back again—she had glided through it all as if untouched, but he had come home stumbling.

The day his father died, his mother had called him at work. It had been sudden, and there had not been time for him to fly home. But he knew exactly what it had been—his thin father, bolt upright on the gurney with his eyes lit, refusing the ventilator again as the long minutes passed. Then his mother alone, weeping, saying her prayers, twisting her hands in the consultation room as they brought her the telephone.

Ann had not gone with him to the funeral. She had given a paper at a cardiology convention in Chicago. The convention met annually, and Ann had spent two solid years of what little free time she had working on the paper she was to give.

Her presentation had gone exceptionally well; she had come back with a prize. Ann and her research adviser had developed a better method for opening very small blocked arteries in the heart. They had used an animal model—pigs—and their initial results had been promising enough that shortly after the conference Ann decided to take six months off to do research.

She had barely known his father, ill as he had been, and Michael had urged her to go to the conference. But nonetheless, when they were home again and she went once more into the intricacies of catheters and pressures and balloons, all he could hear even weeks later was the echo of rifles, and all he could see was his father's flag-draped coffin easing into the ground as the small uniformed crowd stood quietly by. His mother had wept again, and clung to him, and in that moment he had felt more alone than he would have believed possible. He had trembled, and put his arms around her, and the next day he had been required to fly home.

It was remarkable, Ann often said, how similar a pig's heart is to a man's. Even the most expert eyes cannot tell them apart on a tray.

Going to the funeral would have cost her a year and a prize. Cardiology fellowships, particularly at the places she had applied, were intensely competitive. But it had been difficult for him nonetheless.

Many times he took dinner to her in the laboratory. They would eat together, and she would ask him about his day and thank him. Once, and only once, he stayed to watch her work, and though years had passed this scene was what came to mind when he thought of her.

The pig was draped and anesthetized. It was not as large as he thought it would be—little more than a hundred pounds. They were in the basement of the research building, where the animals were kept, but the equipment in the room was identical to that used on human beings.

She wore her lead apron, a blue paper gown, and yellow-white surgical gloves. He stood behind her. The room was dark, and the surgical lamp overhead lit up the pig's shaved and disinfected groin.

The needle was six inches long and half as thick as a pencil, and at first it looked as if she were kneading the pig's flesh. In and out, the skin dimpling, one stick, two, three, and there it was, suddenly—the flash of arterial blood into the clear syringe, as red as a poppy—the femoral artery.

She was deft and quick. She detached the syringe, covering the jet of blood that pulsed through the open throat of the needle with her left thumb. Then the wire, sliding it in through the needle with quick firm strokes of her right wrist—inch after inch—until more than a foot of wire was inside the pig. Another gesture, and she had pulled the needle free, out over the wire. Blood welled from the place the wire entered. She tossed the stained needle on the tray and exchanged it for a hollow plastic dart, eight inches long. She fiddled for a moment, fitting the exposed end of the wire into the hole in the tip of the dart, then pulled the wire back, quickly, until it was through the dart, and the dart lay poised against the skin, the wire hanging out the back of it like a bloody tail.

"I'm putting in the sheath," she said.

She picked up a scalpel from the tray and casually, as if without effort, flicked a gash in the skin at the base of the wire. And then, with force, she drove the dart deep into the pig, twisting it in her hands as she did so, all the way to the hilt. Then she pulled out the wire, so fast it snapped and coiled about itself on the tray.

The catheter, three feet long, so expensive, so thin and perfectly clean, came next. She was gentle, delicate, and calm, easing it in through the hilt of the sheath, past mark after mark on its surface—ten centimeters, twenty—until she was deep enough.

"Fluoro on," she said quietly, and the research assistant—a small, balding man in his sixties, who had prepared the pig and who sometimes cast a brief incurious glance at the monitor, where the pig's vital signs were displayed—swung the X-ray machine over the table and pressed a button.

The television screen hanging above them from the ceiling came to life, and a ghostly image rose up. It took Michael a few seconds to realize what he saw: It was an X ray of the pig's chest. At first it seemed like an ordinary X ray—the brightness of bones, the shadowy lungs, the dark silhouette of the heart—but it moved; the lungs rose and fell, the heart clenched and unclenched.

And there, just below the heart, he could see the waving tip of the catheter, a tendril in the current.

Ann was watching also. The catheter flowed through her hands, rising slowly on the screen.

"It looks like you're in the heart," Michael said.

"I'm in the descending aorta," Ann replied. "It's over the heart."

He was quiet. He was in her world, he thought. The catheter continued, tentative and slow, level with the top of the heart now, waving; then, as if to an invisible hand, it began to curve like a wand, back on itself, down toward the top of the heart. The tip shook visibly with each beat. It was following the curve of the vessel, following it up and then down the arc into the heart itself.

"That's the ascending aorta," she said. "I'm just above the aortic valve."

He found himself holding his breath.

"Contrast in," she'd said, and pressed the plunger of the syringe attached to the catheter.

It was miraculous—dozens of blood vessels leaping from the shadows like lightning, bright off silver, forming a perfect outline of the pig's heart. It reminded him of the veins of leaves, such brief and astonishing detail, gone in an instant as the contrast washed away.

"I'm trying to cannulate a small branch vessel," she said, for Michael's benefit, "without rupturing it."

She moved her hands, turning, Michael saw, little half wheels attached to the catheter. The tip of the catheter bent forward on the screen, then back, left and right, testing.

"Contrast in," she said again, pushing the plunger.

Just a little bit, this time, a flash, filling, and as the vessels lit again the tip was moving, twisting to the wheel, curling into the ostium, just like that, into the mouth of the left coronary artery, and then down, millimeter by millimeter, into the maze. Minutes passed. The thread, deep in the shuddering tissue.

"I'm almost there," she said. "We'd never try this in a human patient."

"Why not?"

"If we rupture the vessel it can be fatal. But this is the thinnest catheter we've developed so far."

We, he thought.

"Contrast in," she said again, and this time he saw the catheter, entering a thread. She was very careful now, easing it forward as gently as possible.

But then, suddenly, there was a tiny bloom of white on the screen, a little white fan, streaming out of the artery into the gray expanse. She stiffened, her lips tight, and shook her head.

"What is it?" he asked.

"I blew the vessel," she said, stepping back from the table. "That's it."

"Oh, well," the assistant said, speaking for the first time, winking at Michael. "Looks like it's pork chops again."

Ann shook her head once more.

"He always says that," she said wearily, when the man had left the room. "He thinks it's funny. He doesn't understand that this is serious."

Michael had asked if she was coming home.

"Why don't you go," she replied. "I have to write this up."

Eighteen months later, just before he finished his training, to her astonishment as well as to his own, he'd left her.

Ronald Gass was drinking again, and doing so quite deliberately. He would come home from work, cast his jacket on the untouched couch of his living room, sit on a side chair, and call into the kitchen.

Nora would emerge with a bottle of gin, a bottle of tonic water, a tumbler of ice, and a glass. They said little to each other. Nora would put the tray on the coffee table and leave the room. He would pour his drink and sip it, letting the gin ease into him until he felt the slightest approach of fog, like the ghost of breath on a windowpane. He was careful to leave it at that. He sat looking out over his manicured lawn and the blooming trees down the street.

If he felt up to it, he would open his briefcase for one of the half dozen or so medical journals he subscribed to and read for an hour or so until dinner was ready and Nora's voice reentered the room, as soft as a bell.

For some time after his wife's death he had stopped drinking. He had determined to himself that it was unwise, that he did not trust himself with it. Now the gin in his mouth felt like a little private risk, but it helped him, in any case, with the insomnia he had always suffered from. Night after night he lay awake in the small hours, and as he aged it had grown worse. Soon, he sometimes thought, there will be no sleep for me at all.

He found himself reading the same article he had seen on Michael Grant's desk the day he had invited him to dinner, a review of elephantiasis. He put it aside after a few paragraphs, the image of Grant rising in front of him: a quiet black-haired man with a facade of arrogance who, for all his pretense of discipline, was, Ronald Gass knew, undisciplined. Look how he had unraveled, look how he had become weak and tremulous, as for the first time he felt a bit of the tragedy that fell so liberally on others. Grant was one of those people, he thought, who have drifted painlessly up to the present, and therefore expect to drift painlessly into the future. Decades of schooling, a thousand well-taken tests, and now all of it rocked to the ground by a squalling black child on the inpatient pediatric ward of a community hospital at the edge of a tobacco field. A child he had only glanced at, at the beginning of an ordinary day, trying to get to the office. He was not even strong enough for that. The sting of the lash did not become him.

The diagnosis of meningococcemia in a black child was difficult only if you didn't look closely. If you looked closely you couldn't miss it. The petechiae were obvious, the black blisters blown out of the skin, little bubbles of blood teeming with the microbe *Neisseria,* the gram-negative rod, the childhood mercenary. In a white child you could see it from across the room in twilight.

Ronald Gass had reviewed the chart, and now he knew for certain what had happened that morning. Grant had come in, glanced at the chart by the bed, glanced at the child in the cot, wrapped in its gown, and simply hadn't paid attention. He hadn't undressed the child and examined the skin. He hadn't checked the labs. And he'd written an indefensible note in the chart—*no fever now, taking liquids, likely viral syndrome*—thinking to himself, Gass knew, Why have they consulted me? What do they expect of me?

Then the pediatrician, a few hours later and far too late, walking by, looking in from the door, the blossoming lesions manifest before her. Anyone could see it then.

The full virulence of meningococcemia is a wonder, a dark and terrible fire. The girl, dead in six hours. Sucking her mother's fat breast that morning.

Gass thought fondly of his own words: Antibiotics probably would not have made a difference. You know that, Michael. Perhaps it was true, but they should have been given nonetheless, and now, for the good of the practice, he was required to consider whether Grant was worthy of partnership after all.

He took another sip of his drink and looked again out over the lawn. Spring was at hand. He stretched in his chair, feeling warm and peaceful, beginning to anticipate the meal whose aromas were spreading through the house, suffusing the drapery and the carpet.

The carpet had been a wedding gift from Clara's parents, one they had always liked. As he sat there he found he could imagine Nora so clearly, as a little girl, taking her new steps into swirling reds and browns as he knelt at one end and Clara at the other. Their little teetering girl, out into the wide expanse, as if she were walking on water.

"Nora," he called, "how is dinner coming along?"

Jonas Williams entered the office shortly before two and took his seat in the waiting room with the others. Michael, on his way back from the bathroom between patients, was expecting him and identified him almost immediately. He was sitting on the chairs with the others, amid background music, by the floral prints on the walls and the tall green plant. The room was furnished carefully, but nonetheless it had the feel of terrible news, and Michael rarely entered it. But now, walking past and looking through the doorway, he saw the figure on the chair and heard Susan's voice.

"Mr. Williams? Dr. Grant's office is the second door on the right. He'll see you now."

Quickly, Michael stepped into his office, closed the door, and sat down at his desk. He waited uneasily, for what seemed like a long time, until the knock came and the door opened.

The man in the doorway was thin and light-skinned, with bright hazel eyes. He was about Michael's height, but he looked nothing like his father; the only resemblance Michael could see lay in the watchfulness of his expression. He wore a dark sweatshirt, jeans, athletic shoes.

"Mr. Williams?" Michael said, rising from his seat.

The man nodded.

"I'm Dr. Grant." Michael extended his hand out over the desk. "Why don't you take a seat."

Jonas Williams took a few steps forward, shook Michael's hand, and sat down in the chair across from the desk.

From a distance, there was nothing out of the ordinary in their meeting. Two figures in a plain white office, a potted plant along the wall, the desk between them. The whisper of blown air, the rustle of papers.

"First let me say how sorry I am about your daughter," Michael said. "It was a tragic loss."

Jonas Williams said nothing.

"How can I help you?"

"I haven't been well," the man answered. His voice was quiet, almost a monotone.

"Why don't you tell me what brings you here."

Jonas Williams looked down at his own feet. "I'm tired," he said. "Sometimes I think I'm going blind. My mouth is white."

Michael felt a click when he heard those words, and the immediate diagnosis of HIV leapt into his mind. CMV and oral candidiasis, malaise, the stuff of bread and butter. The known world.

But the man before him looked outwardly well, with no sign of the wasting he should have seen. The bones of his temples were covered with good fat.

"How long have you been having symptoms?"

"I'm not sure."

"You're not sure?"

"I'm not thinking right," he said. "I'm not remembering."

"Weeks? Months?"

"Maybe weeks. It's getting worse."

"What's getting worse?"

"My eye. My mouth. But it comes and goes."

"What do you mean by comes and goes?"

"Sometimes I see it. Sometimes I know it's there. But other times I don't. Sometimes I feel all right."

"Is it there now?"

Jonas Williams nodded.

"Anything else? Fevers, chills, night sweats, that kind of thing?"

Jonas Williams shook his head. "I just feel weak," he said. "I can't think right. And I see lights."

"What kind of lights?"

"Like fireflies. But they're not there. They come and go."

Michael nodded, writing in the new chart before him. "Do you have any medical problems that you know about?"

The man shook his head.

"Are you allergic to any medications?"

"No," Jonas said.

"Have you ever used any IV drugs?"

"No."

"Have you ever had sex with a man?"

Jonas looked up, eyes narrowed, but then he shrugged. "No," he said.

"Any blood transfusions?"

Again the slight shake of the head.

"Well," Michael said. "Let me take a look."

"I don't have any money," Jonas said.

"Don't worry," Michael said. "It's been taken care of."

"Is my father paying you?"

Michael took a breath. "No," he said. "But don't worry about it."

Jonas considered this for a moment; then he nodded and looked away. "I appreciate it," he said.

Michael rose and walked around the desk, and as he did so Jonas stood up. Michael did not want to go down the hall into an examination room. He could not have said why this was so, but it seemed important to keep the door closed and private. He had the tools he needed here—a stethoscope, an ophthalmoscope—in the drawer of his desk. The details of the history could wait.

"I need to examine you," he said. "Please take off your shirt."

Jonas did so, calmly, and stood bare to the waist. He looked sinewy and strong, tight with muscle. The contours of his back and chest were covered with fine hair, and he gave off the faint metallic odor of sweat. Michael stepped up closely, putting on thin rubber gloves as he did so.

"Turn around, please."

Jonas turned on command, facing the wall, and Michael placed the diaphragm of the stethoscope gently on his back.

"Take a deep breath."

The lungs were clear. The heart was steady and slow, systole, diastole, the shudder of valves closing on blood. A slight murmur, over and again. The belly was soft, with the gentle subterranean rumble of the bowel clear in his ears.

"Please drop your pants for a moment."

Jonas Williams was nearly naked. Michael looked at the skin, the scattered freckles on the belly and lower legs. He felt the distal pulses, and then, for a moment, he pulled the man's underwear aside and examined the coil of his genitals, probing for lymph nodes in the groin. The femoral arteries were strong, leaping beneath his gloved fingers. The man turned his face away.

He took off his gloves and tossed them in the basket by his desk.

"I need to test your reflexes," he said.

Jonas Williams sat down again, his legs loose off the edge of the chair, as Grant tapped his tendons with the hammer.

"It's my mouth," the man said, breaking his silence. "And it's my eye."

He began to feel the man's neck—the firm and pliable muscles, the rise of the thyroid, the grit of the trachea, moved gently left and right against the cervical vertebrae. He pressed deep into the hollows above the collarbones. Everything was normal.

"Good," he said, with the light in his hand. "Please open your mouth."

The flesh was pink and warm, the tongue clear. For an instant he saw nothing other than the shine of saliva. But then, low on the interior of the cheek, down at the back of the jaw, he saw white threads, coiling around one another, and extending into the deep recesses of the throat. He knew instantly that it was not yeast, *Candida,* which is what he had expected. It was a white serpentine pattern, something he could not recall having seen before.

"Is it painful?"

Jonas Williams shook his head, the light in his throat.

Michael took a tongue depressor and ran it gently over the surface of the lesion. He could not scrape it off; it was firm on the gums. The gums seemed otherwise healthy. They did not bleed, even when he rubbed hard and the man started and made a small sound.

He turned off the light and stepped back. The two men looked at each other for an instant, and then Jonas Williams stood and dressed without being told.

"Let me look in your eye."

The man nodded. Michael stepped past him and flipped the switch by the door, plunging the room into nearly complete darkness. At the same time he turned on his ophthalmoscope, and the small light fanned out into the room, like a miner's helmet in the distance.

Almost by feel, as his own eyes adjusted to the darkness, Michael stepped nearer to the man's face. They were so close they could smell each other's breath and their own, swirling together. The discomfort between them was palpable. He shone the light directly into Jonas Williams's left eye, and clicked the dial on the lens to adjust the refraction, swimming down through the conjunctiva, the cornea, through the fine spider of the lens to the retina, which came sharply into view as he held his breath, his right hand steady on the man's moist forehead to brace himself.

There it was again, in the light, the serpentine pattern, coiling in the vessels of the retina, inward from the margins to the center.

He turned on the light in the room.

"Did you see it?" Jonas Williams asked, and Michael nodded.

"I did," he said.

"You know what it is?"

Michael sighed and sat down behind his desk. "No," he said. "Not yet. I'd like to refer you to an oral surgeon for a biopsy, and I'd like to run some tests. You'll need to go across town to the lab and get your blood drawn."

"Can't you do it?"

"You mean the biopsy?"

Jonas nodded. “I don’t have a car,” he said. “It’s hard for me to get around.”

Michael knew he could, though he had not done it in some time. A punch biopsy is simple. He could feel Jonas Williams staring at him, though he did not look up.

“I suppose I could,” he said. “I’ll need to get the equipment. We’ll do it next week.”

“Can you draw my blood here too?” Jonas Williams asked mildly.

Michael rubbed his hand over his eyes. “Fine,” he said, getting up to leave the room. “Fine. I’ll do it now and send the blood over.”

Michael returned in a few minutes with a handful of glass tubes, a thick yellow rubber band, and a phlebotomist’s syringe.

“Give me your arm,” he said, putting on surgical gloves. He wrapped the rubber band tightly around the man’s bicep and tried to feel the veins that rose from the man’s forearm. But it had been some years since he had drawn a man’s blood, and the veins were invisible beneath the brown skin. It was only when he finally removed the glove that he was able to feel the faint roll of the vein with the tip of his naked finger. But the needle entered cleanly, and blood sprang into the clear glass tubes and warmed them.

He filled five tubes. The last tube leaked, just a little, and a few drops of blood fell on Michael’s bare left hand, so warm he didn’t feel them for a few seconds. But then they cooled, and he saw them, and moved quickly with the alcohol pad, wiping his hand several times.

“See Susan on the way out,” he said finally, just before he washed the vials of blood in the sink. “Tell her to make an appointment for you on Monday.”

Nothing further was said between them. Jonas Williams nodded, holding a ball of cotton to his small wound. He flexed his arm, then turned and left, passing through the waiting room, speaking briefly to the receptionist as instructed. In a few minutes he was back in the open air, walking with his head down under the magnolia trees that lined the soft street, full of their sweet odor and the lingering sting in his arm, homeward, as quickly as he had come.

When he was done for the day, Michael took the tubes of blood to the laboratory nearby. He labeled the tubes before he left and handed all but one to the clerk with the gloved hands at the desk.

The last tube he kept in his pocket, lest the lab misplace it.

He did not give the tests themselves careful thought. They were rote to him—basic screening tests, blood and liver and kidneys and antibodies for viruses, the kind routinely ordered in every doctor's office. But later that night he found himself leafing through his textbooks, the color photos of lesions and rashes, faces with small black bars covering the eyes so they would not be recognized. He looked until he was certain that he had no idea what he was seeing in Jonas Williams's mouth and eye. He was thoughtful now, and so, just before bed, he remembered to take the vial of blood from the pocket of his jacket and put it carefully in the freezer beside the trays of ice.

Most Mondays, Michael felt the weight of the week he faced. He would shower and shave, listening for the whistle of the kettle as he did so, and the days ahead would flow into the immediate moment. It was not dread, exactly. It was more nearly oppression, the knowledge that he would do exactly what was expected of him for ten hours of each of the next five days.

This morning, though, the results from the laboratory, which he imagined to be waiting for him, banished the rest of the week without effort from his mind.

He entered the office shortly after seven. He was nearly an hour early, and Susan was not yet there. He let himself in with his key, the key he rarely used, and walked down the hall to the small office library, where the latest textbooks were kept, and the new journals.

For some time, Michael had tried to keep current with the medical literature. He had read, often nightly, and in the past it had been a source of pride for him. He might not be Ann, but nonetheless he had some rigor of his own, and he was as good, he thought, as most in his field. Many physicians slid by, as their knowledge aged, and then perhaps went to a conference or two where the latest therapies were reviewed in the banquet halls of hotels. Over the past few months, Michael himself had not kept up, and now he chided himself. He felt the power of his mind surging as he entered the library and sat down in the overstuffed chair by the lamp. There had been times, in medical school and later during his fellowship, when he had felt the accuracy and sharpness of his own intelligence acutely, almost as if it had entered the tangible world. He had welcomed the precision of his memory and reveled in its intricacies. He had never confided this to anyone. It was a private pleasure, the joy of doing small things well, the exact place on the one page of the book that gave him what he wanted, which was what they wanted, which was the answer.

A library, with its density of pages around him, was therefore a comfortable place. It was perhaps the only place where Michael had been an unqualified success.

He sat down. The small round window opened to the street, and already the sunlight lit up motes of dust rising off the carpet. He was alone for the moment, but he knew that in a few minutes Susan would arrive and make the coffee, and then the telephone would start to ring.

He sat there in the library for a while. Then he stood, stretched, and left the room, feeling the soft carpet beneath the thin soles of his leather shoes, past the water fountain and the glint of the gold handles of the office doors.

Ronald Gass's office door was ajar, and he noticed it immediately, even from down the hall. It occurred to him that the door had been left open over the weekend, but before he took a second step he heard the rustle of paper, the creak of a leather chair. He paused, for an instant uncertain whether he should stop and knock or whether he should continue on, but then his hand was on the knob, and the door opened.

Gass looked up with a start from his desk.

"Excuse me," Michael said. "I didn't know you were here."

"I heard you in the library," Gass replied. "I thought you were Susan."

A textbook lay open on the desk.

"You're here early." Michael felt the need to speak, though suddenly he wanted to be out again in the hall.

"I've been here since four," Gass said.

"Since four?"

"Occasionally I suffer from insomnia. Last night was worse than usual. I use those times to read."

"I know what you mean." He felt his own glibness, uneasy again as he always seemed to be with this man.

"Why are you here?" Gass's tone was weary.

"I was doing a little reading too. I haven't been keeping up as much as I should."

Gass nodded, as if he was expecting such an answer, and Michael felt a flash of irritation.

"It's hard to keep current," Gass said.

From down the hall came the sound of keys and locks unbolted.

"That must be Susan," Michael said, and raised his hand in a little wave as he stepped back into the hall. "Do you want your door closed?"

"Please," Gass replied, turning back to his book.

He smiled and said good morning to Susan, went into his own office, and sat down in the overstuffed chair he used for his interviews rather than at the desk. He rarely sat in this chair, but now he did so, and suddenly it occurred to him that three people who now were dead had sat in this exact place and looked at the desk, and the bookshelf beyond, and the print on the wall, waiting for him to come in. John, he thought, and Christopher. And Roger.

A few minutes later, Susan knocked delicately on his door.

"The lab sent over some results for you," she said. "Do you want to see them now?"

By noon Ronald Gass was feeling his age and his sleeplessness. His body ached, the old ache he thought he had left behind. He stretched between patients, he felt his normally good attention waver. Like Clara's last weeks, when he had been up all night, and the singing kettle those early morning hours had entered his dreams. Another cup of sweet tea, a grape dipped in honey. She was not hungry, but her thirst had been enormous and recurrent and satisfied with only the barest of sips. Then again, and so on, till morning.

He could only remember being so tired during his internship, when as a young man he had looked out the hospital window as the sun rose and felt the approach of another day, awake all night in his short white coat, knowing it would be dark again before he could sleep, before he could fall dreamless into the arms of his new wife in their cheap walk-up, untroubled even by the sound of the nearby trains. But that had been for something, he had thought then. It had been for the glitter in Clara's eyes, or those of his parents, or even his own as he stood in front of the mirror in the early hours and prepared to go in. Chicago, 1962, in winter.

But this was another kind of sleeplessness altogether.

At lunch, he drank two cups of coffee standing up. His belly rumbled, and again a fist passed through his lower chest, settling only when he drank nearly half a bottle of antacid. Indigestion, insomnia—I sound like one of my patients, he thought, full of weakness. He had not showered, and he stood in the odor of his own body, with its thin shoulders and tall man's stoop.

By two he was finding reasons to excuse himself, getting up, walking down the hall to the bathroom, splashing cold water on his face. The mirror revealed him, the drops of water clinging to his hairline, his hollow eyes and thin lips. I am so tired, he thought, and it is so unlike me.

By four, before the last patient of the afternoon, he stood and again went down the hall to the bathroom door. He felt as if he were far above himself; he felt the lightness in his body and the distant ache of his joints and back as if they were another man's.

He opened the door. A man stood bending over the sink. At the sound, the man straightened suddenly and turned to face him. It was a small room. Gass apologized quickly and stepped out again into the hall. The door had been unlocked, and Gass stood outside on the carpeting, leaning against the wall, waiting. For an instant, he was not certain that he had seen what he had seen—a light-skinned black man leaning over the sink, letting a bright thin stream of blood flow from his mouth into the white porcelain, then turning, his lower lip glistening and his eyes alight. In that instant, Gass had the distinct impression that the man was afraid, as if he had been caught in some transgression. Gass rubbed his eyes, and heard the sound of faucets running, and saw again the blood flowing from the man's mouth for what seemed like a long time into the sink.

After a few moments the door opened and the man entered the hall. Their eyes met, and Gass saw that the man had packed his mouth with tissue—a fleck emerged from the corner of his mouth, like a wick, and already it had darkened. The man nodded, swallowed, and continued past him. Before Gass himself turned to enter the bathroom, he watched the man move quickly down the hall to Michael Grant's office.

Gass let the water run over his wrists until the ache of cold reached him, and then he placed his hands over the back of his neck. He felt a rivulet run down beneath his shirt, and he stared into the china sink, trying to gather himself, for a long time.

A FEW MINUTES BEFORE, JONAS WILLIAMS HAD SAT CALMLY IN THE chair and met Michael's gaze directly.

"Your blood work is back," Michael began, willing himself to look directly into the man's eyes. Jonas Williams nodded, his face blank.

"What did it show?"

"It's abnormal."

"You mean it's bad." It was a statement, spoken flatly, without questions.

"Not bad, exactly," he said, "but unusual. I'm concerned, yes."

"What do you mean, unusual?"

"You are anemic. Your platelet count is low. You need more tests."

"What's a platelet count?"

"Blood cells. They allow blood to clot."

"Do you know why it's low?"

"No," he said. "I don't. Not yet."

Jonas Williams closed his eyes and was quiet for a long moment.

"Do what you have to," he said. That was all. Then he looked directly at Grant, and his face changed, and Michael felt a chill, a tensing of muscle, though the man made no other sound and no other movement. His eyes were deep and bright. He could not have put it into words.

Michael was silent for a moment, thinking, looking hard at the man in front of him.

"You'll bleed if I do this."

"I figured I'd bleed some."

"Your platelets are low. They are the blood cells that form clots. You will bleed more than usual."

"Will it stop?"

"Yes," Michael said. "You have enough platelets for it to stop. But it will take awhile."

And so he readied the needle of anesthetic on his desk, and took the silver handle of the tool in his right hand, and then he bent close, and then the man's mouth was open to the metal, and once, twice, three times, the resistance of Jonas Williams's flesh against his thumb, an awl into new wet leather, as the man's mouth began instantly to fill with blood. Three holes in the white coil.

"There's a bathroom down the hall," he said. "Pack your mouth with tissue, and come back when you're done."

During the next few minutes, while Jonas Williams was in the bathroom, Michael studied the numbers again. He reviewed them carefully. Liver and kidney functions, blood counts. Low platelets, a mild anemia. Infection, malignancy. An autoimmune disorder. A toxin. So many possibilities.

He sat back and thought some more, until the knock came and Jonas Williams reentered the room.

It was difficult for the man to speak, with the paper wadding in his mouth, and every so often he swallowed what was filling the back of his throat.

"I'll need to run some more studies," Michael said.

The man nodded and swallowed, and then said, "When will the bleeding stop?"

"If it hasn't stopped in forty-five minutes, come back. I'll be here. Don't take any aspirin from now on, and don't rinse out your mouth for the next couple of hours."

The man stood.

"Come back at noon tomorrow," Michael said. "I want to repeat your blood counts then, and we'll do the other tests at the same time."

"All right," Jonas Williams said, but if Grant heard him he gave no sign, and he remained silent until the man was gone.

A few minutes later, there was another knock on the door. It was Ronald Gass.

Gass looked terrible. The weariness of his voice this morning had risen into his face, his eyes were dark, and his hands trembled.

"Michael," Gass said. "Are you done for the day?"

"I'm just finishing up."

"I was wondering if I might ask a favor."

"Of course, Ronald. Are you OK?"

"I was wondering if you might drive me home. I'm not feeling well, and Nora is not answering the phone."

"I'd be happy to," Michael said politely, as if he were accepting an invitation.

Jonas Williams felt his mouth filling again, more slowly now, as he lay in the half dark of his room. He could not have spoken, with his mouth full of tissue. He did not want to speak but simply to lie here and turn his head to spit in the plastic garbage can next to the bed. He watched the blood flow through his lips, and the bits of darkened paper that went with it. After an hour, the bottom of the trash can was a liquid surface, and his mouth felt like depths of a well.

But it was slowing, and in a few minutes it would stop. The dread he had felt in the doctor's office had been profound, but now, on his own again, he was calm.

He was growing tired. He could feel it gathering him in with its lights, entering his mind like a balm. The earlier fear was gone. He had been afraid, briefly, transfixed, as he stood at the mirror and looked into his shining, bleeding mouth, and then a stranger had opened the door. Now once again he felt soothed, and the flow was only the faintest trickle in his throat. Soon he would be able to sleep. The next step, the immediate ground—these were the only things that interested him now. The distance was lost in cotton wool, in the hum of the fan, in the voices, in the open doors and windows of the neighbors, who sat on the porches of their trailers, fanned themselves, and got up now and then for a drink.

He would sleep for an hour, then get up and take a shower and get dressed.

But he didn't sleep. He lay on the bed and felt the trickle dry up. After a while he worked the clotted mass of tissue with his tongue, gently, until it lifted free from his jaw, and let it fall into the bucket like a plum. Then he stood, entered the bathroom, and turned on the light. He looked at himself, sharp through one eye, misty and glowing through the other.

Some blood had hardened on his chin, and he wiped it away. Then he tucked a wad of tissue paper into his pocket and splashed some water on his face. Suddenly, the effort of a shower and clean clothes seemed far too much.

When the clock on the side of the bed rang at the appointed time, Jonas Williams picked up his key and left the trailer. The warmth of the air met him, and the sound of cicadas from the trees by the streetlight. He locked the door, stepping out onto the unpaved ground, with the high grass in clumps and the bushes thick around the trailer. It was a short way, and the evening filled him as he walked down the bare dirt of the driveway to where the street began, and with it the deeper shadows of the trees.

He heard the car behind him, slowing down and easing over by the curb. He stopped and turned, with his hand up to his face against the glare of headlights, waiting. The street was empty, full of cicadas and now the low irregular engine of the old black car coming softly to a stop. The lights went out, and he heard a soft voice calling him.

REVEREND WILLIAMS FELT HIS SON'S NAME FLOW OUT OF HIM, WHICH he had not planned, and the shadow crossed the hood and opened the passenger door. He heard Jonas's breath beside him, and he reached out, and touched him on the shoulder.

Jonas did not move at all, and if he felt his father's hand he gave no sign. "Do you have it?" he asked.

Reverend Williams handed Jonas an envelope. "There's five hundred dollars."

"I don't need that much."

"It'll last you, then."

Jonas did not thank him but simply held the envelope, white in his hand. Reverend Williams let his eyes adjust to the dark.

"When I was a young man I also did not know what would become of me. I was also uncertain." The Reverend spoke softly, deliberately, muting the power he felt. Jonas said nothing. The windshield was a gossamer surface.

"I also had darkness inside me."

"I don't know what darkness you mean." Jonas spoke slowly, with difficulty.

"Yes, you do, Jonas. I mean sin."

"I don't know what sin," Jonas turned his face, and Reverend Williams felt the bright weight of his gaze. "I don't know anything about your kind of sin."

Reverend Williams took a breath to calm himself. I must be patient, he thought, however difficult it is.

"It doesn't matter," he said. "We'll leave it alone now."

"I don't think clearly," Jonas said at last.

"You came home because you need help."

"I didn't do anything wrong."

"We all do wrong."

"You want to believe I did something."

"You did do something, Jonas. You turned your back on the Lord. You abandoned your family. But it's never too late to return. It's never too late."

Jonas looked down at his hands. "I'm sorry," he said, at last.

"I don't understand what drove you away."

"Sometimes people just don't get along, that's all. That doctor doesn't know what I've got, and neither do you."

"You've chosen the wrong path."

"You can't choose. You either believe or you don't."

Reverend Williams took a deep breath. "Did you care about your daughter, Jonas?" he asked. "Did she mean anything at all to you?"

Jonas looked away, expressionless.

"You didn't even come to her funeral," his father said. "Your own child. I cannot understand that."

Jonas closed his eyes. "I forgot when it was," he said.

"How could you forget? How could you forget when it was?"

"I got sick," Jonas Williams said wearily. "That's all. The Bible's got nothing to do with it."

"What about your nightmares, then? What about them?"

Jonas did not reply but opened the door to the car, leaned out, and let another stream of blood fall from his mouth into the darkness.

Michael started the engine with the unfamiliar keys and adjusted the seat and the mirror. The leather was smooth beneath him; the air conditioner whispered.

"Nice car," he said, to break the silence, but Gass did not answer. Michael glanced to his right, then back again.

Gass was leaning back in the passenger seat, his head high, exposing the brittle structure of his throat. His hair was neatly combed, thin, his face quiet. He might have been sleeping.

"You know the way, don't you?" Gass said.

"Yes."

"Thank you for doing this."

"It's no problem."

Gass was more absent than silent, Michael thought, as he pulled out into the streets, enjoying the feel of the car beneath his hands. He should have been aware of the man's body and his breathing beside him; he should have been wondering whether to speak. But he did not. It was as if Gass were a sack of meal, an inanimate thing. So he drove quietly, even comfortably, lost in his thoughts and the reflections of passing cars. The late-afternoon sun was bright and insistent, and the streets were so clear in it, and the houses, and the people walking on the sidewalks or poised on the curbs, waiting for him to pass. It was rush hour, so he followed the side streets, driving slowly, and it was only as he pulled into Gass's driveway that he realized his own car was back at the office and that he had no way of getting home.

Gass's eyes were open now, and he stretched suddenly, curling his arms out in front of him.

"Thank you, Michael," he said. He got out and stood up on the black asphalt.

Michael felt the heat strike him through the open door, as he too got out and stood up in the sun. Rivulets of sweat began immediately, under his arms and in his groin and on his forehead, as he followed Gass up the driveway to the house. Gass fumbled in his pockets.

"I have the keys," Michael said.

"Oh, yes, of course."

Gass extended his hand, and Michael placed the brass ring carefully in his palm, his knuckles brushing the tips of the man's fingers. The keys were cold from the air-conditioning, and he watched as Gass went through them one after another until he found the right one.

The house was quiet as they entered, and empty, as Michael immediately recognized. The curtains were drawn across the windows, but Gass, to his surprise, opened them wide, allowing sunlight to flood the room. Michael shielded his eyes against the glare, then turned his back, looking down at the carpet. Gass was an angular shadow behind him.

"Can I get you something? A drink?"

"Thank you, Michael. A glass of water."

He made his way to the kitchen and ran the tap, then opened the cupboards for glasses and the freezer for ice. He came back to the living room with two water glasses on a tray. Gass was on the sofa, half of him lit up in the sun, haggard now, and Michael watched as he drank greedily, draining the entire weight of the glass.

"Have the other one," Michael said, and Gass nodded, sipping more slowly now.

"I'm sorry," Gass said. "I don't know what came over me."

"Are you sure you're OK?"

"I'm fine now. It catches up with me these days. I can't go without sleep like I used to."

Michael nodded and sat down also, on the soft overstuffed chair by the coffee table. They were silent for a while, and he watched Gass sip the water and moisten his lips with his tongue.

"Where's Nora?" Michael asked.

Gass shrugged. "Grocery shopping, I believe."

"You should get some rest."

Gass nodded. "Since Clara died," he said, "I've started to feel my age. I'll be sixty-five this year."

"Have you thought about cutting back? You work long hours. Maybe you shouldn't be so"—he thought carefully—"dedicated."

"Dedicated?" Gass smiled.

"Yes. Maybe you're working too hard."

"And what is it you think I'm dedicated to?"

Michael didn't know how to answer. He never knew how to answer this man. "Your work," he said finally. "Your patients."

"My patients?"

"That's what it really comes down to, doesn't it?"

"Were you dedicated to that little girl?"

At first Michael was not sure he had heard the man correctly. "Excuse me?"

Gass smiled and rubbed his temples. "Were you dedicated to that child?"

"Yes," he said, because he did not know what else to say.

"Let me tell you something, Michael. Our business is flesh. We feed it and we water it and sometimes it dies on the vine. And when it does we pull it up by the roots and are done with it. It's not worth thinking about. There is always more."

"I don't follow you." He heard the anger in his voice.

"Don't be angry, Michael, I don't mean to offend you. But I'm being honest. Our patients are strangers."

"I think you're tired."

"I am tired. But I'm also correct. You don't care about that girl. You simply care about the mistake you made and the humiliation attendant to that mistake."

Gass was speaking very clearly and precisely. Michael knew, suddenly, that it was not the voice of sleeplessness he heard but rather the voice unleashed by sleeplessness.

"So you're saying you don't care about your patients? You don't care what happens to them?"

"Abstractly, yes. But I don't care about them as I would someone close to me. In that sense I do not care about them. I'm pleased when they do well, when the disease responds to treatment. I am pleased when the aphids dwindle. But no more."

"And Clara? What about the aphids then?" As he spoke the words, he knew he should regret them. But he did not.

Gass merely smiled and nodded his head. "That is my point exactly," he said. "Clara was beyond the reach of my conscious mind. The conscious mind is not compassionate. But it is where we keep our patients."

Michael was silent for a moment. Now, for the first time this afternoon, Gass looked as if he had regained his strength, though whether it was the conversation or simply the water he could not tell.

"Not always," Michael said.

"Perhaps."

"Have you ever dreamed about them? Your patients?"

Gass thought for a moment. "Rarely," he said.

"I dream about mine," he said. "I dreamed about the little girl."

"And do you think that makes you moral?"

"I don't know. Maybe it does."

"And maybe it's because you have nothing else."

He felt himself flushing. "Neither," he said, "do you."

Gass rose and entered the kitchen. But it was not in anger, he could tell. He heard water running, the ring of ice on glass, and then the man was back. Gass sat down and drank.

Time had passed, Michael realized, and the sun just over the horizon cast a gentleness into the room. "If you are such a cynic," he said, "why do you keep practicing? What's the point?"

"You said it yourself. I have nothing else. It's a pattern. It's occupying."

Suddenly, Michael felt afraid. He felt the gentleness of the twilight and the flowers and the clean smell of the empty house, and it seemed terrible to him. The future: a fine automobile; a man drinking water in front of him.

"I'm not sure I believe you."

"When I was your age," Gass said, "I would not have believed me either."

Michael looked at his watch. "I should be going, Ronald."

Gass nodded. "Yes," he said.

"Do you feel well enough to take me to my car?"

"Why don't we call a cab. I'll pay, of course. Thank you for taking me home."

Michael badly wanted to leave, to feel the air against him, to smell the grass and the spring evening, to hear the sounds of human voices on the street. As they waited, sitting quietly together in the living room, it was all he could think about.

He had not expected to see Gass in the office the next day, but the man was there, immaculate in his soft white shirt and rose silk tie, pale-eyed and steady.

"Good morning, Michael," Gass said, looking for all the world rested and at ease.

"I thought you might take the day off," he replied, as they stood and sipped their coffee, listening to the first murmurs of the day from the waiting room.

"Oh, no," Gass said. Just that. What had passed between them was left unspoken, and remained, as silent as a child in the corner. Gass nodded and started to walk off down the hall to his office, but then he paused.

"Nora will be starting on the books today," he said. "She felt I should have discussed it with you."

Michael met his eye. "I didn't know we had a problem," he said.

"It's nothing that a little arithmetic won't sort out. I thought I'd spare you the details unless you're interested."

"I don't know much about billing," Michael replied, politely, "but I'd be happy to help if you want me to."

Gass nodded, then continued down the hall, entered his office, and closed the door.

A few minutes later, just after the first of his patients, Michael heard her voice. He could not make out what she said, but Susan let out a sudden hoot of laughter, and he opened the door to his office and looked down the hall.

She stood next to Susan's desk, her hand resting on Susan's shoulder. Susan was looking at up at her, chuckling. He hesitated and nearly turned back to his office, but in that instant they both saw him.

"Come out here, Michael," Susan called. "I want to introduce you to someone."

He felt a sudden stiffness as he walked down the hall. They watched him approach, still smiling at whatever had passed between them.

"You look very serious, Dr. Grant," Susan said, peering at him above her half-moon glasses, a look of mock contrition on her face. "We need," she continued, whispering loudly out of the corner of her mouth, "to conduct ourselves in a more professional manner."

"That's right," he said, doing his best to play along. "No laughter allowed."

"This is Nora," Susan said. "She's going to relieve me of my torments."

"We've met," he said, smiling briefly.

"You have?"

"Ronald and Nora had me over for dinner."

"Oh, really?" Susan said. "Was it good?"

He laughed. "It was great," he said. "It was nice to have a home-cooked meal."

"You should come over to my house," Susan said. "Harold never appreciates my dinners."

"Of course he doesn't," Nora said.

"So this is your first day?" Michael asked awkwardly. He was very aware of her, he realized, and did his best to meet her eye, but if she felt any discomfort he could see no sign of it. She was assessing him, a faint smile on her lips.

"I probably won't be here that much," Nora replied. "I think I can do most of it at home."

"After she sees what a mess I've made she probably won't come back at all," Susan said.

"It can't be that bad," Michael said.

"Oh, believe me," Susan replied, "it is."

Nora looked at him and winked.

He expected the morning to go slowly, but the clock moved steadily. The patients shuffled through, one after another—their drawn faces, their mundane and desperate questions—and he went along. Ronald Gass, he found himself thinking, had a lesson to offer after all. The man endured. Of that at least there was no doubt. A rose-colored tie, a clean white shirt, and here he was again, door closed and working.

Nora, for her part, had taken the stack of ledgers into the library, and after several hours passed he wondered if she had gone home.

Jonas Williams did not come at noon. Michael had a strict policy with latecomers. He would wait fifteen minutes but no more. I'm sorry. This is a busy practice. Please see Susan to reschedule. Perhaps at the end of the day or if we have a cancellation. Sometimes, to his shame, he found himself speaking with a dark secret pleasure, though he was careful and deadpan, even when they were angry, even when it was not their fault and they had come a long way.

But now he waited. Part of him, as the minutes passed, was relieved. Nonetheless he remained in the empty offices a full hour, waiting for some further sign. But no one came, and he forced himself uneasily outside, into the open air.

The office was closed from noon until two, so that the morning paperwork could be completed. Susan went home for lunch, promptly at noon, and Gass usually used the time to see any patients admitted to the hospital. For the most part, Michael wrote in the charts as he went, so the break gave him time to go outside and have lunch undisturbed in the park nearby. Sometimes, if he was feeling up to it, he went for a run. The regularity of the park, where no one spoke to him, suited him, with its benches and solid trees and people crossing in the paths.

Perhaps Jonas was simply afraid, he thought, walking toward the park, though in this sense he was unlike the others, whose slow terror could be felt without a word being spoken. Usually it was so simple—

fear colored their every gesture. But after a while they settled back and waited and let him do what was necessary. At times, he had thought of them as actors in a nature show, as wildebeests who lie down, after the first few wild minutes of struggle, in the grass.

Jonas Williams was something else entirely. Absent, or at least a great distance away.

As Michael entered the park, he stretched and took off his jacket and loosened his tie. Squirrels ran up and down the gray trunks of the trees, the grass seemed very green and inviting, and for an instant he was tempted to lie down at the base of a nearby oak. Instead, he found a bench, a hint of rust visible through the bubbled black paint on the iron. He sighed, looking at his watch.

A woman pushing a stroller passed him, smiling briefly. He caught a glimpse of the child's white head, like a mushroom or a rare winter melon, wrapped in cloth. The sunshade of the stroller was pink, with blue flowers that exactly matched the infant's shirt. The infant and the stroller seemed attached to each other somehow. Matching outfits, like those handmade for twins. He heard a faint cry, as they passed him, and the woman's voice, soothing. She was pretty, with blond hair pulled back and white running shoes that for some reason reminded him of seagulls fluttering beneath her legs.

"Michael," a voice said, "didn't you hear me calling you?"

He turned, startled. It was Nora, coming up the path behind him.

"No," he said, starting to rise, "I'm sorry, I didn't."

"Don't get up," she said. "I tried to catch you, but you were walking too fast."

She looked lovely to him, in her jeans and white blouse, her hair dark in the sun.

"I didn't mean to startle you," she said. "Can I sit down? Or should I leave you alone?"

"Of course you can sit down," he replied, moving to give her room. "I didn't know you were still in the office."

"Susan was right," she said, and shook her head.

"It's that bad?"

"Not bad, exactly. The practice is doing fine. It's just that Susan's not too clear on who has paid their bills and who hasn't. She's too nice to think that way. It drives my father crazy."

"I can see that."

"I can't really blame him. He does have a business to run."

"Didn't he have someone doing the bills?"

"Yes," she said, "but she quit around the time my mother died. Susan tried to take over."

"Well," he said, "it's nice of you to help out."

"Do you mind if I smoke?" she asked suddenly.

"Go ahead," he said, taken aback, looking at her.

"Are you surprised?" she said, as she lit a cigarette and blew a plume of smoke into the air away from him.

"A little," he said.

"I know. Doctor's daughter."

"I grew up with it. My father smoked. The smell doesn't bother me."

"Good," she said.

"He died of it, though."

"Emphysema," she asked, "or lung cancer?"

"Emphysema."

She took another drag. "I'm not sure which one to pick," she said. "They both have their strengths."

He laughed. "I shouldn't say this," he said, "but some people get away with it."

"Really?"

"It's true. I've had patients in their late eighties who've smoked their entire lives and have had no problems at all."

"Why are they your patients then?"

"Because they're in their late eighties," he said.

She smiled.

"Do you like it here?" she asked, after a moment, blowing smoke out over the path.

"It's fine," he said. "I'm still settling in."

"What brought you here? Do you know anyone?"

"I needed a change. I thought I'd try someplace new." He glanced at his watch.

"Are you in a hurry?" she asked.

"A patient of mine didn't show up for his appointment, that's all. I was thinking about calling him."

"Remind me to bill him anyway," she said. "Susan never does that."

She ground her cigarette out carefully, then put it back in the pack.

"I don't actually smoke very much," she said. "Maybe five cigarettes a day."

They were silent for a while. She was a tingle in his arm, like static.

"So," he said, after a while. "What kind of bookstore did you have?"

"An unusual one," she said.

"How was it unusual?"

"It was more of a book co-op than a store. People would buy a membership, and then they would get books at a discount and return them if they wanted to."

"It sounds like a library."

"It was supposed to be halfway between a bookstore and a library. The problem is, we couldn't make any money."

"How long did you do it?"

"Much too long. I liked the idea so much I couldn't give it up. I can hardly go into a bookstore now."

"I'm sorry."

"I liked it. It was cozy and quiet and it was mine. But then I blinked my eyes and ten years were gone and my mother was dying." She shook her head, offering him a wry smile. "That's how it happens, isn't it? One day you realize you're not young, and you haven't done anything, and the bookstore you tried so hard to build has become a bakery."

"You're still young."

"How old are you?"

"I'm thirty-five," he said. "I'll be thirty-six in a few months."

"We're almost the same age then. How young do you feel?"

"Well," he admitted. "You have a point."

"You're divorced, aren't you?" she asked a moment later, surprising him again. He had carefully avoided the subject at dinner, just as he had avoided other personal questions. He and Gass had talked mostly about the difficulties of dealing with medical insurance companies.

"Yes," he said. "But how did you know that?"

She shrugged. "I could say that I'm very perceptive, but actually Susan told me."

"I got divorced last year," he said.

"Ah," she said. "Maybe that explains it."

"Explains what?"

"Why you came here."

He didn't know what to say.

"I grew up here," she continued, "and I couldn't wait to leave. They call it a city, but it's actually a small town."

"But you came back." He looked at her, but she didn't meet his eye.

"Maybe it was a mistake," she said, looking out at the grass. "It was home, I suppose. And I felt that I should because of my mother. But I'm not sure I even know why I did."

"Are you going to stay?"

"I'm not sure," she said. "I'm in what they call a transition period."

"What are you transitioning between?"

"Well," she said. "That's a good question. How about this: I'm transitioning between the failed dreams of my youth and the uncertainties of my impending middle age."

He smiled.

"I have no idea why I'm telling you this," she said. "You probably think I'm strange."

"No stranger than I am," he said.

"Why do you say that?"

"Like you said, I don't know anyone here. I took this job on a whim because it was far away."

She glanced at him. "I don't think you're strange," she said. "I just think you're depressed."

Her honesty surprised him.

"Did Susan tell you that also?"

She shook her head. "No," she said. "I came up with that diagnosis on my own."

He laughed. "I suppose I'm also in a transition period," he said.

She brushed a thread of hair from her forehead.

"Then tell me," she said, turning to look at him. "What are you transitioning between?"

He tried with only partial success to keep his tone lighthearted. "I suppose I'm transitioning between the difficulties of my past and the dark realities of my profession."

"A lot of people get divorced, you know," she said. "Things will get better."

He looked down at his feet. It was far more than Ann, he thought. It was his whole life up to this point, the inexplicable emptiness of it and how the prospects of the future seemed just more of the same, endlessly, without a light to be seen. And now the child, fixed and hard, somewhere in the pit of his stomach.

"I'm sorry," she said, and touched his arm lightly. "I really didn't mean to pry. It's none of my business."

"I really don't mind," he replied. It was true, he thought.

"Oh, no," she said suddenly. "What time is it?"

He looked at his watch again and told her.

"I'm late," she said. "I'm sorry, but I've got to go."

"You do?" he asked, and she nodded.

"I have a very important appointment," she said. "I'm getting my hair cut."

"Well," he replied, more formally than he intended, "don't let me keep you."

Both of them stood, and then she put her hand on his arm. "I liked talking to you, Michael," she said simply. "We should do it again."

He felt a moment of pleasure. She walked away quickly, without looking back, and in a few moments she was gone down the path under the trees.

After a while, he rose again, brushed a few ants off his legs, and began a leisurely return to the office. Susan was already sitting behind her desk when he arrived. She wore black-framed half-moon reading glasses low on her nose, her gray hair pulled up in a bun, her thick white arms arranged on the desk around the chart she was reading. She looked up quietly as he entered. Susan, as he had long known, was not easily startled.

"Michael," she said. "You're back early."

He smiled. "I have some charting to do."

"Did you eat?"

"Yes, Susan. I did. Don't worry." He chuckled a little, to let her know, to play along. This was how they spoke to one another—lightly, conveniently. A brushstroke.

"Good," she said. "Run along now."

She was smiling, and he patted her on the shoulder as he passed. He turned in the doorway opening to the hall.

"Did a Mr. Williams call about a missed appointment?"

"No," she said, shrugging her shoulders.

He nodded again and turned away.

The Reverend's card was still in his wallet, so he picked up the phone in his office and dialed.

"First Baptist Church." A soft female voice, smothering a laugh as she answered.

"I'm trying to reach Reverend Williams."

"He's down in the basement practicing his sermon," the woman said. "If you hold awhile I'll go get him for you."

He held. A minute passed, then two. Voices came to him, and more laughter.

"This is Reverend Williams. To whom am I speaking?"

"Michael Grant."

"Ah, the doctor."

"I'm sorry if I interrupted you."

"Interrupted me? No, you didn't interrupt me."

"Your son did not show up for his appointment today."

"He didn't?"

"No, he didn't. I'm happy to see him, but he has to keep his appointments."

"I understand," the Reverend said. "Please accept my apologies."

"His blood work is concerning."

The line was quiet for a moment. He heard music now, in the background, a heavy sound of drums and bass.

"I'll try to find him," the Reverend said at last. "Do you mind if I call you tonight at home?"

"Not at all," Michael replied. "Call my cell phone. I keep it with me. You have the number on my card."

Reverend Williams thanked him and hung up. Michael felt suddenly tired. It was an effort to pick up the chart of the afternoon's first patient.

His telephone rang at 8 P.M. that evening. He knew, even as it chirped like a small bird in the pocket of his jacket, that it was the Reverend.

"I am sorry to inconvenience you, doctor."

"It's no problem."

"I have a favor to ask."

The man's tone was diffident, even soft. He heard the sound of cicadas in the background.

"Are you outside?"

"I'm calling from a pay phone. I'm standing on the corner of Cameron and Assisi. Near the stadium. Do you know where that is?"

"Is Jonas there?"

"Yes. I'd like you to come and see him. He's not himself."

"What do you mean?"

"I mean," Reverend Williams said, "that he's confused. He's better now. But he was confused."

"I don't make house calls, Reverend."

"I understand."

Michael was silent, thinking. "Maybe you should call an ambulance, if you're that concerned."

"I don't think that is necessary. He's improving. But I'm asking for your help, doctor."

A hint of insistence now. The Reverend's hard dry palm, firm on the receiver.

"I know where you are," Michael said. "Give me half an hour."

REVEREND WILLIAMS STOOD QUIETLY BESIDE THE TELEPHONE BOOTH. He was good at waiting and in fact had prided himself on his patience in the past. Where others paced and looked at their watches, where others grew angry in the face of trivial concerns, Reverend William remained calm and dignified in his own eyes. Even now. The minutes passed. The street was empty.

The doctor was good as his word. His car—Reverend Williams knew it was his car, even when he first saw the lights—eased to a stop by the curb twenty minutes later, with the doctor's pale face shining like a lily through the windshield. There was a small electric sound, and the driver's window fell away. For an instant, the two men looked at each other before speaking.

"Good of you to come, Dr. Grant."

The man nodded. "What can I do for you, Reverend?"

"May I?" Reverend Williams gestured with his left hand toward the car.

"Of course." There was a click of unlocking knobs. Reverend Williams walked stiffly through the headlights to the passenger side, then bent, opened the door, and lowered his weight with difficulty into the front seat, holding the roof as he did so.

Reverend Williams was a big man, Michael realized suddenly, and again. He felt the car shift and settle and then felt the door close and the man's presence beside him as Michael looked out into the street.

"It's the rheumatism," he said. "Maybe you can give me something for it."

Michael smiled politely.

"Jonas tried to keep his appointment with you today."

"He did?"

Reverend Williams nodded. "He told me that he could not find your office."

"He's been to my office."

"I know. That's why I grew concerned. He told me he lost his way and it was difficult for him to get back home."

"Did he tell you why?"

"He was not seeing well. He could not remember the streets. He was disoriented."

"Have you seen him? Or did you just talk to him?"

"I've seen him."

"And you want me to go see him now?"

"Yes, Dr. Grant, I do. Would you be so kind?"

There was a sudden change in his voice, in the posture of his body on the seat, and for the first time, Michael felt a hint of weakness. For a moment, the man seemed tired and uncertain; though he tried to hide this uncertainty, it was there. Michael glanced at him again: the lined face, the hair a woven gray at his temples.

"Tell me where to go," Michael said.

The trailer was on unpaved ground, set back from the road, with trash in the weeds and lilac bushes beside it. A cheap place, a worn-out mobile home, Michael realized, the kind rented by the week or month, with an old electric stove and stained plastic sinks. It sat on cinder blocks, surrounded on three sides by a heavy tangle of brush. Fifths of cheap vodka, coughing, blind sleep—a place where business is done. Fans for the heat. Michael's car shone in the streetlight a few yards away, like something wet and newly made, and Michael watched it. They stood at the door, and then the Reverend knocked and called out.

After a moment, the sound of locks, and a slice of yellow light widening across their feet. The Reverend inclined his head toward Grant and entered the room, leaving him in the doorway.

For a few seconds, Michael did not follow. He stood there, with the curious sensation that time had slowed. He was aware of his breathing; he was aware of the wide night and the lights, and the sound of low voices flowing out of the half-open door, even as he walked forward and closed the door behind him.

The main room of the trailer was simple: an unmade single bed, brown shag carpeting, faded white walls. Over the bed hung a print—Monet's *Water Lilies,* he realized abstractly, incongruous as it was. A duffel bag in a corner. The odor of unwashed clothing and something else, acrid. A stranger's room. A place where the poor traveled and into which the homeless sometimes rose.

Jonas Williams sat in the corner on a stained green armchair. There was no television, only a low table with an ashtray. Two dead white cigarettes lay there. A third burned, uncoiling its gray threads up the drawn curtain over the window. As Michael entered, Jonas leaned forward, lifted the cigarette to his lips, drew on it once, and quickly, then ground it out. The bloom of the coal. A single cough, his hand to his mouth. He looked up.

The man's face was expressionless, with wisps of smoke easing from his lips. Michael couldn't see anything there, at least not now—no fear, no anger. Nothing but absence.

"Be respectful, Jonas," Reverend Williams said, from where he stood across the table. There were no other chairs in the room.

Jonas glanced once at his father and then stood. "Thank you for coming, doctor," he said calmly, looking at Grant.

"Please don't get up."

Jonas Williams shrugged and sat down again. The smell of smoke came to Michael strongly.

Jonas looked no different from the last time Michael had seen him. As both men looked at him, Michael stood awkwardly, walked over to the bed, and sat down on the tangled sheets. They were damp beneath his hand.

"So what happened today, Mr. Williams?"

"I don't know."

"You don't know?"

"I got lost. I couldn't remember where I was."

"Do you remember where my office is?"

"I remember now."

Michael thought for a moment. "What do you remember about this afternoon?"

"I remember going to your office. I remember the sun was real bright."

"The sun was bright?"

The man nodded. "Bright," he said. "Different colors."

"And you lost your way? Could you see?"

"I could see. But there were too many streets. Like a spiderweb."

"Like a spiderweb?" Michael felt himself growing calm.

"Streets going everywhere. I couldn't read the signs. I felt like I'd never been there before."

"How long were you out walking?"

"I walked a good while," Jonas said quietly, as he looked away. "I almost didn't get back."

"But you did get back."

"I guess."

"How did you get home?"

The man rubbed his eyes. "Fire hydrant," he said.

"Fire hydrant?"

"I saw a yellow fire hydrant. It's on the corner. It led me back."

Michael was silent again. He stroked his chin, holding his arms close to his chest as he sat on the bed.

"Has this ever happened before?"

"No," Jonas said.

"Mr. Williams, is there anything else? Have you been seeing things? Have you been hearing any voices? Do you know what I'm asking?"

"I'm not crazy. I know what you're asking."

"Well?"

"No. But I've been having dreams."

"What kind of dreams?"

The man shook his head, smiling a bit now. So he is not so stoic, Michael thought.

"Bright dreams."

"Bright? You mean colorful?"

"No. Bright. Bright lights. Shadowy too."

"And you've been sweating."

"How did you know that?"

"The sheets," Michael said, gesturing. "They're damp."

"I wake up wet."

Reverend Williams was watching intently, back and forth, as if at a tennis match. "Tell him what you dream about, Jonas."

Jonas looked up and met Michael's gaze directly. "Sometimes I dream," he said, "that the Devil is bathing me. I dream that I'm wet from the Devil's tongue."

Michael might have smiled or even laughed. But the Reverend was looking at him with the face of certainty, and therefore he allowed himself to feel the brief chill that was required. The Devil bathing him. Damp sheets.

"You're probably having fevers at night," he said lightly, "that's all."

The three of them were quiet again, until Jonas spoke.

"You don't know what I've got. But my father thinks he does."

Michael looked quickly at Reverend Williams, who did not respond or give any sign that he had heard.

"Mr. Williams, do you mind if I ask you to do a few things? They may seem strange."

"You're going to test my mind?"

"That's one way of putting it. I want you to start from one hundred and subtract by seven. I want you to keep subtracting seven from each number and say it out loud."

"Ninety-three," Jonas said.

"Go on."

"Eighty-six."

"Keep going."

"Seventy-eight."

Reverend Williams watched him.

"Seventy-two."

"I want you to remember three objects," Michael said, looking around the room. "I want you to remember that painting. I want you to remember the doorknob on the door. And I want you to remember a coin." He held a dime from his pocket up in the air, where it shone for a moment.

"All right."

"Good. Please continue."

Jonas Williams rubbed his eyes again. "Where was I?"

"Seventy-two," his father said.

"All right." He took a breath. "Sixty-seven."

"Jonas, were you good in school? Did you graduate from high school?"

"I graduated."

"He could easily have gone to college," the Reverend said.

Michael nodded. "Keep going."

"Sixty."

"Good. One more."

Jonas Williams looked as if he were making a great effort. "Fifty-two," he said.

"Good." To pass a little more time, Michael stood and approached. "Do you mind if I look in your mouth again?" he asked.

Jonas glanced at his father, but then he shrugged and stood and opened wide.

Michael did not have a penlight, and the lights in the room were not quite strong enough, but when he bent his head, and peered into the recesses of the man's throat, it was clear that the white lines had receded significantly. He could barely see them now.

"Your mouth looks better," he said, looking again.

Jonas closed his mouth and stepped back. "It comes and goes," he said. "Like my eye."

Michael looked at him for a while, letting his mind wander back through the many textbooks he had read, but again nothing came to him.

"Jonas," he said, finally, "those three objects I asked you about. Do you remember them?"

"The flowers in the water," Jonas said. "Like in the painting."

"And the others?"

"The door," he said. "The doorway. The door."
"That's close enough. And the last one?"
"Money," he said.
"Money?"
"A coin," he said. "I think it was a coin."

Michael and Reverend Williams walked out together toward the car.

"Was Jonas really a good student?" Michael asked, as they crossed toward the pool of light.

"He was, doctor. He could easily have gone to college."

"Do you think under normal circumstances he could have subtracted more accurately?"

"There's no doubt in my mind. None at all."

Michael felt his mind working in the dark as they walked toward the car. "I want to see him in the office," he said. "Can you bring him?"

"When?"

He thought. "I can fit him in the day after tomorrow, at noon. Can you do that?"

Reverend Williams nodded. "It's affecting his mind," he said.

"Right now, Reverend," Michael said, "you know as much about this as I do."

"It might be that I know more."

"If you do," he said, "now is not the time to keep it from me."

"Jonas . . . ," Reverend Williams said, as if he meant to continue. But then he was silent.

"Where's your car?" Michael asked, after a moment.

"I walked here. Sometimes I go walking at night."

"In that case," Michael said, "let me take you home."

He drove, following instructions—right here, two blocks down on the left—stopped by a small house with a rose garden out front, and turned off the engine.

Reverend Williams sighed and ran a hand again across the tightness of his hair. "Why don't you come inside," he said at last. "Unless you have someplace else to be."

"I don't have anyplace else to be," Michael said.

Reverend Williams looked over at him, and Michael again saw a hint of vulnerability, a sadness. It was not what he expected, and with it he felt the authority he had gathered—the interrogator's authority—begin to wane.

He felt intensely alert as they got out of the car and walked up the neat path to the door. The roses shone in the darkness.

"You're a gardener, Reverend," Michael said.

"It's a hobby of mine."

"They're beautiful."

"Thank you."

As Reverend Williams opened his front door with a heavy ring of keys, Michael thought he could smell the roses—delicate, almost unnoticed.

A short hall led into the living room. The walls were paneled with dark wood, and stood out in relief behind a cream-colored couch and dark red carpeting. A fireplace, with ashes, which struck him somehow as strange. He imagined the Reverend, in winter, reading in the leather easy chair by the television. Against one wall, a bookcase, filled to the ceiling. It was clear that Reverend Williams spent most of his time in this small room.

What struck him most were the photographs on the wall above the couch: two girls and a boy on the grass, dressed in their Sunday best, a smiling woman, and Reverend Williams beside her, recognizable still, though many years had passed. His arm around her shoulders. The fading green of the grass behind them.

He stood for a moment, aware that the Reverend was watching him, aware of the inspection and the questions it would bring.

"Your family?"

The Reverend nodded. "My wife," he said. "She died eleven years ago."

"I'm sorry."

The Reverend nodded again.

"Your children?"

"My girls are doing fine. They're married now. Moved off."

"You haven't changed much."

Reverend Williams smiled. "Oh, yes, I have," he said. "I was stern back then. I thought that to be stern was to be strong."

"You still seem stern."

"Maybe I do sometimes. But back then I meant it."

The boy on the grass, wearing a suit, standing with his sisters, squinting into the sun, even then revealing nothing. After a sermon or before a sermon, who could tell.

"And that's Jonas?"

Reverend Williams nodded once more. "That's my son," he said. "I had hopes for him."

Michael was silent for a moment. "And what was it," he said, "that made you lose your hopes for him?"

The Reverend did not answer directly. "I'm going to have some orange juice," he said. "Can I get you anything?"

"Maybe a glass of water."

The Reverend made his way toward the hall and the kitchen beyond, briefly filling the doorway. Michael felt more awkward standing alone in the room, somehow, than he did with the Reverend beside him. There was plenty of time to look now: a brass lamp in the corner with a red shade, books on the shelves, photographs on the wall. Jonas as a boy, behaving well. He studied them for a while longer and then sat down on the couch against the wall. From the far room came the sound of cupboards, of liquids being poured, and a few moments later the Reverend returned carrying a tray with two glasses, one of water, the other of orange juice the color of sunflowers, which he raised to his lips.

Michael felt a sudden thirst as he lifted the glass in his hand. The water was cold enough to make his throat ache, but nonetheless half the glass was empty when he put it down again.

"Every so often I need sugar," Reverend Williams said, wiping his mouth with the back of his hand. "I'm a diabetic."

Michael looked down at his own hands, pale, with a dusting of dark hair on the knuckles. He held them together for a moment before looking up again.

"Are you OK? " he asked.

"I'm fine now. Earlier I was a little shaky."

"Why isn't Jonas staying with you?"

"He wants to be by himself."

"I don't understand."

"Let me show you something," the Reverend said, rising from his chair. He walked to the bookcase, withdrew a thick notebook, turned, and sat down next to Michael on the couch.

"We did this for each of our children," he said. "This is for Jonas."

Michael took the volume in his hands and opened it. It was an album, each page neatly covered in plastic. A birth certificate, with its little footprint, on the first page. And then the first photograph—black and white, a woman holding an infant in her arms, looking shyly into the camera. A time and date, with a fountain pen. He looked up.

"Are you sure you want me to see this?"

"You said you wanted the story," he said.

A child's crude drawing, the colors of the crayon untouched and new. A first report card. *Jonas is a good boy. He is very well behaved.*

Later on, a red ribbon, by itself on the page.

Sunday school. *I feel sorry for Joseph. It was hard for him to get out of Egypt on the donkey, with the devil after him.*

As a slightly older boy, with a toy sailboat. Tenth birthday. His mother smiling in the background. She wore a uniform, a white dress, with a name tag, as if she was going to work.

"My wife," the Reverend said.

"Was she a nurse, Reverend?"

"Rosemary was a head nurse at the university hospital."

Junior high. *Jonas is an intelligent young man. But he has trouble concentrating.* The last sentence underlined in red.

A ninth-grade report card, As and Bs.

Jonas crouching in a football uniform, his right hand planted on the grass, the helmet beside him.

"Jonas," the Reverend said, chuckling, "was never much of an athlete."

Standing beside a pond, turning, smiling at the camera. Pines on the far shore.

"Our summer place," he said. "Jonas loved it up there. My wife died about then. It was harder on Jonas than the girls. They were older."

"Did she make this album?"

"Yes. But after a bit I started keeping it again."

Toward the end of the book, among the last few pages, was a letter. The handwriting was neat, and clear, and began with the words *For my father*. The pages were well worn, as if they had been handled over and over again.

"Jonas wrote that," the Reverend said.

Michael looked up. "Is it important?"

"It's how he told me he was leaving the church. That he had lost his faith. He wrote me a letter." Reverend Williams shook his head. "We lost touch for several years. I didn't even know where he was. And then he sent me this letter."

He paused.

"Do you know what it is like, doctor, to minister to people, to comfort them with scripture and pray alongside them, when your own son has turned his back on everything you know to be true? When you yourself have that terrible knowledge in your heart? Do you know what that is like?"

"No," he said.

"It is difficult, doctor. It is very difficult."

"Why are you telling me this?"

"I am a good judge of character, Dr. Grant. I can feel the Lord in people just as I can feel the darkness in them. And I feel the darkness in Jonas, though he is my son, and though I love him."

"Whether or not Jonas left the church doesn't mean anything, from my perspective."

"But it means everything from mine, Dr. Grant."

He's so absolute, Michael thought. It's all so clear to him. In that moment he pitied Jonas, whoever he was, and the burdens he must carry.

"It must be hard for him too," Michael said.

The Reverend nodded. "Judgment is hard," he said. "It's like grace. It works in mysterious ways. And we are all judged for our sins, Dr. Grant. Look at the last page."

It was the child.

"He didn't care," Reverend Williams said. "And that is something I can't forgive."

Jonas listened to them leave; he listened to their feet on the dry ground until they were gone. He felt relieved, free to do what he wanted, which was to sit in the dark and light another cigarette and smoke it slowly down to his fingers, peacefully, without thought. Thought, he knew, was coming with greater effort now. Where once his mind had tumbled and remembered, now it was a stone, a sleeping animal in its den, asking only to be undisturbed. It wanted to sleep, and he saw no reason not to let it, not his father and not the doctor, with his numbers and his assessing gaze from the bed. He watched the smoke flowing out of him, and it reminded him of winter, the quiet houses in the nearby countryside, his grandmother's cabin when it was cold, with maybe even the rare ghost of snow.

Another part of him knew this was not right, that the calm he felt was in itself something strange and wild that had come over him, along with his eye and his mouth and the growing weakness in his hands. His eye was often nearly blind now.

He wondered if the doctor would find it. The question hung there before him, like a jellyfish in deep water, before it too drifted out of sight. As far as questions went it seemed like any other, without power of the kind that catches you by the throat. It had been awhile since he felt this. Only the ache of his daughter reminded him—his little girl, her eyes shining under the mobiles, the way her mouth worked on whatever it was given. She had sucked on his knuckles, and he could feel her mouth there still.

He ground out the cigarette, rose and crossed to the bed, and lay down on his back. The ceiling was above him, with its cracks and faces. The line of yellow light under the door, the way it entered the room like a liquid and played across his feet.

After a while he fell into a kind of half sleep, barely aware of where he was. For the moment it was enough, it was more than enough, simply to lie there, and he would have, had the sound of voices and drunken laughter not woken him.

"I ain't got my shoes," a woman shouted, laughing, just outside his door. They were walking by, he thought, passing through. Then a man's voice: "Come on, honey, you won't need 'em. I'll carry you."

The woman laughed again, pausing to draw breath. The sound of footsteps. He wondered if the man, whoever he was, was carrying her now, down to where the dirt turned to asphalt. With difficulty, he squinted at the watch on his left wrist. It was nearly nine o'clock.

Time, he had begun to notice, no longer passed for him as it once had. The irregular leaps of time in the everyday world were now magnified to the point where he could not say if a minute had passed or an hour. And sometimes there were longer stretches, several hours, that passed with the speed of seconds. They were gone; they didn't even appear to him as gaps unless he examined them closely.

Something like that had occurred as he was trying to find the doctor's office. He had left a full thirty minutes beforehand, and then he had simply forgotten not just where he was but *when* he was. It might have been another day entirely, or another year. The appointment had seemed far away, and there were many streets and many reflections off the glass of passing cars. The faces of pedestrians had seemed irregular and fractured, as broken as mirrors, and there were shadows flowing by him on all sides, though it was a clear morning, with only the promise of heat distant over the rooftops of the houses. He might have tried to explain, but it was difficult; it was an experience unlike any other he had had. So he had walked and, after a while, found himself back by the corner of the street leading to his room, with the yellow fire hydrant as shining and glorious as one painted by a child. The sky was blue, with only a whisper of clouds, and the sounds of the street, of the morning life of workers and schoolchildren, had come to him as if from the bottom of a well. Though he was in it, though it was all around him.

Now the odor of the sheets came to him, the odor of his body where he had lain. The sheets felt as cool as tears, cool as his mother's arms, when she had held him as a boy with a fever. After a while he drifted off to sleep. In the morning she would be gone. Though he would call out to her.

Lying by himself, full of slow, icy thoughts—this was what he had come to. It was enough not to think, not to speak, not to listen. He imagined snow falling onto the roofs of houses all around him, though it was nearly summer now. Snow in the summer, with the boys who opened the throats of the fire hydrants and danced through them, their shorts soaked through and darkened to the same color—bare feet, ice on the streets. It was at once freezing and mild. He remembered how the mist had hung in the air and given them its blues and greens, little private rainbows. Oil in the puddles, or the shining dead wings of pigeons. Fish scales. Bruises and thunderstorms. My sisters.

Or years earlier: his father, calling, with his arms crossed at the other side of the pond near their cabin in the woods. *Go on, Jonas. Let it go*. And then in the gentlest of winds, its one sail filling like a handkerchief, the little boat eased out past the shallows, a growing wrinkle of water at the bow, steady and straight, crossing the fifty yards of space between them toward the green rushes of the far shore. They had watched it.

His father had taken off his shoes and socks, rolled up the legs of his pants, and entered the water, his feet slick and shining with mud. He had bent down and lifted the sailboat gently from the rushes and carried it back to shore. Here you go. A hand on Jonas's shoulder, steadying himself. Wiping the mud from his feet with a handful of grass.

Or his father's voice, late at night, when no one should hear. *Rose-*

mary. His voice, full of weeping and shaking. *Pray for your mother, Jonas. She died that you might live*. That's a lie, Reverend. She died because she died, no reason at all.

Or even other things: water, the drip from the sink. Sitting in the grass. The taste of beer on Sunday, the vague shame still with him after all this time. Things that did not matter, not even then, but that he remembered anyway.

It went on and on, and there was none of the release of sleep.

He felt a trickle begin in his mouth, as gentle as a feather. He swallowed, casually at first, like a sip of water at a public fountain. His blood was not warm exactly. It was almost cool, without any heart behind it. The blood of afterthoughts, of casual openings, of stopped drains in sinks left standing. It was easy enough to swallow, in little sips. A glass held up to his mouth, a thimbleful at a time, coating the softness of his throat.

A few minutes later he rose, went to the bathroom, took the roll of toilet paper from its bar, and brought it back to the bed. The bucket beside him was dry and clean—he remembered, vaguely, that he had washed it at some point not long past. He had poured its contents down the bathtub drain, washed it out with a yellow piece of soap, and then scrubbed the ring off the plastic walls of the weak tub, feeling it flex and bend on its mountings as he knelt there in the yellow bathroom light.

He packed his mouth again, the tissue tight against the unhealing wound inside his cheek. There was no pain. The doctor had said it would stop. And so it had, for a while. He thought of sprinklers, his father's expensive sprinklers for the roses, and how the heads rose at the push of a button out of the grass, and how they left little palm-sized glittering pools afterward.

Time passed, until again it was a plum he held in his mouth, dark and blue and sweet. The pit somewhere deeper, where he could not feel it. So it was wells and plums, prisms reflecting. This is only a room, he thought, with a hot plate. I am lying here listening. Nothing else.

After a while it occurred to him that he had not eaten. How long it had been, exactly, was unclear. It was important to eat, though, so he got up, with effort, and filled the pan with water from the bathroom tap. He turned on the hot plate by the window, wondering, for a moment, what to place in the water. There was a gust of wind, and the cheap curtain swelled against his face, waving gently over the pan. Something would come to him soon, something to sip, to quiet his belly, he thought, as he lay back on the bed. Don't worry, it doesn't matter. Go back to sleep, son. You were having a bad dream, that's all.

It was the Devil bathing me.

You have a fever, that's all it was. The Lord will protect you.

Like he protected your wife?

She was your mother, Jonas. Don't speak of her like that.

The plum was swollen to an orange now, and soon he would have to spit it out. Only one line to walk, one exact straight place to stand, and even then a slip was all it took. One slip, one small act. There is no such thing as innocence, Jonas. Remember that. No such thing. Not for you or anyone.

The feather began again, elsewhere. It was awhile before he reached down, knowing what he would find. A trickle of blood between his thighs, as slick as oil. I've wet the bed.

It was this sense, more than any other, that moved him, and he stood abruptly, with one hand on the side table, feeling the red line go loose and runny down his legs. There was no pain; none of this had been painful. But he felt light and strange. His eyes darkened and flickered and nearly went out. He stood there, feeling the weight of his hand against the bedside table, pushing down hard to keep himself from falling. Then the steps to the bathroom, one after the other, his eye steadying again, his socks darkening already.

The light was on, and he fumbled with his pants. A glimpse of his slim brown legs, his red-streaked calves. The sucking sounds of his shoes. He turned, then half fell back onto the toilet. The startling cold of the black plastic seat against his thighs. His body, relaxing, though there was no need, because it gasped out of him anyway. Someone else's hoarse voice, like a cough, and then it ran as straight as a faucet into the water. One minute, two . . . ten seconds, fifteen . . . he couldn't tell. His face felt shiny, his forehead and his lips and the tips of his fingers tingled. He felt himself sliding backward, sliding though he pushed his legs straight out before him, and reached out toward the sink, though it was too far away to steady him.

Then a pause, as if to give him a few more seconds to compose himself. Just a little while. It was happening fast now. He was in the blinding moment, it was all around him and inside him, where only a few hours before it had been as distant as hills. There was nothing to do now but sit and gasp. He waited, looking down at his slick feet and ruined shoes. With an effort he toed them off, slid them toward the corner. *You won't need 'em, I'll carry you.* His feet were wet. He felt himself settling, his breathing coming down to rest, the gurgling in his belly receding. So he had a little more time. He felt alert now, more alert than he had for weeks. In a few more minutes he would be well enough to stand.

He stood slowly, pausing for what seemed a long time before bending down and pulling up his pants. He took a few steps and came to rest against the sink. There it was, in the mirror: his face, his bloody lips, and his dead left eye. He stepped up closer, then closer still, until the bad eye grew clear in the good. The surface was covered in white threads, twisting in and out of the depths. The pupil did not move, whether he closed it or opened it. Whether he looked up or down. The white was bone china. The eye of a doll, an inanimate thing.

His mouth was full, his cheeks bulged. He bent his head down and spit, gagging for an instant. The clot fell out of his mouth into the sink with the sound of a hand flat against a cheek. He felt his teeth again, his thin tongue along the ridges.

When he looked up again he saw it completely: the blue skin; his lips, black and red; his eye; the floor behind him. The bruises even now blooming on his hands where he pressed down.

It came as suddenly as thunder or an animal's cry, which is what it was. He was crying, he was making sounds. It was the clear part of him, not the cloudy part that had taken him here; it was crying over what it saw, a pure flush of terror through him, a blown open door, a red flower in a field of snow, a siren, a knife through a fingertip. Desperation, which even as it filled him, finally and completely, he knew would pass, and flow off, and be done with him.

After a moment, his fear eased. He was standing in the bathroom, his hands sliding on the countertop. He saw this clearly. And then he turned and made his way back to bed. He walked as if drifting. One step, another, a third. Two more to be there. Maybe there is nothing liquid left. The pot on the hot plate began to tick, and the curtain floated back and forth above it.

He half fell, his torso on the sheets, his knees on the stained carpeting. Another effort, and he was fully above the floor, rolling over, his mouth leaving a dark smear on the pillows, just visible in the half dark. The skin of his knees ached and tingled and blossomed. He was lying down now on his back. The sheets beneath him, the bedspread he found the strength to pull across his chest and belly. His feet, wet in the cold, drawn up. The light from the bathroom cast out into the room. No one can see me now. No one can look at me. Vaguely, it occurred to him that his face was back there in the mirror. He had left it, like a photograph suspended from a fishing line. A clear tendril, one made visible only by reflections.

Dial tones, the hint of other voices, other conversations. The battered telephone of the bus station in town, where he had walked down from the woods in the morning. A place where small and desperate things were asked, where news was given and received. The memory of it. I want to come home. Seat 5A. A window.

Probably, he slept.

Late that night, the Reverend Williams's telephone rang. He had been sleeping deeply, and for long seconds he did not understand what he was being told. He realized only later that Jonas must have given his number to the landlord.

The glow of the fire rose through the trees. It grew brighter as he turned into the narrow street, the tires of his old car shrieking, and when he reached the rough dirt end it was so bright he could no longer see the beams of his headlights.

Then the fire trucks, the ropes of water from the hoses, the lights, red and blue and red again, the men in their gear, the man with the torch, trying to wave him by, then turning it in his face through the windshield, even as he threw himself out of the car and the fireman moved to stop him.

Most of the trailer was engulfed in flame. The remainder steamed and smoked and trembled under the cold weight of the water, and he could hear it, twenty yards away—the sound fire always makes, the sound of arrival, like a baby's cry. The thundering hoses swept back and forth in the lights, and the mist from the hoses filled the air and beaded the sides of the pumpers.

A crowd stood by and watched.

"My son is in there," he said again, to the firemen, and the faces of the crowd around him changed, like a ripple from a stone cast in still water, and they looked at one another and eased away from him, and finally one of firemen touched his shoulder and spoke, gently.

"I'm sorry, sir. No one is allowed past the tape."

It seemed dreamlike, impossible—the fantastic shapes, the half-lit faces of curious neighbors, the roar of the hoses, the heat on his face, and the shining puddles in the ground around the trailer. Even the final collapse of the roof, with its cascade of red and yellow sparks and the sound it made, the *whoosh* like that of a man being struck in the belly—he could not believe it even as he believed it, even as he stood there and watched the fire keep burning until it stopped. They played the water—a single hose—so casually, then, into the smoldering coals, and the supply of hisses seemed endless.

Somehow, hours later, he had found his way back home; somehow his own car carried him away. He could not remember the journey or their questions. The world: stopped utterly and struck dumb. *I'm sorry, sir. No one is allowed past the tape*.

By morning he lay in the double bed he had shared with his wife, feeling the emptiness of the sheets, remembering the smell of her perfume. There were times, though many years had passed now, when she came to him so strongly he believed her to be real. But this was not something one spoke of, so he kept it to himself. Now, though, he wanted to feel some echo, however slight, of her presence, though what came to him was only his own body on the clean and empty bed. He had done a wash only two nights before. How time passes.

The telephone rang several times. It was determined, an old rotary made from dark green plastic that he had never seen fit to replace. It had a true bell, loud enough to hear through the roar of a shower, and now it rang on and on until whoever it was saw clearly enough that no one was coming. It stopped for a few minutes, then began again. He did not answer. He did not trust himself to speak. In a few hours he would be able to trust himself again, he believed, a few more hours, but at the moment there was no respite, nothing that could save him. I will think only of Rosemary. Only of her and her gentleness, and of how much I miss her, and how happy I am that she is gone on this day.

Images were falling all over him—random, like the shuffling of cards. He was a very young man, on the lawn with his friend Isaac. Isaac had a new .22 rifle and sat a few feet away, working and unworking the bolt, popping the little bright bullets out of the magazine and onto the mown grass. A sunny day. Then the sudden crack of the gun, the look of surprise and fear on Isaac's face. He saw this first, before he saw his own hands, reaching down, from far away, to his thigh. The little black hole in the center, the blood coming up as if from a tiny well. That moment, suspended, and only then the sear, the brush of a hot iron and the ache beginning, and his terrified friend rushing toward him, long after he himself knew it was not serious. Through and through, the bone untouched. A slip, nothing more, healing in a week. He had not even gone to the doctor. It was another age. But there was something about that moment, as he'd looked down at his wounded leg, before any pain at all, something about the look on his friend's face and the sweet smell of the cut grass and the sound of bees, that called him back across forty-five years. He thought of this, and he thought of Rosemary, his sweet wife, and it was all he could do to center his thoughts on her face and her hands and the way they held him still in his dreams.

There was a knock on the door, then another. The brass ring, almost never used. Silence for a while. He got up then, not to answer but to open a slice of light in the blinds, watch the man head back for his car and get in. The doctor. For a moment he felt his anger begin, but just as suddenly it was gone. Across the road, the doctor sat in his car, blinking with uncertainty.

He sat back down on the bed. The lash of judgment—and when, Thomas, do you turn it on yourself? What could I have done? Let me lie down with my wife now. How much is that, among all the wishes in the world, to want? The doctor was gone. He would call again, and sooner or later they would have to speak. He felt the hours passing, though he did not look at the clock again. The telephone rang three separate times. The room was shuttered, but nonetheless he sensed the lengthening shadows of the afternoon, the presence of others on the street as the day ended. He heard the slamming of car doors; he heard the voices of neighbors. His heart felt slow and steady in his chest, and his breath came easily, and from this he was forced to conclude that it would not stop, that it would go on no matter what had happened or what was yet to happen.

It was dark. He could barely see his hands outstretched before him. Nonetheless he lay awake, thinking of his wife and of his son, as the streetlights spilled off-yellow in the driveways. The pond in the scrub pines by their summer place, spring-fed, muddy nonetheless, and Jonas as a small boy, dark and sleek, swimming out, his tiny head crossing between the patches of sun and shade, as Rosemary watched anxiously from the shore.

My son, my young man. Your gentleness, your hands and eyes and footsteps. Your shyness in rooms, in kitchens. Your cries in the night.

That morning, Michael had woken early, with the sense that he had not slept at all. He lay there, knowing he had hours before daybreak. The sounds that came to him were dim and inhuman. He might be, he thought, the only person awake at this moment, and the notion pleased him. To be alone in a crowd of sleepers, his thoughts untroubled by voices. The breeze lifting the branch of the oak, dew in the grass below. It felt like childhood, and for a while it felt almost like comfort.

The sky outside grew lighter, and with daylight came a red glow in the east. With a start he cast off the bedclothes and stood up. He was shirtless. Stepping up to the window he felt the cold of the glass. He stood just close enough for his breath to cloud his view of the street, and the houses on each side, and the indistinct fields in the distance, as the sun glided out of the low trees.

He realized, as he stood there, beginning to shiver, how tired he was. Nothing he could do today would matter much. There was no urgency that he could see, unless it was to call the pathologist about the biopsy results, which he could do just as easily from home. He thought of coffee and rolls, of newspapers, and the quietness of his house. I am not, he thought, Ronald Gass. Because look where it got him.

He turned away from the window, walked back to the bed, and slid under the sheets again, his bare back against the headboard. He reached for the telephone on the nightstand.

The recording came on—you have reached the offices of . . . our office hours are . . . if this is an emergency, hang up and call 911—and he waited patiently, pressing the black buttons on the telephone with his thumb. *Susan, it's Michael Grant. I won't be coming in today. Please tell my patients I will reschedule.* He took pleasure in the fact that he did not lie, which was nearly the same, he thought—though not quite the same—as telling the truth.

He wondered if it had been a mistake not to go to work. It was too late now, of course. I'm waiting, he realized, I'm waiting and waiting, and I'm thirty-five years old, and there will be more of it, great reams of it, to come.

I need to put Jonas Williams in the hospital.

The thought hit him with force. He wasn't sure exactly why—the man had looked all right in his trailer, and his mouth seemed to be improving—but now it came to him powerfully. At times he had relied on this feeling with his patients and had been correct, wondrously correct in at least one case he could recall. Other times it had failed him. Nonetheless it was the kind of feeling that was impossible to ignore.

He waited awhile, until the church would be open, and then finally found the card in his wallet and dialed the number. The telephone rang.

"First Baptist Church."

"Reverend Williams, please."

"The Reverend is not in today. Do you want to leave a message?"

"Do you know where I might reach him?"

"I can take a message."

"This is urgent. Do you have any idea where he is?"

"Who is calling, please? Are you a member of the congregation?"

"Dr. Michael Grant. I'm not a member of the congregation."

"Well, you could try him at home if you have the number."

"Do you have the number?"

"I'm sorry, we don't give out his home telephone number without his permission."

Michael glanced down at the card and it was there, in pencil, scrawled in a thick hand. He remembered, suddenly, the Reverend, touching the pink tip of his tongue to the point before writing.

"Never mind. Please tell him I called."

"All right. Yes, sir. He'll be here tomorrow."

He listened to the dial tone for a few seconds, the deepness and distance of it, with the brush of static. The Reverend's telephone rang and rang. There was no machine, which did not surprise him. He would try again later, and again after that, he thought, and then he would probably have to get into his car and find him. He imagined Reverend Williams outside weeding, wearing knee pads.

He dressed hurriedly and went downstairs to the kitchen, where the coffeepot waited. He spooned the black powder into the paper filter, poured tap water into the white plastic of the machine, and flipped the switch that lit the red light and began the first stirrings of vapor and heat. In a few minutes the kitchen filled with the smell of coffee as it dripped into the glass pot. He drank it black, sitting in the light of the living room, which just now was letting in the warmth of the day. Grains of dust lit up over the carpet, and he watched them drift and boil in the faint currents. Silent, so close to stillness, and yet they moved, they tumbled as if through water, like coins fluttering to the bottom of a pool. The coffee was both bitter and pleasant in his mouth. He felt awake now, fully awake and alert, with the barest touch of guilt for where he was and for where he was not. A child, home from school. Just old enough to be alone. Long ago, but he could feel it, he could imagine the sound of his mother's key in the lock, her coat smelling of winter as she bent down to him, her cold hair falling against the heat of his cheek.

"Dr. James, please." He spoke casually into the phone. It was nearly ten o'clock.

"This is Dr. James."

"Sam, it's Michael Grant. I'm glad I caught you. Have you looked at the specimen I sent you?"

"Yes, I did it yesterday. Unusual specimen."

"What did you find?"

"Nothing malignant. Just some inflammatory changes. But are you sure it was an oral lesion?"

"I'm sure."

"Well, that's puzzling, because the cells looked almost like osteoblasts. It looked more like periosteum than epithelium."

"Did you see any organisms on the gram stain?"

"No, I didn't. No bugs at all. I sent it for culture, though, like you asked."

"Viral cultures also?"

"Yes, and fungal. But you know that will take weeks."

"Osteoblasts? Are you sure?"

Osteoblasts, laying down calcium. The cells that create bone.

"I'm not positive. It was a small specimen, after all. It would be nice to have more tissue to work with. But that's what they looked like. Mixed in with epithelial cells, of course. I'd recommend repeating it. Do a true excision, not just a punch biopsy. It would give me more to work with."

"Do you know what it is?"

"With such a small sample it's hard to say. But I don't think I've seen anything like it."

"Do you know of anything that could cause osteoblasts to form in an oral lesion?"

"No," Sam James said, after a moment of thought. "I don't think I do."

Two hours passed. Reverend Williams did not answer. Finally he put on his shoes, his suede jacket. He glanced at himself in the mirror by the door and ran a brief hand through his unwashed hair, parting it roughly.

He found the house without difficulty, though he had been there only in darkness. He got out, walked the few steps to the door, knocked with the brass ring, waited, and knocked again, peering cautiously into the kitchen windows. The room was empty, as best he could tell. Dishes, drying in the rack. Blinds drawn on the other rooms. The car was gone, unless it was inside the small garage. No answer. Nothing to do but get back in his own car. He sat there, considering, and after a while he drove home again.

Article after article, abstract after abstract, back ten years, then fifteen, then twenty. The whir of the machine. He typed. He felt like running, but he did not want to leave the telephone. Why he felt such urgency, such restlessness, he could not exactly say. Nonetheless it was there; it was with him all through the afternoon. And so he searched the computer, and paced, and watched the shadows of the trees lengthen outside his front window and the yellow folds of sunlight flow up the flat surface of the lawn toward the bushes.

At six o'clock, when he knew that Ronald Gass would have just arrived home, he picked up the telephone once more, fumbling in the black leather of his address book as he did so. Even as he dialed, he wondered. But he needed another opinion, he knew, he needed it from someone experienced, and the only person he could think of who could provide this on such short notice was Ronald Gass, though he wished it otherwise.

"Hello," Gass said. Michael suspected that he rarely received personal calls these days.

"Ronald, it's Michael. I'm sorry to call you at home."

"That's quite all right, Michael."

"I know this is a bit unusual, but I was wondering if we might discuss a patient of mine. I'd like to ask your opinion."

"A patient of yours?"

"Yes. It's a long story. It would be difficult to do over the phone."

"I see. When would you like to discuss it?"

"Well, I'm wondering if you'd be willing to do it now. This evening, I mean. Unless of course you have other plans."

"I have no other plans. Unless by plans you mean to watch the news and go to bed."

"I don't mean to impose."

"Not at all. Why don't you come over? I'd be happy to offer my thoughts, though I'm not sure they will come to much."

"Thank you, Ronald."

"You weren't in the office today."

"I was working on this case."

"Well, that's interesting. You're appealing to my curiosity. Why don't you come over in about half an hour."

"I think I should have asked you earlier."

"Well," Gass said, with a hint of dry amusement in his voice, "it's never too late."

Gass met him at the door and took his coat. Michael held a manila folder under his arm as he stood in the carpeted hall.

"Can I get you anything? A drink?"

"No, thank you."

"Well, I'll admit I wondered where you were today. You didn't seem ill."

Michael sighed. "I needed to work on this. I felt that it was important."

"So you canceled your appointments?"

"There was nothing that couldn't wait."

Gass nodded somberly and stroked his chin. "It is not something I would have done. But then, to each his own."

He felt a flash of anger. "I almost never do this."

"No offense, Michael. It's good to take a day off every once in a while. It's just that I'm of the old school. The world is different now."

"I did not take a day off. But maybe you should every once in a while."

"What do you mean?"

"Just what I said. Do you remember, when you were so tired that day, and I took you home?"

"Of course."

"Well, the next morning you came to work as if nothing had happened. I would never have known it. That's what I mean."

"So you think I shouldn't have come in?"

"Of course you shouldn't have come in. It was all you could do to get home. It was obvious you needed rest."

"Michael, for me work is rest. Perhaps that's the difference between us."

Michael did not know how to answer, so he simply shrugged and looked away.

Gass wore a gray cardigan, brown corduroy pants, leather loafers. He must have changed, after the office.

"Well, Michael," Gass said, after the moment had passed, "who is this patient you wanted to talk to me about?"

"Can we sit down?"

"Of course."

He followed Gass into the living room, which was as immaculate as ever. Again the sense of absence, the emptiness of rooms and space.

"Where's Nora?"

Gass turned suddenly, as if Michael had touched him on the shoulder. It was startling, so abrupt was his movement, and Gass must have realized it also, because he took a moment before answering.

"She's out," he said. "She's seeing an old friend from high school."

"Oh."

"Nora," Gass continued quietly, "has always been—how should I say it?—somewhat independent. It's caused problems."

"For you?"

"Well, yes, for me. But mostly for her."

"What kind of problems?" He couldn't help himself now, though he knew he was being impolite.

Gass smiled, but he was uneasy, it was clear, shifting from foot to foot, looking out over the room toward the curtained windows.

"She's disappointed me," Gass said finally. "She's intelligent. She is even, at times, industrious. But she's done nothing at all with her life."

"Most people don't."

Gass nodded. "Yes," he said. "That's true. But she might have tried."

"She told me about her bookstore."

Gass snorted. "She went to an excellent college, which I was happy to pay for. She almost finished a master's degree at an excellent university, which I was also happy to pay for. But she gave it all up to start a bookstore."

"What's wrong with that?"

"For ten years? To do nothing else? It was hopeless from the beginning."

"I'm sorry. I didn't mean to pry."

"Yes, Michael, you did mean to pry. It's quite all right. Is there anything else about her that you would like to know?"

"I was curious, nothing more. I'm sorry I asked."

"Don't be. I'm happy to tell you."

"I just wondered where she was, that's all." Michael looked angrily down at his hands. This odd man, full of unguessed calculations.

Gass seemed to be enjoying himself, smiling, rocking so slightly, back and forth and back again. "Well, Michael," he continued, after a moment, "tell about your mysterious patient. Can I get you a drink? I'm having a gin and tonic."

"Sure," Michael said wearily. "I'll have one of those."

As he sat on the wide gray couch, listening to the sound of ice and refrigerator doors, it struck him that this was exactly the position he'd been in at Reverend Williams's. The day before. How like and unlike both men were, strangers, from different worlds, both men gathering ice, coming back into the room. The death of wives or husbands, the troubles of children. The same story, again and again. Sooner or later everyone can tell it.

The gin stung a bit in his mouth as he sipped it. He placed the glass carefully on the coaster on the coffee table before him. Gass sat across the room in an easy chair. Michael picked up the manila folder, pulled out the history and physical that he'd typed himself, only a few hours ago.

"I might as well read it to you," he said.

"I'm listening."

"The patient is a black male in his late twenties," he began. "He came to my office a few days ago complaining of vision loss in his left eye and oral lesions. This had been ongoing for several weeks to months. He also reported night sweats and unusual dreams."

"I believe I saw him," Gass said.

"You saw him?"

"Yes, in the office. But don't let me interrupt. Go on."

Michael nodded. "His past medical history is unremarkable. He has no allergies. He takes no medications. His family history is significant only for diabetes. His mother died of ovarian cancer in her late forties. His father is a non-insulin-dependent diabetic who is otherwise in good health. He is married with one child, now deceased. He smokes approximately one pack of cigarettes per day. He drinks alcohol rarely. He has no identifiable risk factors for HIV infection. He has never had a blood transfusion. Review of systems is positive only for some mild confusion.

"On physical exam, he is an alert, well-nourished black male who appears in no distress. His vital signs are normal.

"His right pupil appears normal and is reactive to light. Fundoscopic exam on the right is normal. His left pupil is partly opacified and minimally reactive to light. There is an afferent pupillary defect. His retina appears grossly intact, though there is a notable weblike serpentine lesion involving both margins of the retina and extending centrally to the macula. Cranial nerves are otherwise intact. There is a notable serpentine lesion involving the posterior hard palate, the soft palate, and the buccal mucosa on the left side. The lesion is elevated, white, and does not easily scrape off with a tongue blade. The remainder of the head and neck exam is unremarkable. There is no cervical adenopathy.

"Both lungs are clear to auscultation. Cardiac exam is entirely normal. His abdomen is soft, non-tender, with good bowel sounds. No masses are present. There is no organomegaly. The genitals are normal. There is no cyanosis, clubbing, or edema of the extremities. There are no rashes.

"The neurologic examination is normal.

"Mini-mental status exam is significant only for poor serial sevens. He was able to remember three objects at five minutes with some difficulty.

"Laboratory examination is significant for profound thrombocytopenia, with a platelet count of thirty thousand, and a mild anemia. The remainder of the lab work is normal. HIV serology is negative, as is the RPR. A punch biopsy of the oral lesion is inconclusive. Cultures are pending, as is an MRI of the brain, a PPD, and a chest film."

He'd been reading in a monotone. He closed the folder and put it down on the couch beside him.

"Well," Gass said, "that was certainly a thorough presentation. It reminds me of grand rounds."

Michael took another sip of gin. "What do you think?"

"I'm not sure what to think. I would have thought of HIV, of course. But the serology was negative, you say?"

"Yes."

Gass stroked his chin. "It sounds infectious to me."

"That's what I'm thinking also. It's indolent. And it's systemic."

"If his platelets get too much lower he might bleed."

"That's what I'm most worried about at the moment."

Gass nodded. "What about a spirochete?"

"Possibly. But that should have shown up on pathology. I asked him to look."

"Nothing on microscopy? No organisms?"

"No."

"What do the lesions look like?"

"I wish I had a photograph. They look like little coils of white lines. Like worms, almost."

"I suppose it could be a parasite of some kind. Not one I've ever heard of, though. Cysticercosis, something like that. Any foreign travel?"

"Apparently not."

Gass was silent, thinking, stroking his chin again, almost in pantomime. "It's certainly an interesting case."

"Yes. It is interesting."

"Well, Michael, right now I have to say I'm at a loss. You say the pathology was inconclusive?"

"Yes, pretty much. Though he did say that some of the cells looked like osteoblasts."

"Osteoblasts?"

"That's what he said. I think the white lines might actually be bone."

"I've certainly never heard of that. I'm sure I would have remembered, though my memory is not what is used to be."

"I've never heard of it, and there is no record of it in the medical literature that I can find."

Gass looked up. "Are you certain about the osteoblasts?"

"No, I'm not. I need to get another specimen, more tissue to work with."

"Well, this is probably a case report."

"I think it's more than that. I think this may be a new disease."

"A new disease?" Gass chuckled. "I think that is premature, at the very least. Why don't you see where you are when you've finished your work-up?"

"I'm not making any announcements, but I think this will end up being something new. It's like nothing I've ever seen or read about, and I've been doing a lot of reading."

"Common things are common, Dr. Grant. It's much more likely an atypical presentation of a common thing. You know that as well as I."

"Maybe so."

Gass chuckled again, softly shaking his head. "I understand," he said, "that after the unpleasantness with the child your confidence was shaken. But don't you think you might be taking this a bit far?"

"I don't follow."

"Michael, there's no new disease here. How often is a new infectious disease identified? Once every twenty years, if that? And you think it will be by you? You think you will be the one who discovers it?"

"It happens."

"No, Michael, it doesn't happen. You're chasing shadows. It's an interesting case. But an interesting case is not a new disease."

Michael felt suddenly ashamed, deeply so. The ridiculous formality of his presentation, when a few words would have been sufficient. His phone call, after hours, his childish need to impress. All of this, and by proxy all of himself, splayed out in front of this man, all of this for Gass to mock and smile as he sipped his drink.

"It has nothing to do with the child."

"Well," Gass said, rising from his chair, "thank you for coming, Michael. If anything occurs to me I will let you know. And I'd be interested in what you find. You've got a fascinating case there. I'm sure you'll be up to it."

Michael stood also, by reflex. He didn't look at Gass but held the manila folder in his hands, listening to the words now flowing from the man's thin mouth, feeling utterly foolish. And beneath it a hint of despair, which is always, it occurred to him, what a fool feels.

"We'll see, Ronald," he said, as mildly as he could. "But thank you for listening."

"Of course. It was much more interesting than the news."

They were in the hallway now. The brass knob was in his hand, the door was open. The sound of cicadas was strong in the surrounding trees. Gass was a presence behind him.

"I may be wrong, Michael," Gass called after him as he crossed the lawn to his car. "Maybe you have discovered Grant's disease."

For a while, as he sat in his car, he considered going home again. But he felt Gass's mockery intensely, and the need to dispel it.

The lights were on in the windows of Williams's house. His knock was louder than he intended.

It was a few seconds before the door opened. The light above the door lit up the man's face and cast Michael's shadow behind him on the grass.

Reverend Williams looked exhausted, terribly old and worn, as he peered through the crack in the door. In an instant Michael knew that something had happened, that the telephone had gone unanswered for a reason.

"Reverend," he said, "I've been trying to reach you all day."

Reverend Williams opened the door wider, stepping out. He seemed to be squinting, and Michael realized that his eyes had not yet adjusted to the dark. But then he saw the change in the face, the tightening about the mouth, the sudden stiffening of the shoulders, as if bracing for a blow.

"It's you, doctor."

"Yes," he said. "Where have you been?"

"What do you want, Dr. Grant?"

"I didn't hear from you or from Jonas. I was worried."

The Reverend rubbed his eyes. His breath was shallow and quick; Michael thought he would speak, but he didn't. Instead, he turned away and walked back into the house, leaving Michael alone on the small porch.

Only a few seconds had passed, but the Reverend was already sitting in his chair when Michael followed him inside. A book lay open on the floor by his feet: a Bible. There was a scent of burned food in the house. Otherwise, the room was exactly as it had been.

"What's happened?" Michael asked, his voice rising; he felt his heart begin to race.

"Will you do me a favor, Dr. Grant?"

"What's happened?" he said again. It must be Jonas, he thought, it must be.

Revered Williams acted as if he had not heard the question. "Will you get me a glass of orange juice?" he continued quietly. "It's in the refrigerator."

"Are you all right?"

The Reverend nodded. "Yes," he said.

So he did as he was asked, and went into the kitchen, and found a clean glass in the drying rack by the sink, trying to calm himself. Something terrible had occurred, that much was clear. Again, he thought, here it is again. But nonetheless he poured the orange juice to the rim and carried it carefully back to the living room.

"Thank you," the Reverend said. He drank deeply, his throat working, as Michael watched him.

"Your blood sugar?"

He nodded. "It comes on fast," he said.

"Are you feeling better?"

"Why don't you sit down," the Reverend said.

Reverend Williams turned to him now, and Michael saw the face he had seen so many times, on so many people, just outside of doorways—the look of hallways, of hospital waiting rooms, the look of early morning hours, when the worst of all bad news is heard.

"They think he left his hot plate on," the Reverend said finally.

For a moment it seemed as if he would begin to sob, but he composed himself, wiped his eyes with the back of his flat brown hand,

and took another swallow of juice. Then he put down the glass, and turned to Michael, and told him.

Michael could not clearly remember the minutes that followed. What he had said in return, what gestures he had managed—he knew he had done these things, as one automatically does—but what he did remember, as he stepped out into the night air, was the sense that the ground was opening up beneath him. It was all falling on him, he thought, showing him his own failings in the clearest of lights. I should have put him in the hospital right away, he thought. I should never have waited. And why did I wait, when he was so obviously confused, so obviously not himself, when I left the trailer full of questions, what stopped me from doing the single necessary thing, which was to pick up the telephone and make a few calls, which now, in retrospect, was all that stood between that moment and this one?

He found the street easily and stood there a long time. The hoses must have run for hours, he thought, because there were pools of water where the trailer had been, filled with clotted ash. Cinders stained the grass, and forms were visible: a twisted length of pipe, a cracked white sink, a blackened, erect refrigerator, and there, in the corner, the skeleton of a bed frame, as dark as a winter branch.

Michael felt lost and weary when he arrived at work the next day. He was precisely on time, vaguely noticing that Gass's car was not yet in its accustomed space. He had not slept well. He'd been up all night, thinking about Jonas and his father and the fire and the little white tracks of bone. It was an effort to nod to Susan, and smile, and say good morning.

"Well, Michael," she said. "You must be feeling better."

"I am."

"I almost brought you some chicken soup."

He forced another smile. "No need for drastic measures," he said, and then patted her on the shoulder before making his way down the hall to his office.

He felt his face go blank again as he closed the door behind him and sat down at his desk. A neat pile of charts lay waiting for him. He thumbed through them quickly, and as he did so the contours of the day fell in place before him. Ten before lunch, eight after. Perhaps he could leave early. As soon as the thought occurred to him, he realized that he would do so, if at all possible. He would leave; he would walk and think. It was eight-thirty in the morning. In fifteen minutes, the first patient would come through the door. He picked up the phone and fumbled in his Rolodex for an instant before dialing.

A moment passed. A trickle of sweat fell from beneath his arm against his flank, inside his shirt, where no one could see it. Though he did not feel warm.

"Sam, it's Michael Grant."

"Yes, Michael. Do you have another specimen for me?"

"Unfortunately, I don't. But I was wondering if you might do me a favor." He was careful with his voice.

"Sure."

"You're one of the county coroners, aren't you?"

"I am."

"Yes. Well, this is an unusual request. One of my patients was just killed in a fire."

"I see," Dr. James said, in puzzled voice.

"He was the patient I biopsied. The one we discussed."

"You mean the one with the osteoblasts?"

"Yes. His name was Jonas Williams."

"If he died in a fire, there will have to be a post. It's state law."

"That's why I'm calling you. I need to know what the autopsy shows."

"That shouldn't be a problem."

"I think he had some sort of infectious illness, and it was progressing rapidly. I have no idea what it was. A detailed post could be extremely helpful."

"I'll give the morgue a call and see what I can find out. What was his name again?"

AS MICHAEL LOOKED AGAIN AT THE CHART HE HELD IN HIS HAND, IT struck him that there were at least two kinds of waiting. There was the waiting of silence, the waiting of an empty house, where the slightest sound—a ringing telephone, a knock on the door—was infused with significance. This was another kind, where he had to act in the world as if he were not elsewhere. To smile, and shake hands, and speak to his patients, coming through the door at fifteen-minute intervals.

During a quick break, he walked down the hall to the bathroom and washed his face. He dried his face with a rough brown paper towel and stood for a moment, at the mirror: He looked exhausted. He could see his own tiny reflection in his eyes, his white shirt shining in the corneas. Then he glanced at his watch and had to return to his office.

The minutes passed slowly. He knew these people or, rather, he knew the numbers that applied to them. The viral loads, the regimens. I'll see you in three months. You're doing very well. Thank you, Dr. Grant.

Right on schedule, almost two hours to the minute since they had last spoken, Sam James called.

"Well," James said, after the pleasantries, "they haven't done the post."

"When will they do it?"

"Today. But it doesn't sound like it will be very helpful."

"Why not?"

"The body was almost completely reduced to ashes. They said the only thing they had to work with is a pile of charcoal and two feet."

"Two feet?"

"Everything else was burned."

"But why didn't he escape? Smoke inhalation?"

"Probably, but we'll never know. No way to tell whether the fire came before or after he died."

Michael was silent, thinking. "Do they know the cause?"

"They think a hot plate was left on. It was by a window, near some curtains. But they also said the bathroom was full of blood."

"What?"

"The firemen tried to get inside. They said there was blood all over the bathroom floor and in the toilet, but they didn't see a body, just bloody footprints. But the whole thing was on fire and they had to leave. Those trailers go up fast. Turned out he was on the bed."

"When should I check back?"

"In a couple of days. I'll call them again."

"Thanks, Sam. I appreciate your help."

"Sure. Just don't send me any more referrals."

Michael chuckled, as was expected, and hung up the phone. Softly. Such a studied darkness, men like Sam James, who were, he knew, neither more nor less dark than anyone else. Pediatricians wore bow ties; pathologists spoke laughingly of darkness. It was expected of them.

When the last of the day's patients had left the office, he placed their charts in his OUT box for Susan to collect, put on his jacket, and went out into the hall. Again his thoughts returned to Jonas.

Just then Nora emerged from the library, with a notebook in her hand.

"Michael," she said immediately. "What's wrong?"

It must be clear to everyone, he thought. You never knew how close or how far you were from the world. Your own suffering was an intricate marvel of workmanship and craft, a jeweled puzzle of locks.

"I'm fine," he said.

"You don't look fine."

He hesitated. "A patient of mine died," he said.

"Oh, no." She gave him a look of concern.

He shrugged. "It happens."

"What did he die of?" They were standing in the hall, and he felt her gaze.

"I'm not sure," he replied.

"You're not sure?"

"His mobile home caught fire, but he might have been already dead."

"Why was he already dead?"

He looked away, wishing he'd said nothing. But she was staring at him, so he took a breath and continued.

"I think he was bleeding first, and couldn't get out of the trailer. It's a long story."

"Bleeding from where?" She looked troubled but also curious, as the well always are when contemplating the dark end of a stranger.

"From the intestines," he said, and she wrinkled her forehead and looked down.

"That's terrible," she said. "When did it happen?"

"Two nights ago. I talked to the pathologist about the autopsy this morning."

"I'm sorry, Michael," she said sincerely, and reached out and touched his arm. He realized she thought highly of him in that moment, that she believed he was a compassionate man.

"Well," he said, to change the subject, "how are the books going?"

"Who cares?" she replied. "Are you done for the day?"

He told her that he was.

"Do you have any plans for dinner?"

"No," he said. "I was going to pick something up on the way home."

"Good," she replied, looking at the small silver watch on her wrist, "Let's go get something to eat. I'm hungry."

The restaurant was a short drive from the office, a place she knew, and he followed her. The air smelled of broiled meat as they walked together from their cars across the parking lot, and he felt his mouth begin to water. He had not eaten all day, he realized, feeling a sudden intense hunger. His pants were loose around his waist and thighs; he had been losing weight, he knew, and now he felt his thinness, the lightness of his body.

They stepped into the foyer, allowing their eyes to adjust to the half-light. The dining room was to his left, full of low conversation and the whispers of eating. A woman laughed, high-pitched and long, and though he could not see her he imagined a head thrown back, a mouth open to the ceiling. Lipstick.

"May I help you?"

She was young, early twenties at most, and pretty, with short red hair and a thin black dress.

"We'd like to have dinner," Nora said.

"Do you have a reservation?"

"No," Nora said.

The woman looked down at a book. "Well," she said, "you're in luck. We have a table. Please follow me."

Michael watched the girl's body in her thin black dress, the line of her underwear just visible, as she seated them in a booth along one wall. He could see across the table into the bar from where he sat and, to his left, the expanse of the dining room. Candles, reflections, waiters in white shirts.

"Your server will be with you in a moment," the young woman said, giving them a bright disinterested smile as she walked away.

Nora snorted. "This place is never full," she said. "You never need a reservation. I only picked it because it's close."

"Is the food good?"

"It's adequate," she said. "Overpriced, anonymous, and average. Just like every other restaurant around here."

She looked around her.

"I used to work here, actually," she said. "A long time ago, but it's still pretty much the same."

"You did?" he asked politely.

"One of my college summers I waitressed here," she said, inclining her head toward the receptionist, who now stood tapping her pencil at her booth by the door. "I was exactly like her."

He nodded, placing his hands on the table before him. At the far end of the room a band was setting up to play. A flash of light caught the flat surface of a guitar; he could see the shine off the strings from the spotlight overhead.

There were three men in the band, a drummer, a bass player, and a guitarist. They were middle-aged men, two with hair going gray, one still dark, and they wore dress shirts and well-pressed pants. An earring sparkled. A few whispers into the microphone, a nod from the guitarist, the drummer tapped his sticks together once, twice, three times, and they began.

It was a slow, easy song, played softly, under the murmur of voices. A few bars passed, and then the guitarist began to sing in a clear tenor voice. It was a song he'd heard before, Michael knew, one whose chorus he remembered in that part of his mind which recalled such things, the part where he put half-forgotten faces or the rooms of childhood homes.

"Oh, my God," Nora said suddenly, turning in the booth. "He's still here!" She was looking at the band and shaking her head. "Ricky Blakewell," she said, as if in wonder.

"Who is Ricky Blakewell?"

She turned back to him. "He's the one singing. He was a couple of years ahead of me in high school."

"You should say hello," he said vaguely.

"He was going to be famous."

"What do you mean?"

She shook her head again. "He had a band in high school, and everyone thought he was going to be a rock star. He used to play when I worked here, and that was fifteen years ago."

"He's got a good voice," Michael said.

She nodded. "He thought he was going to be a rock star too," she said. "It's depressing, isn't it?"

Ricky Blakewell's black hair was carefully groomed, his face was expressionless, lips against the microphone, and his eyes were closed. Michael could have read anything there, but suddenly he felt pity for this man, nearing forty, keeping the volume low so the customers could eat.

As he looked down, he caught a glimpse of a woman's profile. She had turned her head for a moment, though she sat with her back toward him, at a small table down at the far end of the bar, at the edge of the few square yards of dark wood laid out as a dance floor. For a flash, for a heart-stopping moment, he thought she was Ann. But then she turned her head again, and she was a stranger.

"I was at your house again," he said. "Your father said you were out with a high school friend."

Nora looked at him, amused, and ran her hand through her hair. "He told me," she said, with a hint of a smile. "I was out with a friend. She's married and has two kids."

He looked down at his plate.

"Was that a subtle way of asking if I'm involved with anyone?" she said, smiling at him openly now.

He laughed uncomfortably and looked up at her. "Yes," he admitted, "I suppose it was."

She nodded. "I'm not," she said. "I've had a few serial boyfriends and left the last one approximately a year ago."

"Why did you leave him?" Michael managed.

"I think it was because he was a lot like Ricky Blakewell," she said.

"He was a musician?"

"No," she said, and smiled. "He was a banker."

It was nice, he thought, to be out in the world.

They ordered a bottle of wine with dinner. He drank the wine and felt it quickly, and when the food came he was ravenous.

"Well," she said finally, when they were done eating, "do you want to tell me about your patient?"

He shook his head, because suddenly he didn't want to think about it.

"It's not the best dinner conversation," he said.

"OK, then, tell me about your ex-wife."

"Do you really want to hear about her?"

"Would I have asked you if I didn't?"

"I'm not sure where to begin," he said, after a long pause.

"Did she leave you?" Nora asked bluntly.

"No," he said. "I left her."

Nora looked surprised and took another sip of wine. "Really?" she said, after a moment.

He nodded. "Why are you surprised?"

"I don't know. I just thought it was the other way around."

"I'm not sure it really matters," he said carefully. "We were very different. It was amicable."

"That's the kind of thing everyone says."

"All right," he said. "She's a cardiologist. She's extremely driven and very good at what she does. She's done well for herself. But I realized that I married someone I could never have."

"I'm not sure I understand what you mean."

He thought. "She was elusive. I'm not sure how to say it. She was unreachable. I liked it at first."

"You liked it?"

"In a way I did. Unreachable people are mysterious. Or so I thought."

"She was mysterious?"

"No," he said. "She was just unreachable. I didn't want to be my mother." He paused.

"What do you mean?"

"My mother was always trying to reach my father. She spent her whole life trying to find him, and I don't think she ever did."

"Are you in touch with her?"

"My ex-wife?"

She nodded.

"No," he said. "We've gone our separate ways."

Nora took another sip of wine and watched him. She smiled.

"You haven't told me about your mother," she said.

The question pained him, and he looked away. "She has Alzheimer's," he said. "I think she had the beginnings of it even before my father died. She's very confused now."

"Does she recognize you?"

He looked down. "Sometimes," he said.

"Where is she?"

"She's in a nursing home. I was going to move her here next year, if things worked out with your father. Physically, she's fine. She's not that old."

"I'm sorry, Michael," she said sincerely, reaching out and touching his hand, "That must be very hard."

"As your father said," he replied, "it's the way of the world."

"So what?" Nora said, taking a large swallow of wine. "That's no comfort at all."

He thought of his mother, smiling sweetly in her chair by the window, turning toward him as he entered the comfortable room. Only a month ago, on his most recent visit, she had stood and introduced herself.

"Did you and your father get along?" Nora asked, changing the subject, because it must have been clear on his face.

"We never understood each other," he said. "We were cordial."

"What did he do?"

"He was a navigator in the air force. He flew B-Fifty-twos. Later he flew for an air freight company."

"So you moved around a lot."

"Yes," he said. "Usually it was a new base every two or three years."

"Dr. Strangelove," she said, but he smiled and shook his head.

"Actually, they're just like everyone else."

"That's the problem, isn't it?" She fumbled in her purse. "Oh, well," she said, as she withdrew a cigarette and lit it, "at least we're in the smoking section."

Then she looked him in the eye, and blew a stream of smoke sideways out of the corner of her mouth.

"How do you get along with your father?" he asked

She inclined her head but didn't answer directly.

"I thought his heart attack might actually help him," she said, "but it didn't."

"He had a heart attack?"

"You didn't know?"

He shook his head.

"I guess I'm not surprised," she said. "He had a heart attack a couple of years ago. A mild one. Now it's his big secret. You probably shouldn't tell him I told you."

"Why does he keep it a secret?"

"Because of who he is," she said. "I was naïve to think it would change him."

It was uneasy ground, he realized, so he left it alone. But the news troubled and surprised him.

"Here," she said, reaching for the wine bottle and filling his glass. "Why don't you finish it."

"I'm no expert," he said, as he took a sip, "but this is pretty good."

"That's why I ordered it. I've always liked wine."

"It tastes like slate," he said, without thinking.

"Slate?"

"When I was a kid we had a slate porch. The sun used to warm it up even in the winter. I used to lick it. My mother hated that."

"Why did you lick it?"

"I liked the taste. It had this wonderful taste. The wine reminded me."

She smiled. "How old were you?"

"I was probably four or five. I've haven't thought of it in years. I can barely remember the house. We didn't live there long. But I remember licking that slate porch like it was yesterday."

It was true: the deep gray of the slate in the afternoon sun, half in the shadow of the eaves, the vast white rope hammock he lay in, which hung so low to the ground, and how he would drape his head over the edge and touch his tongue to the warm stone, swinging so slightly. And the marks his tongue made, little brushstrokes through the finest sheen of dust.

"What do you remember," he asked, "from when you were a little girl?"

"Oh," she said, "I don't know. I think I remember learning to walk."

"Really? You remember that?"

"I'm not sure. It's probably impossible. But I remember walking on the rug we have in the living room. I remember wearing a white dress, and walking from my mother toward my father across the rug."

"Could it have been later?"

"It probably was. But I remember my father calling me. He was calling my name, and I was walking toward him. And then they both clapped."

"It's a good memory, then."

"Yes," she said. "I think so. I suppose it doesn't matter when it was."

Later, after the check, which he insisted on paying, they stood together in the parking lot by their cars. It was a clear night, and the lights of the city flooded up into the sky. Only a few stars were visible. Her face was in shadow, and he could not see her expression.

"Thank you," he said, after a moment. "That was nice."

He caught a white flash of teeth as she smiled, and then, calmly, she stepped up and kissed him lightly near the corner of his mouth. He smelled perfume, and lingering smoke, and felt the warmth of her body as she stood close to him.

"I liked it," she said simply, as she stepped back and got into her car. He stood for a moment, watching her drive away, feeling a delicious tingle at the corner of his mouth, and as he drove home he realized that he felt better than he had in a long while.

But later that night, alone in his house again, the tingle slowly faded. The world felt strange now, kaleidoscopic, the easy flow of ordinary days mingling with the burned, blackened forms of the trailer, and the Reverend's face in the doorway, and Jonas, somewhere beneath it all, in ashes. An underworld, he thought, a place where things do not make sense, a place of patterns and forces, just beneath the surface of the everyday.

He would come to think of the days that followed as an island, a little island of time, the place between what had happened and what was yet to happen, a place to breathe and consider.

It had been one of those summer showers, brief and furious, spending itself in a few minutes and then letting the sun pick up after it. The morning had passed uneventfully, and it was lunchtime. He carried his umbrella, which he didn't need, out to the street, where the cars hissed and flung sheets of water onto the sidewalks. Underneath, the dim roar of the sewers, trailing off as the sun came out to work. His leather shoes were loud on the grit of the sidewalk, and already a dark line of water rose up from the soles.

There had been no further word; it was as if Jonas Williams had never existed. He exchanged pleasantries with Gass. Days passed, and he came to realize there was nothing more he could do. He could go to the office. He could carry on. But there was nothing else to be done at the moment, which was stretching out into days, and from there to weeks.

So there was a third kind of waiting. The waiting for the story to continue, the story that has begun, that has caught you, but that you can only partly see. The story that may go on without you.

These thoughts, and others, carried Michael to the park and through it. The streets and the passersby and the facades of the narrow brick townhouses in this part of town drifted through him without conscious awareness. It was as if he had become transparent, though his legs carried him along and he paused on the corners and looked left and right and waited for the correct moment to cross. No matter that he could not remember these simple acts only a few minutes later. He had experienced this while driving his car many times but rarely when walking. Walking bred close attention. Yet here he was, as if without warning, on a quiet side street, looking down at his watch. His watch told him he should have been in the office fifteen minutes ago, and he realized from this that he had been walking for the better part of an hour. Which meant that he would be late and there would be people waiting for him.

He stood in front of a yellow two-story clapboard house with white trim, a tiny square patch of green grass in front, and the facsimile of a picket fence. On both sides, other houses, much the same, ran off down the street. This part of town was full of such streets. Suddenly he realized that he had no idea where he was.

It shocked him. He had a powerful sense of vertigo, even of panic, as he stood on the quiet street with its neatly clipped lawns and good paint. He felt as if he might fall. He felt his breath coming suddenly and fast.

A woman was walking toward him. She was slightly stooped, with gray hair and thick white walking shoes of the kind that a certain generation of nurses wear. She wore gray khaki pants with many pockets, like those worn by tourists, and a blue blouse. The light caught her glasses so that for an instant it looked as if she were winking at him.

"Excuse me," he called, as she approached. She stopped, looked up, and smiled in that characteristic, tremulously inviting way of old women.

"Yes?" Her eyes were strikingly blue against her hair.

"I'm afraid I've gotten turned around. Do you know how I can get back to the park?"

"Do you mean Johnson Park?"

"Yes. I was trying to take a shortcut."

"Oh," she said. "Certainly. Just go down this street two blocks and turn left. It's about half a mile down on your right."

"Half a mile?"

"About that. Maybe not quite so far."

It was much farther than he thought. He had imagined only a few hundred yards, and if anything her information simply disturbed him more.

"I didn't realize it was so far away."

"Well, I'm afraid it is. But it's such a nice day for a walk."

He smiled politely.

"The rain was lovely, wasn't it? So good for the flowers." She looked, he thought, like a happy woman. Though she, not he, was of the age where people wandered away from home and couldn't find their way back. She was the one old enough to be lost.

"Thank you," he said.

"Not at all," she replied, and raised her hand in a little wave before continuing past him.

As he walked the opposite way down the street, following her directions, which soon, he knew, would reveal the park and thus the way back to the office, he felt a gathering unease. He felt as if someone were following him, as if he were being watched, and though he tried to shrug it off as nonsense, he nonetheless found himself stopping and turning around.

The street was empty, save for her tiny figure in the distance. She was walking away; she was not following him or looking at him. She was paying him no attention at all. Yet he couldn't shake the feeling, as he walked, like a residue, an oddness, a familiarity he could not precisely describe. It might have been something in her voice, or in her blue eyes, or the brightness of her hair. An old woman, out for a walk after the rain. The sun shining now in earnest, causing threads of steam to rise from the pavement.

He kept going, and in a few minutes, just as he expected, he saw the green expanse of the park, with its trees and benches, largely empty now that lunch hour was over. He knew where he was, and though it would take him a few minutes more to reach the office, the way was so familiar it felt like no time at all. Soon he found himself in front of his building, ashamed of his lateness, a few feet from his own car, which he was suddenly tempted to get into and drive away. Gass's car was there also, shining and luxurious, with beads of water on its flanks.

It was only then that he realized why the woman had troubled him. She looked exactly like Clara Gass.

That evening, when he finally left the office, he could not shake the sense of dread that followed him home. It was not powerful. If anything, it was gentle and soft, like a sound just at the threshold of hearing. But it was there, and he could feel it as he went about the business of dinner, a frozen tray in the oven. The cold foil against his bare fingers and the sound it made as he slid it across the wire rack made him shiver. The oven ticked as the heat rose.

It was quiet. Almost eight, with darkness fallen and the moon beginning—a waxing moon now, which he could see high above the rooftops through his kitchen window. Early in the month, weeks before it was full again. He believed the term was *gibbous*. The word came swimming across a distance of years—fifteen, to be exact. Fifteen years ago, from his college astronomy course. He had taken the class on a whim, hoping to learn something about the names of stars, the history of constellations. Instead, he had found himself required to calculate the percentage of hydrogen in the sun or, in one case that he could recall, the expected duration of an eclipse expected in another hemisphere, which no one in the class would therefore see. He had learned only one thing that he could clearly remember: the red shift. Which now, after all this time, a waxing gibbous moon had led him to.

The red shift, as he understood it, is the only real evidence we have for the origin of the universe. Even at the time it had struck him as weak, but there it was. The stars and the galaxies are moving apart from one another. This we know from the light the farthest stars emit: it is shifted, toward the low red end of the spectrum, in the same way that a car, blowing its horn, approaches, passes, and moves on, the tone of the sound rising at first, then falling. As the car approaches, its speed is added to the velocity of the sound waves it makes, which is the same as frequency, and therefore the pitch of the note is high. As the car passes, its speed is subtracted from the velocity of its sound waves, and therefore the pitch of the note is low. Light is a wave as well, and thus the color of what we see depends on the speed of what we see. This difference is invisible, of course, unless there are great distances, and great speeds, and great reaches of time.

These thoughts came to him with an odd formality. He felt them as if he were standing at a lectern and speaking instead of sitting at the kitchen table, waiting for the stove to cook his meal. But they continued, so he followed them, discovering a kind of solace there even as he indulged himself. He articulated them carefully in his mind. And suddenly, without warning, he found himself speaking out loud as well, as if to an imaginary audience: a crowd, a classroom, of patient listeners. He did not speak loudly, but it was enough; his voice was in the air, and someone could have heard it had they been standing next to him. He knew what he was doing was strange, yet it did not feel so. Instead, it felt comforting, as if he could speak free from the possibility of being heard, and therefore he could say anything at all. A small transgression, which would forever pass unjudged. At first, it felt liberating.

Everything is moving away from everything else. This we know. This, in turn, means that at one point, at one unimaginably distant moment in history, everything had to be together. More specifically, everything was singular. Then, the Big Bang, the origin of the universe. This is our best evidence—the stars are moving away from one another. This, and our faith in cause and effect, in unbroken laws, which, it seemed, must have been there beforehand. So there was something before the origin of the universe. Cycles, continuing. Out of conscious thought. Entirely out of reach.

After a while, it was not the act but the sound of the act that stopped him. His own voice, muttering and low, startled and disturbed him. He stood up, knowing as he did so that an independent observer of the scene might think him out of his mind.

He glanced at the clock on the stove. Twenty-five minutes had passed, though twenty-five minutes was only accurate if one were traveling at the exact same speed as the clock. If the clock were traveling at even a fraction of the speed of light, it would not be twenty-five minutes at all but some other mysterious portion of it. It all depended on where you were, and where you were going, and at what velocity.

He stopped himself again. He ran his fingers over his face, then through his hair, and for a terrible instant he felt as if his mind were accelerating uncontrollably away from him. But then it was back, and his once more, and the aluminum tray was steaming beneath his fingers on the plate as he peeled off the foil. The food bubbled, and he blew it where it lay on the fork.

He ate slowly, taking sips of sparkling water from a glass. He concentrated on the task before him, the knife through the white meat, three green beans on the tines, the roll into brown gravy. It was enough to fill him for a while, the work of eating, the sensation of the food entering his belly. He washed it down, taking his time, because he did not know what he would do when he was done. He was reaching that point where the hours before him were not empty after all. Rather, they were full, full of his own mind and the wildness of his thoughts.

It was not Clara Gass. It was simply a woman who bore a passing resemblance to the photograph that hung in Ronald Gass's hall. So what was interesting about her was not who she was but who, for a moment, he had thought her to be. He was playing tricks on himself, for reasons he could not see, no matter how clearly and dispassionately he thought about it. It was only an old woman on the street, smiling, talking about rain.

He had stayed late at the office, though it was unnecessary. He'd offered excuses to his patients, who had tapped their feet and checked their watches again in the waiting room. And then, when he had seen them all and given each his absolute, undivided attention, and the afternoon had passed into early evening, he'd found himself reviewing charts. It was true that he generally did this every few weeks, to remind himself of those who were in his care. In the past, he had prided himself on his ability to recall his many patients from memory, the details of their histories, so he might provide answers to anyone—other physicians, usually—who might call him with questions. He knew them well, of that he was certain. But on this afternoon stretching into evening, he had pored through the charts with an unusual rigor. He had studied them, chart after chart; he had remembered their faces with an act of will. Even when everyone else—Nora, Ronald Gass—was gone from the office. Even when Susan, on her way home, had tapped on the door and spoken to him.

"Michael, you should go home. You shouldn't worry about being late this afternoon."

"Oh, I know, Susan. It's not that. I'm just getting caught up."

"Well, take it home with you then. Eat some dinner. You're making me worry."

He had smiled, suddenly feeling a great affection for her. "Don't worry, Susan. But thank you. That's very nice."

She'd blown him a kiss from the doorway before disappearing.

He was done with his meal now. He tossed the empty tray into the trash and placed the knife and fork and empty glass carefully in the sink. The cleaning lady was coming tomorrow, so he left them for her. There was little else for her to do.

After a while, he found himself next to the sliding glass window of his living room, which opened to the small back yard. For a moment he was tempted to go outside, though he did not. It was a clear night, and while houses were close around him and the lights of the city were nearby, the moon was faint, and the stars stretched out by the million before him. Fifteen years had passed since his wish to learn their names, fifteen years of school and nights, of work and sleep. A handful of women, two cars, three new towns. His father's death. This empty house. So much of what is true is hard to believe. He looked out at them, the still lights of the sky, thinking how mysterious they were, how unblinking and quiet. Even after all this time they told him nothing.

Michael was between patients when Sam James called the next morning. The man's voice was jovial as ever, but also puzzled.

"I asked them to do a couple of things on a hunch. I'm not sure if what they found is helpful, but it's interesting."

"What did you ask them to do?"

"I asked them to debone the feet."

"To debone the feet?"

"I figured if he had some kind of process going on, the bones might tell us something."

"Did they?"

"There were markings on the bones. Little lines. Very unusual."

"Did they look almost like worms?" He felt his voice rising.

"I guess so. Though they were depressions, really. Almost like the tracks of worms. I don't know what to make of it. If it was an organism, the fire would certainly have killed it."

"I suppose so."

A brief pause, both men listening to the crackle of the other's breath.

"Why weren't his feet burned also?" Michael said, as it came to him.

"I wondered about that too. I think his feet were hanging over the edge of the bed. The fire burned through his calves, and his feet dropped off onto the floor. The bed was burning above them and covered them with ashes so they never got that hot. They were only charred. That's my best guess, anyway."

As the hours passed, Michael could not get the image out of his mind. The feet, bending like rubber, then falling off.

Another day now, asking things of him. Prescriptions called to the nearby pharmacy. *Certainly. I will be happy to. Thank you, Susan, would you pull that chart I asked you about? I haven't seen that patient in months. You're doing very well, Mr. Johnson, and I'll see you in three weeks.* Footsteps on soft carpeting. The rustle of pages being turned. People in the waiting room, sitting on soft couches and chairs, though it was a line nonetheless, and they got up to go in, one after another. Two feet, bowing down, bending where they should not bend.

The light in his office seemed very bright on the papers of the desk, the off-yellow folders of the charts, the gunmetal cabinet in the corner. The window, opening to a parking lot behind the building. The lit particles of dust, clinging to the varnished oak surface of the desk, and the green felt blotter, and his pens—clinging to him also, he imagined, though he could not see them on his clothes. He rolled back on his wheeled chair, lifting his legs, and there they were, on the surface of his shoes. He stared at his own feet for a moment, the swell of his ankles in his brown socks. He was sitting with both feet lifted in the air, which would look ridiculous to anyone opening the door. So he put his feet down again and slid forward to the desk. He felt feverish.

This is how the day passed. At times he was there, with a patient before him, and he felt the intensity of his concentration, their faces seemed magnified, with every blemish, every black grain of stubble made clear. Their faces rose out of the background like the surface of the moon through a lens, saliva glistening on their lips as they spoke. He listened, and when he answered he could feel his own lips forming around words, slow and exact, as if he were speaking under water.

Other times, they receded into the distance, they blended like leopards in the undergrowth, so he could see them only when they moved. Nonetheless, he spoke, suspecting even as he did so that no one save him could tell the difference. He felt as if he were standing on the edge of a cliff, looking down into the depths below, and had suddenly lost his balance. He clung to the railing, which was sense, which was a reasonable tone of voice. He was speaking clearly, that much he knew. But even as he spoke, he wondered how long he could continue.

After a while, he became aware that his office was empty. I must be between patients, he thought. Though suddenly he wasn't sure. Some time must have passed. And now there was a knock on the door.

"Come in," he called. For a moment, he glanced down at his desk, at the pile of charts that lay there. They should be in order, which meant that the chart on top of the pile should belong to the owner of the knocking hand. He shuffled quickly through it, but it was too late to be ready, because he looked up to see a figure in the threshold.

"Just a moment, I'll be right with you," he muttered, then looked down again, quickly thumbing through the pages for the name.

"Michael, it's me."

He looked up again. It was Susan, wearing a look of concern.

"Oh," he said.

"Michael, what's the matter?"

"What do you mean?"

"The last patient you saw said you were acting strange."

"He did?"

"Yes. He said you were rambling. And I must say, you don't look well."

For the life of him he could not remember who the last patient had been.

"I'm fine."

"No, I don't think so." She approached the desk, reaching, and he felt her palm against his forehead.

"You feel warm to me," she said.

"I'm fine, Susan."

"Michael, you don't look fine. I think you have a fever."

"I'm OK. Really." But as he said it, he wasn't so sure.

"I'll be right back," she said, and disappeared.

Dimly, he wondered where she was going. Though what seemed most interesting to him, suddenly, was the white wall, with the single dry rivulet of paint down at the baseboard, and how it cast the tiniest of shadows in the light from the window.

Susan returned a moment later with a digital thermometer in her hand.

"Hold still," she said, before he could protest, and deftly placed the tip inside his left ear.

There was a pause and then a beep.

"You see?" she said. "I've been doing this for a long time and I know. You have a temperature of 101."

"I feel fine."

"No, you don't. I'm going to send you home."

"I'll be fine. There are only a few more patients to see."

"Michael, I hate to tell you this but you've only seen three patients. You're backed up. There are ten people waiting for you out there."

"I've only seen three? Are you sure?"

"Yes. I was wondering what was taking you so long. So don't argue."

He was about to protest, but suddenly he felt terribly tired. What he really wanted to do, and now the desire was so strong it astonished him, was go home, and open the bed, and slide between the linen sheets, which would have been freshly washed by the cleaning lady. He wanted nothing else, he realized, and he gave in to it so willingly it surprised him.

So he nodded to her. "All right, Susan. Whatever you say."

"Good. Get your coat. I'm taking you home." But she looked surprised, as if she were expecting him to protest further.

Out through the waiting room. It was crowded; Susan was correct. So many half-familiar faces, their eyes turned toward him. Their heads like nuts. Their voices. His little half wave, his chagrined smile, as he followed Susan out into the parking lot.

"Susan," he said, beginning to shiver as he stood in the sunlight, "you don't have to take me home. I can drive."

The air against him moved; it felt alive.

"Are you sure?"

"Yes. It's not far."

She was looking at him, he realized, with the experience of years. He felt as if he were naked before her, as if in that moment he had no secrets she could not see. So many sick people had stood where he stood, in front of her heavy, concerned face, her curled brown hair shot through with threads of gray, the small pale pouches under her eyes. Her reading glasses, hanging from her neck from a string of little plastic beads. Red and green and yellow, lined up in a row. He realized that she was perhaps the only person who felt this way toward him. He felt close to tears, though he knew, even as he mastered them, dried them before they formed, that they were a self-indulgent, sentimental weakness. A collection of salt and fluid, in the narrowest of passages, which even as they flowed raised further questions. She did not know him, not really. Therefore she was concerned about the idea of him. The ritual, again, though this time it stirred him, this time it made him weak, and gave his lips and hands a new trembling life.

"OK," she said, "but I want you to call me when you get home. If you don't, I'm going to come and get you."

"You don't know where I live."

"Yes, I do. I've driven by your house."

This surprised and pleased him. To think that she had driven past, going somewhere else, with this knowledge. As if he had been watched, from a distance, by kindly eyes.

"I'll call, don't worry."

"Good. Run along now."

He wondered, as the car took him home, what she would tell those who waited. Dr. Grant is unwell. He had to go home. He's sorry for the inconvenience. His body ached; the air flooded against him through the open window. Only a short distance, and he was nearly there now. The light was so bright where it fell, and the streets, though they were utterly familiar to him, seemed strange and lovely. They looked as if they had been washed and dressed, like a child to dinner. So I am a dinner guest, he thought, though my tie is undone. I need to straighten it before I call Susan and tell her I've arrived. I need to get out of the car. I'm in the driveway. The keys in his hand now, the engine silent. He watched them shine, for an instant, and then they fell together with the sound of bells and found their way into his pocket. He felt luminous.

"Susan," he said, a few minutes later, "I'm home."

Sometime late that night, he washed his face. He stood in the bathroom, let the water fill the sink, and brought it up in his cupped hands, again and again. The hiss of the tap, which he had the presence of mind to turn off before his journey back to bed.

Or later, the electric clock's winking numbers on the nightstand, green and irregular: two and three and four. His own breathing, which for a moment he confused with a stranger's. *There is someone here, there is someone else in the room.*

I'm dreaming, or I was dreaming. Night sounds, from the depths of the house, nothing more. His ragged breathing, on and on. A sound for visitors, for mothers to the childhood bed. *Go back to sleep. It was a dream, that's all.* Which is how morning came, the black of the room giving way to gray, and soon it was enough to see.

At first he barely noticed them, but they gathered in numbers: a cascade of tiny lights, a few at first, then dozens, and then hundreds. Grains of dust, in the darkness over the foot of the bed, and the floor, and the dresser in the corner against the wall.

They might have been fireflies. It was the right time of year, he thought. He watched them for a while, considering. But they were too small, and they were too many. His thoughts came with a deep slowness.

He closed his eyes. They were there. He knew then that it was not the room, not an open window, it was nothing at all outside of him. It was inside. It was his left eye, and it was sparkling like a wand, and showing him its new trick, and letting him take his time, and making certain beyond any question that he saw it.

Gradually they faded, each star moving away from the other, until there were only a few and then none at all. It was only a room again, and it would soon be day. The chair, the bureau, his robe where he had cast it on the floor. A single black sock, like something washed out of the sea.

He was nearly certain. Nearly, but not quite, and so he gave himself a little more time. His skin was moist and cold as he sat on the bed. He did not want to get up and go into the bathroom, though he knew he had to. The room brightened around him.

Then it came again, a few brief sparks, nothing like the shower of moments ago. Something which, under normal circumstances, he might not even have noticed. But now he could wait no longer, and he was in the bathroom, turning on the light, with his face in the mirror.

He looked into his own eye as best as he could, past his own reflection, past the glint of light on the surface of the cornea. His brown pupil, narrowing as he focused. But he could see nothing. It was as calm and steady as its twin.

So he opened his mouth, as widely as he could, until the joints of his jaw began to ache, and he kept his tongue flat and stepped up to the mirror, holding his breath to stop it from clouding the glass.

He saw pink flesh, the interior of his cheeks, his teeth lined up in their sockets; at first, he could see nothing strange. His uvula, hanging straight down. Nothing was there. Then he inhaled once more, and stepped up close, and turned his head slightly away from the mirror, with his eyes pointed straight.

Which is when he saw it. On the left side, far back, just behind the tonsil. Almost invisible, in a place no one ever looked. A single white thread, no wider than a human hair, too far back to touch. The tail of it, no more, as if the rest were coiled back in the dark.

In that moment, the mirror, the light, his own body—all of it stopped. It was only a tiny thread, a single coil, so small and delicate, but he could see it clearly, and now he imagined that he felt its touch.

He was shaking, he was sitting on the toilet with his head in his hands. Time passed.

Sometime later, when he finally left the bathroom, it was full morning. He heard the sound of birds, of cars starting in driveways. It was difficult and took concentration, but he sat down carefully on the bed, and found the telephone, and dialed the number, and waited, as the minutes went by, until Gass came on the line.

It was only with difficulty that Ronald Gass dissuaded Susan from accompanying him.

"Someone needs to be here," he pointed out. "We do have other patients, after all. It shouldn't take that long."

Susan drew him a map. It occurred to him, as he pulled up to the curb, recognizing Grant's car in the driveway, that this was the first time he could ever remember going to a patient's house. Not that Grant was a patient, of course. He again considered the possibility that he would have to replace the man. Though he had done his job well enough, he supposed, up until his mistake with the child. But in recent weeks there had been too many missed appointments, too many absent days. It could be tolerated for a while. And Grant had accumulated a good deal of vacation days and sick time, as accorded to him through his contract. He had checked. So for the moment there was nothing to be done.

Grant, when he finally answered the door, was unkempt, his hair in tangles.

"Thanks for coming, Ronald."

Grant held himself tight, Gass saw, blinking and clutching his bathrobe against himself. Gass could smell the man's body.

"Not at all," Gass said. "What can I do for you?"

Grant turned and walked back into the house, inviting him to follow. Gass did so and immediately felt the stifling warmth of the interior. The heat was on, he realized, though it was already warm outside. The blinds on the windows were drawn, and the house was nearly in darkness.

"Michael, do you mind if I turn on a light?" he said mildly.

"No, no. Of course. I'm sorry," Grant said, his hand fumbling along the wall for the switch.

An end table by the couch lay on its side. A glass lay a few feet away, on the tan carpet, in a dark circle. Liquid had spilled. Near the glass, a small pile of clothes, brown corduroy pants, a blue dress shirt, a red tie, a pair of leather shoes. Otherwise, the room was neat, with books in precise rows in the bookcase and the bare coffee table wiped clean.

"It's warm in here."

"Warm? Oh. Yes, I turned on the heat."

Grant was sitting now, on a leather chair. Leaning back, with his eyes closed. Gass stood and watched him for a moment.

"So, Michael," he asked, "what seems to be the problem? Do you have a fever?"

"I think so."

"Anything else? Cough, congestion, that kind of thing?"

"No. No cough."

"Any GI disturbance?"

Grant shook his head.

"Well, Michael, you know as well as I that it's probably just a viral syndrome. As long as you're holding fluids down, I doubt there's anything else to do."

"I think it's more than that, Ronald."

"Why don't you take the rest of the week off. See how you feel over the next couple of days."

"I've been having visual symptoms."

"Such as?"

"I've been seeing lights. I think I have a retinal process of some kind."

"Are they there continuously?"

"No. They come and go."

"Are you seeing them now?"

"No."

"Well, perhaps you should see an ophthalmologist."

"I have a lesion in my mouth."

It began to dawn on Gass then. For an instant, he struggled with a smile that continued inside him.

"All right, Michael, why don't I have a look at you. Though my ophthalmoscope is in the office."

"I have one here," Grant said.

He stood and walked over to the wall, bending down to the electric outlet. A battery-powered ophthalmoscope, Gass saw, protruded from it. With effort, Grant pulled it free and turned, handing it to Gass.

"The battery should be charged," he said.

"Let me turn off the light," Gass said, and did so, plunging the room in darkness. It took a few moments for his eyes to adjust. Both men stood facing each other now. With the ease of long practice, Gass turned on the scope and rolled the dial down to zero. There was no refraction now. The light entered the room.

"Which eye is it?"

"The left."

"Let's have a look. Stand still."

Gass stepped up close to Grant, as close as the two men had ever been to each other. As he did so, he raised the ophthalmoscope to his own left eye and shone the light directly on Grant's face. They were so near that only half of Grant's face lit up, and now he moved closer still. The eye, brown and white, with a touch of swirling red in the conjunctiva. The man's breath behind it.

He brought his left hand up to rest on Grant's forehead, stooping a bit, and focused on the cornea. Then deeper, into the red distance, down through the vitreous, his index finger rolling the dial down to the retina. The blue of tiny veins, the red of the arterioles. All of them converging on the disk, where the optic nerve courses out of the brain.

Michael stood silently, with his eyes fixed on an imaginary point on the wall. He felt Gass sweep the light back and forth across the depths of his eye. Their faces were so close they almost touched. Michael held his breath as best he could, letting it out of his nose. His eye was so full of light he could see nothing else. A few moments passed, and then Gass stepped back to a comfortable distance.

"I don't see anything unusual."

"Nothing at all?"

Gass shook his head. He seemed, Michael realized, distinctly amused.

"No, Michael. Of course, I can't see your entire retina. We didn't dilate your eyes. But what I do see looks fine."

Michael looked down. The light lingered, an afterimage of circles and smoke. He blinked a few more times.

"Good," he said finally. "That's good."

"Still, I'm no ophthalmologist. If you're concerned, you should get a complete exam."

"Yes."

Grant brought up his hands to his temples and rubbed them.

"Now," Gass said, "what's this about your mouth?"

"I have a lesion in my throat. I saw it this morning."

"Let me see."

Michael opened his mouth then, as wide as he could. Though as Gass approached again, the light rising from his hand, Michael suddenly felt his heart begin to tumble and skip.

His throat was full of light. He stood with his head thrown back, his tongue protruding. He felt as if he were opening himself.

"Where did you say it was?" Gass asked.

"Behind my left tonsil," he replied, before opening his mouth again.

Gass craned his neck. "I don't see it."

Michael closed his mouth then, and stepped back, letting out his breath, which he realized he'd been holding.

"It's there, Ronald."

Gass nodded. "I'm sure it is. Let me look again."

Michael felt something bubbling out of him now, something strong, like the desire to shout or break glass. He said nothing. I must be careful, he thought. I need to control myself.

"Maybe I should show you. In a mirror."

"All right." Gass spoke calmly, though he was studying him closely. Michael turned and walked the few feet to the bathroom off the hall, and Gass followed.

Both men were in the bathroom now. Gass, in his creamy shirt and dark tie, the buckle of his belt sparkling above his pressed pants, revealing nothing. Grant stood beside him, unshaven, unwashed, his body aching beneath his robe. Shorter. His hands were trembling.

Michael stepped up close to the glass once more. As he did so, he watched Gass, just behind him, bending over his shoulder. He opened his mouth again, and pressed his tongue flat, arching his neck. A ridiculous posture, he knew, even as he assumed it.

But now Michael could see nothing there. Gass was staring intently, bending forward, his hand on Grant's shoulder to brace himself.

Michael turned away from the mirror to face him. "I don't see it now," Michael said.

Gass sighed. "I don't either. Your throat is normal, Michael. There are no lesions there."

"I saw it clearly just a little while ago."

"Perhaps you thought you saw something."

Michael felt a swirling inside him, as if he were standing inside a ship, on the gentlest of swells.

"I think you've let your imagination get the best of you," Gass said.

The news should have comforted him, Michael realized, it should have soothed him, and calmed the wildness he felt now. But it did not.

"Michael," Gass said, "do you really think you have Grant's disease?"

"His blood was on my hands."

"What?"

"I drew his blood. I spilled some of it on my hands."

"Did you have a break in the skin? A cut?"

Michael shook his head.

"You didn't stick yourself with the needle?"

"No. I washed it off immediately."

"Then it's extremely unlikely you caught anything, Michael. You know that."

"That's what I've been telling myself."

Gass sighed. "Michael," he said, "I need to get back to the office. You do not have Grant's disease. Take the rest of the week off. It will do you good."

"I'm sorry, Ronald." He was mumbling now, utterly confused, following Gass into the hall, where Gass was turning on the lights. He was preparing to leave, and the thought filled Michael inexplicably with dread. Gass, with all his certainty, walking out the door, driving away, back to the office, talking to Susan. Full of questions.

He blinked again and tried once more. Desperately, he felt. Though he spoke quietly. "I know what I saw, Ronald."

Gass was smiling now, patting Michael on the shoulder like a frightened child. "Don't worry, Michael. You'll see. You'll be fine in a few days."

As he heard the words, he could not bring himself to do what he knew was expected of him, which was to agree. So he was silent and stood looking at the floor. Shame flooded through him, a great sense of abject humiliation. Though there was something else as well, in the sound of the central heating clicking on once more, in the sound of Gass's voice, in the opening of the door, and the smell of fresh air—a sense of absolute solitude, which is the same, he considered, as being lost.

"Goodbye, Michael."

He looked up, but he could not meet the man's eye. The smile again. The world in order.

"I'm sorry, Ronald," he said, as calmly as he could. "Thank you for coming."

The next morning, he turned the water on full blast and sent billows of steam into the bathroom. He stood in the shower for a long time, washing his body and hair again and again. It was very early, and he had plenty of time to reach the office and do what he needed before Susan came. I will think no further than that.

The madness of recent hours—he did not delude himself, he recognized it for what it was—seemed to have gone. He felt clear now, though tired. With deliberate patience, he dressed: pressed pants from the closet, a white button-down shirt. Short sleeves, so that he would not have to roll them up. No tie. Loafers, brown socks. A windbreaker, for the chill of the morning. His keys and his wallet. Holding himself tight. The snap of the comb through his wet hair, in brief firm strokes. The hum of the electric shaver against his cheek.

With a last glance in the mirror, he folded the windbreaker over his arm and left the bedroom. Yesterday's imbalance, the vague need to hold on to walls, was also gone, and he walked easily down the stairs and into the brightness of the morning.

He knew, as he quickly crossed the short walk to the driveway and slid his hand carefully into his pocket for his keys, that anyone, looking through any window, would think he was going to work. But it was difficult, as he turned the key in the lock, not to notice the oak tree above him, like a vast green whispering sail. He did not look up. It was important to keep his mind fixed, his intention clear, yet already the tree above him, and the metronome of the neighbor's sprinkler down the street, and even the sound of his key in the car door threatened to carry him away. Part of him knew that if he paused even for a moment, or nodded to someone walking past, he would be lost. He thought of Clara Gass, whom even now he imagined strolling only a few blocks from here, smiling, with her blue eyes and white hair, like the old woman she was. He felt as if he had only a few more moments before she came around the corner, only a few moments before she would stop and turn to face him.

He got into the car and started the engine. He clung to the sound of the motor, the trembling wheel he held in both hands, the jolt of reverse, and the lawn sliding by as he backed out into the street.

Accelerating carefully away from his house, he kept his attention exactly where it should be, which was the next turn, and the next, and the stoplight. A few minutes passed, and even as he felt the strain of his concentration begin to build, and his hands whiten on the wheel, he knew he could reach where he was going.

And there it was, his office, just as it had always been, the space waiting for his car as if he had never been away.

He had to be quick. He had thirty minutes before Susan would arrive. He fumbled with the keys before entering, crossed the waiting room, and turned down the hall to the supply closet for what he needed. Three clear glass tubes. The needle, alcohol pads, a yellow rubber cord. Then into his unlocked office.

It was brighter there; the sun fell through the window and lit up the room. He draped his jacket on the back of the chair, far enough from the desk. He laid out the vials, one after another, on the desk, and then, with difficulty, tied the rubber cord around his upper arm, pulling it tight with his teeth. He worked his hand then, back and forth, clenching and unclenching, watching the blue veins fill, one after another. The alcohol tingled as it dried on his skin.

The correct angle of the needle was difficult to find, and on the first try he was too gentle, easing the bright point in. His chosen vein slid away, and he knew he had not been quick enough. His arm stung nonetheless, but when he withdrew the needle only the tiniest speck of blood rose from the mark. Weakness, he thought, and then touched the tip directly to the full blue cord. A flick of the wrist now, a little strike, and there it was, a stream of blood, no wider than string, firm into the vial, and he released the rubber with his teeth, watching the string melt to a hair as he did so. The needle ached in his arm, and he struggled to keep the point from wandering through the walls of the vein. Another vial, and another. He took a curious pleasure in it, and for a moment he wanted to make vial after vial red and full and warm. But then he was done, and the last tube lay full as a tick on the desk. He flicked the needle out, and it left a tiny arc of beads across the green blotter, dissolving into the green felt. Eleven minutes had passed.

The tubes of blood clicked against one another in his hand as he placed them carefully in the pocket of his jacket. The clear desk, empty of papers, dusted, the empty black leather chair—in a few moments there would be no sign that he had been here at all. With another glance at his watch, he left his office, crossed through the shade of the waiting room, and locked the door carefully behind him.

Cars passed on the streets as the beginning of the workday approached. He was in the distractions again—the glint of rooftops, the smell of green grass, the whisper of traffic—and he felt the strain immediately. Fifteen steps to his car, the engine starting. Back into the street, down the block, around the corner, where he could not be seen.

The lab was not far. It was open now, he knew, or should be. And though he knew the way, each turn brought the deepening sense of vertigo, as if he were wandering into a maze of hedges. He was careful, signaling each turn with a blinking light, until the low building appeared.

The fat technician seated behind the window looked up at him briefly, then back down at the computer on the desk. She raised one finger in the air as she did so. He did not know her. There was no one else in the room. He stood, shoulders hunched, with his hand around the bundle of tubes in his pocket. He looked at her finger: the way it hung suspended in the air for a moment before drifting away out of sight, the ring around it. Seconds passed. One foot in front of the other. The rattle of buttons, of numbers, passing through an expert hand.

"Can I help you?"

"I'm Dr. Grant. I'm dropping off some blood work for a patient." He was speaking calmly, each word measured, though his head was lowered. As he spoke he felt a brief flash of terror go through him, and the muscles of his jaw flexed and clenched, as if to squeeze it away.

"What is the patient's name?"

"Williams," he said.

"First name?"

"Jonas."

She nodded. Her fingers ticked on the keyboard. "Date of birth?"

"I don't know."

"I need a date of birth or a social."

He gave his own.

She pushed a lab slip through the window between them. "Fill out the tests you want."

He did so, as best he could, squinting at the scores of tiny black boxes before him. Blood counts, electrolytes, clotting functions. His kidneys, his liver. He watched the hand below him, working the pen. It continued, checking and checking, one after another. He let it go for a while, hoping it would be enough, but then he stopped because he had to, because already he could see the attention in the clerk's eyes.

"That's a lot of lab work," she said. He did not answer immediately, because he was looking away and handing her the vials from his pocket.

"Just run them, please."

"You're the doctor."

"When will the results be ready?"

She glanced at the form. "Some of these are sendouts. But we should have most of it back by Monday."

He nodded. Her face, he saw—the heavy lids, the dark mascara, the coils of her bleached yellow hair—her face had begun to sparkle. Her moving mouth, the underside of her chin as full as a woman's breast.

"Excuse me," he said, and nodded to her, and turned and hurried out to his car. The world had begun shimmering again, and flowing, and there were spots and lights everywhere he looked—in the asphalt beneath his feet, in the white side of his car, which he half ran for now.

For a moment he wondered if he were going blind. It was all he could do to make out the silhouettes of the other cars in the lot, and the yellow lines on the concrete, and the exit sign, whose letters were half eaten away. There were gaps between objects: not spots but absent places, where he could see nothing. He felt a great wave of nausea, and he fumbled along the dashboard for the air conditioner, flipping the lever as high as it went. The air washed against his face. He was sweating and panting, and he bent his head close to the little grate, letting the air flood against his cheek and down his collar against his damp neck. The engine shifted beneath him, and he sat there, with his eyes closed, until the cascade of little stars finally began to flicker and go out—a private shower—and he breathed, as slowly and as deeply as he could, until the wave of nausea passed. His hands left streaks on the wheel.

After a while, he felt well enough to continue. He was shivering and welcomed it, because his shivering, more than anything else, seemed likely to carry him home. And it did. He shivered out of the parking lot and down the street to the avenue; he shivered past the park where he walked at lunchtime, past the flat brown pond and the black iron benches, down past the corner, left and right again, his teeth chattering, the air hissing against his knees and chest. A blue dot where he had drawn the blood oozed all the while on his forearm, until finally his house came up beside him.

He stood in the hall with the door safely closed behind him and walked past the kitchen into the living room. He felt terribly warm and reached for the thermostat on the wall, finally turning it down. Somewhere he heard a click, and the ducts went silent for the first time in days. He threw open the sliding glass doors that faced the back yard, and the curtains swelled against him as a breeze entered. Finally, he loosened his collar and lay down on the couch. His feet tingled, and he closed his eyes, and his hands felt their way under his belt to the heat of his groin. He held himself as tightly as he could. The air from the yard rustled against him.

At the lab the machines would be doing their work, and now it was his own blood flowing through the coils, illuminated in secret interiors—calcium, magnesium, phosphorus. The click and whir of measurements, of lights going on and off and on again, automatic and anonymous. He imagined the fat technician feeding the vials like coins to a slot machine, pulling the lever, watching the wheel fly, before reaching for the next. The machines went on with their digestions. He lay there and slowly, after a long while, began to feel somewhat better.

Ronald Gass was done for the day; the afternoon's charts lay in a neat pile on his desk. It had been a slow afternoon, and now he had several hours of daylight left to go home, to thumb through his bills—it was nearing the end of the month—and ensure that his accounts were in order. His affairs, as he liked to think of them, were a source of calm, a small comfort, and each month he made it a point to sit down and balance his checkbook. In another life, it had long since occurred to him, he might have been a banker or an accountant. He enjoyed the whisper of his pen on the paper, the feel of the calculator's buttons beneath his fingers. The sums were always close, or close enough, and he knew this was an activity he could easily do without; nonetheless, the ritual of it pleased him, the easy knowledge, the world of simple numbers coming precisely into focus. He would sit at his desk and work for an hour or so, and then, after dinner, he might watch television for a while until it grew late enough for bed.

With these thoughts in mind, he left his office and entered the bathroom off the hall, where he washed his hands with the yellow soap from the dispenser. He dried his hands carefully, on the rough brown paper towels laid in a neat stack by the sink. He wondered why they were not in the metal box on the wall—he would ask Susan about it—and then, patting his pocket to make sure his keys were there, he made his way back into the hall to the back entrance and out of the building. This was his routine—to enter through the front door and leave by the back. There was no reason he could think of why he did this, but over the years he had fallen into the habit. He was, as Clara had joked early in their life together, a man of personal tradition.

It began as he descended the stairs. There was no one in front of the brownstone, just the sun of the late afternoon and his car, though he knew Susan was still at her desk. He might have called out to her, he might have turned and reentered the office, and he would have done so had the arrival been announced more clearly. But it was a tentative sensation at first, just below the threshold of alarm, so he continued on to his car, got in, and turned on the air conditioner. His breathing, just beginning, just barely, had the faintest rustle. It was warm outside, warmer still in the closed interior of the car, and he lowered the windows with the button as the air conditioner blew hot air against him. Pulling out into the street now, for his short trip home, going about his business.

In the few minutes it took him to drive home the announcement was more formally made: pressure, a presence in his chest. Not entirely clear, not beyond doubt, but he was sweating now; he could feel the sweat rising in little beads on his forehead, on his chest and belly. Just then his belly uncoiled inside him, with no warning, making his teeth clench, and he pulled the car violently to the curb. His hand on the knob, so quickly, the door was open, and he was leaning out, and bending down, the heat of the asphalt flat against his lowered face, the sound of the idling engine, the air from the vents, his silk tie dangling into the street. A few more gasping moments, and then it came, the burn in his throat and in his nose, as the fluid rose out of him and crackled and slapped against the pavement. He threw up again and then a third time. He had not done so in years. His stomach was empty, his tie ruined where it lay trailing in the gray fluid. There were specks, he saw dimly, on the interior of the car, on the leather seats and on the left leg of his pants. He was breathing hard, and he reached up to his throat, loosening his tie. Just a few seconds had passed, but he was white, he could feel it, and now there was a bed of coals in his chest, and it was for real, it was in earnest. It left him no time to think at all. An enormous band tightened around his chest and his back, a black belt that even now drew in another impossible notch. There was nothing else to think about, nothing at all; just like that the everyday world was gone, as fast as the flick of a pen.

Somehow he made it the few blocks home. His car left purring in the driveway, a few steps to the door, panting, soaking wet, his stinking stained shirt. He held on to the railing on the roof and leaned on the bell. His keys behind him in the running car, too far away—the bell, the bell again. For the first time in many years, a small part of him—the part that remained his own, the smiling part—realized that he was afraid for himself.

The door opened.

"Nora," he said, between gasping breaths, "call an ambulance."

"What's wrong?"

"I'm having another heart attack. Call an ambulance right now."

"Come inside."

He felt a great weariness, as he leaned against her, as he felt the foreignness of her body, close against his own, as she held him and guided him to the couch. He wanted only to sit down, and lean forward, and breathe, and breathe again. He heard her voice, from the kitchen, from a distant room, low and quiet into the telephone. He heard their address, their telephone number. Repeated. Then she was back, standing before him.

"Take this," she said.

A single white pill lay in the center of her outstretched palm.

"What is it?"

"Aspirin. Take it."

He did so, without question. His chest had settled a bit, but not nearly enough.

"They're on their way." She spoke evenly.

They waited, in silence, together on the couch, a foot between them. He noticed a smear of his vomit on her dress. She was looking at him steadily. The minutes passed. He could not think. His chest was a vast thing. He was nearly sick again, and already he could feel the hiss of his own breath. His lungs were filling with fluid, he realized, which meant his heart was failing. Just like that, with no warning at all. *I was coming home. It was just another day.* In the distance, he heard the wail of an approaching siren.

He was very afraid, as afraid as he had ever been in his life. Already his lungs were crackling like the end of a fire—the heart failing, starving, letting the pressure build in the spidery lungs, which began to leak and swell. This much, in the space of seconds, occurred to him. An artery, plugged by the oyster's pearl, risen from a grain of sand.

They were entering the room now and they were carrying things—an orange box, a brown wooden board with straps. Their hands were nearly upon him. They were speaking. He felt an immense weakness. It was all he could do to turn his head and look at her.

Michael did get up, finally. There had been no word from the lab, and hours had passed. He would call Monday. They should have something ready for him then. That they had not done so already probably meant there was nothing remarkable to report; remarkable values were acted on quickly. They would have called. His tongue was sticky and sour against his teeth, but for the moment he felt clearheaded again.

The telephone rang, frightening him. Perhaps it was the lab after all. Someone, an indifferent stranger, to whom the numbers meant nothing—someone was calling him. A few quick steps out of the kitchen to the living room.

"Hello."

"Michael?"

"Yes."

"It's Nora. My father is in the hospital. He's having a heart attack. I thought you should know." She spoke quietly, with composure.

"Where are you?"

"I'm at the hospital. I'm in the waiting room."

"I'll be there as soon as I can."

"Please," she said, and he heard it then—a catch in her throat, her voice beginning to break.

"Give me half an hour."

"Thank you," she said softly, and was gone.

He drove quickly, combing his free hand roughly through his dripping wet hair. He had not taken the time to dry himself thoroughly from the quick shower, and as he drove he felt the shirt go dark against his back. It was only a short distance, and in a few minutes he had pulled up in the hospital parking lot and was walking toward the door beneath the red neon sign: EMERGENCY.

Nora, when he found her, was sitting in the far corner of the waiting room on an orange plastic chair bolted to the wall. At this hour, early in the evening, the room was full, and next to her a small child twisted and screamed in his mother's arms. There was a cut on the child's lower lip, bleeding slightly, and every so often the boy would reach up with his hands and smear the blood all over his face. His mother sat exhausted, holding him, tapping her foot, no longer making any effort to stop him. Her plain white blouse was speckled and stained; her hair hung limp. They must have been waiting for hours—already the blood on the mother's blouse was hard and black.

Nora sat still, leaning away from the mother and child. She was staring out into the space in front of her. Her arms were crossed, her back hunched. She looked like someone prepared to remain there all night.

She had not seen him come in through the door, and he made his way through the lines of seats.

"Nora?"

She looked up, then, and saw him above her, and smiled. The smile, more than anything else, surprised him, shocked him even—it had a wildness to it, a distillation of grief and anger, rising up, then gone again, as quickly as it had come.

She stood now. "Thank you for coming," she said hoarsely.

"Where is he?"

She gestured toward the door of the emergency room. "In there," she said. "The cardiologist is with him now."

"Which cardiologist?"

She mentioned a name he did not know. "They're going to do something soon. An angioplasty, I think."

He nodded. "He must be infarcting, then."

"What?"

"He must really be having a heart attack."

"That's what they said. They asked me to wait out here."

The child beside them began screaming again, a piercing shriek, and Michael winced and looked down.

"Sshh," the mother whispered, trying to juggle the boy on her knee. "Ssshh." The woman was looking at the floor.

"Let me go see what I can find out."

He touched her shoulder, briefly, and turned to leave. The child's mother looked at Nora.

"I'm sorry," she said. Nora did not answer.

It took him a few minutes to talk his way past the glass window and the locked door leading to the emergency room. But then he was through and inside the large white space. There were curtained gurneys along each wall, and nearly all of them were full. In the center, like an island, a ring of desks and computer screens where the clerk sat.

"I'm Dr. Grant," he said to her. "I'm looking for a patient named Ronald Gass. He's a physician."

"Let me see," she said, turning to look at the large gray board behind her on the pillar, where names were written in black marker. "Cube Twelve," she said.

But Michael had seen him already, or rather had seen the cluster of activity around him. A man in a long white coat, with a heavy black stethoscope around his neck, stood at the foot of a gurney. The curtains were half drawn, obscuring Michael's view. A nurse dressed in lavender scrubs was doing something to a bag of IV fluids suspended from the pole overhead.

He could see only the foot of the bed and two pale legs emerging from the hem of the hospital gown.

He struggled with the urge to walk directly to the curtain and draw it aside. As he hesitated, looking at the legs, and their stillness, the cardiologist turned from the bedside and came purposefully back toward the clerk's station. He spoke to the nurse, over his shoulder, and Michael heard him clearly.

"Start the dopamine at ten mics."

He felt a little click when he heard those words. Dopamine, to drive up blood pressure. Gass's heart was failing.

The cardiologist—who must have been new, because Michael did not know him—sat down only a few feet away and picked up the telephone.

"Is the crew here yet?" he asked quietly. Then: "Please call me as soon as they get here." The man put down the phone and sighed.

"Excuse me," Michael said then, and the man looked up. He was young, nearly Grant's age, and dark-haired also. From a distance, Michael realized, they could be mistaken for each other.

"I'm Michael Grant. You're seeing my colleague, Ronald Gass."

"Oh," the man said. "You're a physician also?"

"I'm an internist. Infectious disease, actually."

The man handed Grant a piece of paper from the desk. It was an EKG. The pattern was unmistakable.

"It's an anterior MI," he said, handing the EKG back to the cardiologist, who nodded.

"A big one."

"The cath lab?"

"They're on their way."

Michael was silent. "What do you think?" he said, after a while.

The cardiologist shrugged. "If we can open the vessel he's got a chance."

Just then, the monitor screen next to the clerk began to ring and flash, and both men turned. There was no mistaking the sawtooth pattern, the green waves in front of them. Two seconds, then three, and then, just as the cardiologist leaped from his seat, it was gone and the pattern was normal and steady once more. A lethal rhythm, a sly wink, gone in an instant, and the nurse in lavender scrubs was beside them.

"He just had a run of V tach," she said.

"I saw," the cardiologist said. "Give him a hundred of lidocaine now and start him on a drip."

"How much?"

"Two milligrams per minute. Let's get the pacer pads on him too."

She nodded and was gone just as quickly, back to the bedside, pulling the curtains behind her.

"Do you mind if I see him?" Michael asked.

"Go ahead. I'll be over in a minute."

Michael paused at the drawn curtains. Though only a few minutes before he had wanted to fling them aside and walk right in, now that the moment was upon him his strength was nearly gone. He wondered if he should go find Nora. There was no way to knock, no way to announce his presence, so after a few seconds he simply parted the curtains and stepped inside.

The figure on the gurney bore only a passing resemblance to Ronald Gass. Michael was reminded of a fish, silvery in the water, its gills the only sign of life. Gass was laboring for breath, despite the clear plastic mask that cradled his face, through which the oxygen poured. He looked straight ahead, his eyes fixed on the ceiling. They were pale gray and rose out of his face like polished glass. Tiny beads of sweat lay on his exposed shoulders, his flat hair was tangled, shot through with black. His hands were clenched tight, and if he noticed Michael step through the curtain he gave no sign.

The nurse shot a questioning glance his way.

"I'm Dr. Gass's colleague, Michael Grant," he said stiffly.

"Oh," she said, gave a little shrug, and rolled the tiny wheel attached to the IV tubing. He watched the drops tumble through it.

"Lidocaine," she said, and he nodded. A drug to quiet the heart.

The monitor over Gass's head was all green and red lights: the heartbeat for all to see, his blood pressure, his oxygen level. It took a moment to interpret them.

"His pressure's low," he said, and she nodded.

"I just started the dopamine."

The world was going strange once more, spinning and turning, and now, in just an instant, it had turned on the figure before him, it had knocked him flat with the most casual of gestures. And here he was, the pale-eyed man, the endurer, gasping and clenching his hands on the thin sheet.

The nurse was looking at him. She spoke. "Are you OK?"

"Yes," he said, taking his own deep breath, feeling the refrigerated air of the room enter his lungs like a ghost.

"The cath lab is on the way," she said, sympathetic now. "It'll only be a few more minutes."

Michael stepped up closer to the gurney, until he was bending down, and now Gass turned his head and their eyes met directly.

"Michael," Gass said.

"The cath lab is almost ready," he replied.

Gass was silent for a few moments, breathing heavily, before speaking again. His breath was white on the surface of the mask.

"How did you know I was here?"

"Nora called me."

"Nora," Gass said, then paused, as if he were going to continue. But he did not.

"Do you want to see her?"

"No." He was adamant now, trying to sit up.

"Try to relax, Dr. Gass," the nurse said. "It helps to be calm."

Gass smiled an odd soft smile then, and in that moment, in the time it took for Gass to smile, Michael saw the man's whole life, in all its empty reaches, spreading out before him. Believe the worst, so you may master the world, so it cannot touch you—and it had come to this, a clot the size of a pea, which no amount of endurance could endure. A clot the size of a pea, nothing more—a child's thumb, pressing down on the point where all the arguments wear thin.

The cardiologist was at the bedside now. "The lab's ready," he said. "Let's go."

Nora wasn't in the waiting room. She was outside, in the darkness. A light rain had begun, falling gently on the heat of the pavement. It was almost too soft to be heard, and soon it would be gone. It was common, this time of year—a light rain, whispering for a while, then moving off, like an animal grazing in a field of grass. And it was this, more than anything else, that allowed Michael to collect himself.

He walked toward her, and in the few seconds it took for his eyes to adjust to the dark, he realized that she was watching him with great intensity, as if afraid to speak, and her hand was curled in a little ball up to her mouth. No words came to him, and he stopped before her, feeling the rain on his exposed arms.

"How is he?" she said, letting her hand drop.

"Not so good." He struggled to speak in a normal voice; he drew himself together to do it. But he sounded shaken, he knew. He could hear it in himself.

"Is he dead?"

"No. They're trying to open the blockage." He thought briefly of Ann and her pigs, one after the other.

"That's good then, isn't it?"

"Yes. But his heart is badly damaged. It's not pumping very well."

"Oh." She was quiet for a moment, looking out past him. Her face was wet, but whether it was rainwater or tears he could not tell. She reached up then, covering her face with her hands, bending, just slightly.

"Will it get better?" But she was crying, he saw clearly, her tears falling down her face in patterns; she was crying after all.

"I don't know."

"What do you think?"

"I don't know, Nora. I really don't. I'm sorry."

"Tell me," she said, looking at him now. "You're a doctor."

He wanted to avoid her gaze, but he was looking at her directly.

"His heart may get better. Sometimes when heart muscle is starved of oxygen it doesn't completely die. It just gets weak and then it comes back. They call it stunned myocardium."

She turned away from him, leaned back against the wall. The concrete was starting to go dark.

"They have a name for everything."

He didn't answer. He thought, *They don't; they don't have a name for everything*. But he was quiet also. It was all he could do to stand there. He wanted to take her in his arms. He wanted to bring her close to him.

"When you were in there," she said, "I thought, I'll know when he comes back. When I see him I'll know. And when I saw you I did."

He did not answer.

She turned toward him, bowing her head until it rested on his chest, and started to sob, and he put his arms around her, and for a moment he rested his cheek against her black hair, beaded with rain, smelling of soap. She shook against him, and it was so intimate that for the briefest moment he was lost in it, in the darkness of her hair, and her shaking shoulders, and her hands on his back, and his own arms tightening around her.

Hours later, they sat together in the cafeteria. It was a wide room with fluorescent lights, made for hundreds, but at this time of night there were only a few people there. Nurses working the night shift, coming and going. Some others also, in ordinary clothes, looking weary, talking quietly. Families waiting for news.

They drank coffee from Styrofoam cups at a large round table. They had not spoken for some time now. The coffee was lukewarm and weak, and he spent a few seconds watching the powder of the creamer dissolve into the surface, stirring it with a thin red straw. The powder had gathered in the center, a little off-white disk, spinning slowly.

Gass was still alive. He lay a floor down, on a ventilator now, with the others. The room had been quiet, the nurse just outside the door on her stool, writing down numbers on the flow sheet—blood pressure, heart rate, ventilator settings—each hour, over and again as they passed. The catheter, a gold tube of urine, ran out from beneath the bedclothes into the bag: Five cc of urine per hour, she said. Paralyzed now and sedated, little balls of fluid tumbling one by one into his arms, Gass could not speak or move. Everything was being done. The cardiologist had long since gone home to sleep. It was the nurse alone now, used to waiting. "You look exhausted," she'd said to Nora. "Why don't you go home and get some rest. Visiting hours are over now. I'm sorry." Then, taking him aside, "You're a physician, so I'll tell you what I think." Out of earshot, as Nora walked slowly away.

So they were in the cafeteria, another way station, drinking coffee, silent for a while, Nora holding the cup close to her mouth, hunched and sipping. He watched her and felt the warmth of the cup in his own hands. It felt good, in the chill of the early morning hours, to hold the heat of the cup close.

Nora put her coffee down on the table and stretched, putting her hands over her head, arching her back, and the outline of her breasts pressed against her gray sweater for an instant before retreating again.

"You should go home," she said.

"I'm OK."

"There's no point in your staying here."

He took another sip of coffee and did not answer. It was the third time she had said this.

"I'll be back in a minute," he said, standing, running his hand through his hair.

She looked up at him suddenly, as if to get up and follow.

"I'm going to the bathroom."

"Oh," she said, pausing. "I'm sorry." She smiled briefly before looking away.

He urinated for a long while, it seemed. The tightness in his belly eased, and his back began, gently, to ache. The men's room was empty at this hour, so he took his time, washing his hands and face at the sink.

Nora was waiting for him, and as he left the bathroom, he clung to the knowledge of her presence, sitting alone at the table with her cup of coffee, a place to focus and begin. His hands were warm from the water.

Just as he reached her, they heard it over the PA system. It came again, the woman's voice calm and impersonal, and he sighed.

"It's his room," Nora said. "Ten-twenty-five." She started to run, taking the stairs two at a time, and he followed her down the hall to the ICU.

Gass's room was at the far end of the ICU. The glass doors to his room were open, and a small crowd stood outside. They could not see into the room.

"I'm not sure you should see this," he said, turning to her.

She was staring down the hall, the scene, whatever it was, just out of sight.

"Tell me what's happening," she said.

"I'll be right back." He turned, moving quickly away from her, until he was there. The earlier twilight of the room was gone; all the lights were on now, and they spared nothing. He craned his neck to see above the shoulders of the others—there were six or seven people crowding into the room and more arriving, called by the operator from throughout the hospital.

The bedclothes were gone, pulled to the foot of the bed. Gass lay naked upon it, so white he seemed nearly translucent. Already his fingers and toes were blue. The catheter ran up from the floor into his penis, which lay wrinkled and gray and small, stained by Betadine. Only the wound in his groin was covered. His fingers lay curled, the triangle of hair on his thin chest shot through with white. Wires were stuck there on circles of cloth; his face above them utterly expressionless, a clear tube entering his mouth. The machine still hissed. He was there for all to see.

A male nurse knelt on the bed beside him, his arms rigid, hands locked together. He was up there for leverage, Michael knew, nothing more, but it looked monstrous; he towered over the body, rhythmically driving the heels of his palms into Gass's chest, again and again, the chest bending under the force of it, then springing back. The nurse was fat, wearing loose scrubs that let his pendulous belly fall out and swing, the white line of his underwear just beneath it. In that moment, Michael saw something give beneath the man's thick hands, and there was a faint sound, like green wood broken underwater.

"I'm popping ribs," the man said, to no one in particular.

"Not so hard, Gary," a woman said, entering the room behind Michael. He turned. It was Gass's nurse, with a syringe in her hand. They stood facing each other.

"What's going on?" He knew already, of course.

"He was doing OK, and then he coded. The cardiologist is on his way."

The room was unflinchingly bright, leaving no detail unspared. The flesh on the bed, kneaded and broken. So this, he thought, is how it will end. He imagined Gass's smile, thin, as bitter as the world. And what do you think of me now, Ronald? Which one of us is chasing shadows?

"Stop CPR," the nurse said, her eyes on the screen. The green line there, flat, like rolling countryside. "Asystole," she said. "Get the pacer pads on him."

The two nurses rolled Gass roughly on his side, slapping the flat electrode to his thin well-lit back. For an instant, he could see the bones, the tent of the shoulder blades, the buttons of the vertebrae, and then they let go, and Gass rolled loosely back. His head followed the rest of him. Another pad now, on his chest, and there was blood, just a touch, on Gass's lips, his eyes half open, his gray and yellow teeth, moist and shining, with the tube between them.

"Start pacing."

"One hundred joules," she said.

Gass started to twitch, the muscles on his chest wrinkling and unwrinkling, his hands pulsing as if on strings and even his lean jaw, his teeth, again and again, seventy times per minute.

The nurse was shaking her head. Gass lay there, close enough to twitch, close enough to be warm, but gone, without question.

"Should I restart CPR?" The fat man, panting and sweating.

She shrugged. "Why not?" she said.

So the kneading began again, and the hiss of air out of Gass with each compression, the bed squeaking also, the force of it, the lolling head, the empty open eyes, the naked body, pulled this way and that, his chest loose and broken and wet inside. The ventilator continued.

Michael turned away for just a moment, but it was enough, because he saw who was standing behind him. It was Nora. The pallor, the stains, the caved-in chest, the hissing breath, the empty eyes that all the mockery in the world could not fill—she stood there and watched it all.

Finally, the cardiologist burst into the room, out of breath also, in his white coat, speaking. "What do we have? Have you tried pacing him?" These words, and others, the man's lips moving, the nurse's lips moving, so close, as if through a lens, magnifying their faces, the man shaking his head now, both of them shaking their heads, and then the man bending over the figure on the bed, looking in his eyes, listening with his stethoscope, motioning, looking at the screen. He must have spoken, because the fat man got off the bed, heavily, with effort.

Gass lay alone. There was silence everywhere, and bright lights. The crowd began to file out, one after another, quietly, which is how the dead are always left. The cardiologist turned toward Nora, murmuring, his hand on her shoulder. She stared at her father, naked and stained, as thin as a boy; she stared as if to be absolutely certain, giving no sign that she heard or felt the man's touch, or Michael's, until he led her away.

"My father," Nora said, before she began to cry again, "was so hard. He was so hard."

They sat together in the consultation room. Time had passed, arrangements had been made, mortuaries had been discussed. The chaplain had patted her hand and left, and through it all her tears came and went like gusts of wind. Nora wiped her nose with her fingers. Her eyes were red at the edges, her nostrils raw and pink already, her hair in strands. It seemed very important that he look at her.

"He loved you, though," he said. The words felt flat. What we offer, what we require—say this; this is what you do at such times.

"I don't think," she said, after a bit, "that he loved anything."

"That can't be true," he said, wondering if it was.

"He was so hard," she said again.

"He was disciplined."

She laughed, short and bitter and brief. "Yes," she said. "And now he's dead. He was disciplined and pretended he knew everything and then he died. Look where it got him."

He did not reply. *What can I say to that?* But there was something more, of course, that was left unspoken, that could not even be described. The withholding figure, with his faint annihilating smile, looking out into the world as if untouched . . .

"I'm sorry, Nora."

"There are some people who shouldn't have children," she said. "There are some people who are empty and try to fill that emptiness by denying love. By judging everything. By mocking everything."

"I don't know you very well," he said carefully. "And I didn't know him that well. But he was concerned about you. I know he was."

"That's because he was disappointed in me. Not because he loved me." She was sobbing now.

"I don't think that's true," he said, as gently as he could.

"Well," she said, "he never told me. He never made it clear. And it seems to me that's the one real responsibility you have in life."

He was clinging to her now, he could feel it. He was clinging to the certainty of her grief and her bitterness and her struggle. It was giving him focus, a kind of rough clarity. He thought this consciously: *Stay here with her, listen, give her what you can, before you are in the wilderness again*. She wept, and for him it was a place of rest.

"When I came into the room," she said, "and I saw what they were doing—"

"He wasn't there anymore, Nora. He wasn't feeling it."

"But what that man was doing to his chest—"

"I know."

"I will never forget that. I think I'll always remember him like that."

"That wasn't him. It wasn't."

"He didn't think much of me, Michael. It's hard."

"Nora . . ."

"He didn't think much of you either. Not at all."

It wounded him—deeply, he realized—even as she spoke. It was so unexpected that he had no time to brace himself. Not that it mattered. But even from the dead, it wounded him, and it must have been clear on his face.

"No," he said, after a while. "I don't suppose he did."

"I'm sorry," she said. "You've been very kind to me."

Suddenly, he felt his eyes fill with tears, and though he blinked them away, he was certain she had noticed.

"I tried to impress him, I think," he said. "In a childish way. He lost respect for me."

"My father," she said, "was never impressed by people who tried to impress him."

"I can see that."

"Do you? Do you understand what I mean?"

"Maybe not."

"What my father did his whole life was withhold. He withheld from my mother. He withheld from me. He had contempt for people who wanted his approval and his love because he thought that meant they were weak."

"I thought he loved your mother."

"When she was dying he acted as if it didn't touch him at all."

"Did it?"

"I don't know. I really don't."

"He told me she was precious to him."

"And I'm sure he said it like he was talking about the weather. Or like he had a meeting."

"Maybe so," he said. But he couldn't remember, not really. Had so much time passed? Was it true?

"What my father hated," she said, "was weakness. He couldn't stand weakness in any form. And he was a cruel person because of it."

"You don't have to tell me this, you know," he said. "I don't mean to pry."

"Sometimes," she said, after a moment of thought, "it's easier to talk to people you don't know that well. Do you know what I mean?"

He nodded.

"It was normal for you to want to impress him, Michael," she said. "I'm sure you looked up to him. He must have been a father figure for you. And it was just like him to throw it back at you."

"Maybe he was right. He wasn't my father."

"No, he wasn't right. He wanted to throw it back at you, do you understand? He wanted people to try to get his approval so he could deny it. It was power for him."

She was speaking with great intensity, looking at him as if it were terribly important that he believe her. It was a desperate story, and through it he could see the depth of her sadness, her losses, unspoken, there in the past. Damage and insight and intelligence and anger and darkness: all of it together, all of it boiling just beneath the surface, rising now, vaporous, half controlled. That, and a dead man, lying nearby.

He shook his head and blinked, as if to clear his eyes.

"Do you remember when he asked you to dinner?"

"Yes."

"Why do think he invited you over?"

"I don't know. I thought it because I was going through a bad time."

"It was about a patient, wasn't it?"

"A child died. It was hard for me."

"Well, you were right. That is why he invited you over."

"I don't understand."

"He was pretending to comfort you. But what he was really doing is drawing you in. He wanted you to turn to him for help so he could deny it. He saw it as an opportunity."

"Your father and I had an odd relationship," he said slowly. "I'm not even sure exactly what it was. There was some tension between us. But I can't believe that he would do that consciously. I'm sorry." He spoke wearily. It didn't matter to him, he thought, one way or the other. But to her it did matter, it mattered a great deal; that much was clear.

"I don't mean consciously," she said. "I mean unconsciously. That's the point. My father thought he could endure everything, he thought nothing touched him, and underneath he was completely deluded. He had no idea why he did the things he did. He found reasons, but they weren't the real reasons at all."

"How are any of us different?"

"We're different because we don't take pleasure in the pain of others."

"Do you think he was evil?"

"Do you think he was good?"

"I don't know what he was," he said, thinking of Gass in his bag, six floors down. He must be warm even now, clinging to the ghost of life. It would take hours for him to be as cold as the others. Nora bowed her head and began to rock slightly, back and forth.

"You should go home, Nora," he said, after a while. "You should try and get some sleep."

She nodded, finally. "I'm going to get cleaned up," she said. "I'll meet you in the lobby in fifteen minutes."

So he sat alone in the consultation room, looking at the plants, the pastel prints hanging on the wall. He felt very alone, looking at his watch, and a few minutes later there was a knock on the door. It was the chaplain.

"Excuse me," he said, looking at Michael. "I didn't know you were still here."

The chaplain was an older man with a warm, quiet voice, gray, a little stooped. He had told them he was a retired pastor, and now he looked down awkwardly.

"I'm sorry, Dr. Grant," he said. "There is another family . . ."

"Of course," Michael replied, realizing that their allocated time in the room had expired. "I was just leaving."

There were others waiting to come in. Vaguely, he wondered who they were and whom they had lost, as he stood in the hall, and pressed the elevator button, and watched the numbers grow nearer.

There was a *ping,* and the elevator doors slid open before him. Standing there, looking directly at him, stood a small, very black child. She was perhaps six, wearing a white-and-blue-striped dress, with high white socks and shiny black shoes. Her hair was cornrowed, a blue or a white bead at the end of each strand. Their eyes met, and she smiled at him shyly.

For an instant, he believed she was alone. Impossible, he thought—such a young child, by herself, at this early hour of the morning, dressed as if for church—but there she was, smiling at him before looking down. Then he saw a man's shoes, just visible to one side, and realized that someone was leaning back against the wall of the elevator, hidden by the doors, which did not open entirely.

"Going down?" he called, into the elevator, standing a few feet away and to one side.

"Going up," a voice replied.

The girl stood there for just a moment, shining and new. She is too old, he thought, she is far too old, and then the doors closed with a hiss and left him watching the numbers—four, five, six, and seven—with the briefest pause between.

Nora was already waiting in the lobby, looking at him closely as he crossed the carpet toward her. For an instant, he'd wondered whether she would be there at all, whether any of these recent events had occurred. They seemed so difficult to believe, in the unease of the elevator as it drifted down to a stop. But she was there, waiting, and the sight of her drawn and reddened face filled him with such relief that he nearly ran toward her. She looked like grief, she looked exhausted and distraught, and this alone reassured him.

"Are you OK?" she asked, standing.

"I'm fine."

"You don't look fine."

"I know." Speak to her, do not think. Never mind the shifting periphery, faces passing left and right. It was morning now, and people were starting to arrive. He could see the strong light of day over her shoulders through the lobby windows. The lobby, he thought. As if this were a hotel. Though perhaps in a way it was, now that he thought of it, because it was for travelers, and was full of rooms, and food was served, and messages were left, there were appointments and meetings everywhere—

He stopped himself then, before his thoughts could continue, and tumble, and carry him even farther away. She was speaking to him, looking into his eyes.

"Did you hear me, Michael?"

"I'm sorry."

"I asked if you wanted to get something to eat. In the cafeteria."

"I'm not hungry."

"No. I guess I'm not either."

"We should go home," he said.

"They're going to come and get him. I should stay for that."

"You mean the mortuary?"

She nodded.

"You don't need to be here. They do it all the time. It'll probably be this afternoon."

She looked as if she might start crying all over again.

"Yes," she said. "They do come a lot, don't they? I suppose it's routine."

He had seen the hearses, many times, by the service entrance of hospitals. Almost every afternoon, sometimes for his own patients. Now they would come again. He said nothing, but he pictured it clearly: the bored driver, reading a newspaper as he waited in the long black car.

"You need to go home," he said.

"I know. It's just that I don't want to go home. I don't want to go back there." She paused. "Do you know what I mean? I know he's gone, but as long as we're here it almost seems as if he isn't. Almost as if it isn't over. I'm not making any sense." She raised her hand quickly to her lips and then let it drop.

"You *are* making sense," he said.

"It was his house."

He nodded, and then, gently, he took her arm. "I'll take you," he said. "I'll drive you."

She didn't answer, but she followed, and together they walked out through the wide automatic doors into the sunny morning. To either side stood little clusters of smokers, and the smell of cigarette smoke mingled with that of clean, fresh air. The sky was clear, with only a few clouds on the horizon over the city.

"It's such a beautiful day," she said. She seemed her age, he thought, and exhausted, but now she was looking around with the eagerness of a child.

"It really is," he replied, because he was taking it in also—the beads of water on the blades of grass, the sound of a lawn mower in the distance, the air smelling of last night's thunderheads, and the wind moving just slightly, as if waking.

"Where's your car?" he asked, after a while.

"Oh," she said, as if coming back. "Over there, I think."

She inclined her head in the direction of the emergency room parking lot a few feet away, and they both started walking.

"Where's yours?" she said.

"Same place." And he could, to his surprise, remember where it was exactly, as if he'd parked it only a short time ago.

They stood by the cars, which were only a few spaces apart.

"I'll drive," he said, gesturing.

"Why don't you follow me?" she replied. "That way we don't have to come back."

So he did. It was much easier, he thought, to simply follow, and keep her small car full in the windshield, and let her lead him where she would. She could have driven anywhere in the city; he ignored everything but the black knot of her head in the car in front of him, fading and growing in the ebb of traffic.

She parked in the driveway, next to her father's car, and he pulled up along the curb just beyond her, directly in front of the house. She was sitting in the seat, as if waiting for him, so he got out. She was crying again, he saw, as he opened her door.

"Nora," he said.

"I'm sorry." She wiped her eyes and nose on her sleeve.

"Come inside."

She nodded, took a breath, and stood. "It keeps coming over me," she said. "One minute I think I'm OK and then it just comes again."

"I know."

She was quiet.

"Do you have the keys?"

"What? Oh, yes. Here." She handed them to him. Her tears had stopped, though her face was still damp. He thought, Only so many tears are possible.

She followed him up the walk and up the steps and stood quietly as he fumbled for an instant with the lock.

"It's the square one," she said.

The house was quiet. It is only an echo now, he thought, but you would never know it. The furniture, the deep reds of the carpet. The curtains open to the yard, the whole room full of light. On the wall, the clock said it was nearly eight in the morning. They had a full day ahead of them. He thought of how it must look to her—her father's medical journal open on the coffee table, articles unread, pages unturned. And it struck him how the next few days would be an endless repetition of this moment. A pair of shoes left out on the floor, letters with his name on them, telephone calls, his dishes in the sink—all the small details of life and now of death.

But she walked past him, into the kitchen, and he followed.

"I want a cup of tea," she said. "Do you want one?"

"That would be nice. Thanks."

She nodded and busied herself with the cupboard, taking out matching cups and saucers. She turned the knob on the stove, he heard three quick clicks, and then the flame of the burner went up like an umbrella being opened. He watched as she filled the kettle from the tap and placed it on the burner. Soon the kettle began to tick. She set the cups on the table, a teabag in each one, and sat down.

"My grandmother's china," she said, gesturing.

They were thin and delicate, off-white, with tiny yellow circles around the rim. She stared at them.

"It's funny," she said. "I remember these from when I was a little girl."

The kettle began to sing. She stood, lifting the kettle off the burner, turned, and poured the clear hot water into the cups. The tea stained it instantly, and he reached out and lifted the bag by its string, feeling its small weight in his fingers as the water slowly darkened.

The tea was hot and sweet.

"It was horrible, wasn't it?" she said, as she sat down. "It was so horrible."

"They were trying to save him, Nora."

"I realize that. And that was almost the worst thing about it. What they had to do."

"It was necessary."

"I'm sure it was."

They were silent for a while, sipping their tea.

"I've seen so much of this," he said, after a while, "that I forget how difficult it is. It has to happen to someone you know to remind you. Someone nearby."

"Was my father near enough?"

"Yes," he said. "He was."

"Well, then, I'm glad for you."

"I didn't mean it like that," he said carefully. "What I meant was, you learn to let it go past you. But when it doesn't, nothing is any help."

"So what have you learned, Michael? From all your experience?"

"To be an actor, I think."

"To be an actor? What do you mean?"

"To be an actor in my own life. Or a tourist. I'm not sure exactly how to say it."

She laughed bitterly. "You're deluding yourself if you think that. None of us are tourists in our own lives."

"You don't think so?"

"No, I don't. We're not tourists, because underneath we're all afraid."

They were silent for a while, finishing their tea.

"Do you want something to eat?" she asked.

He shook his head. Soon, in only a few more moments, he would have to leave, to go back to the emptiness of his own house and the parade of days to follow. The thought made him ache. There is nothing there for me, nothing at all except stillness and hours, waiting for whatever was yet to happen, and the results from the lab, which suddenly he could almost feel, like the brush of a hand on his shoulder. His desire to stay here, in this kitchen, and drink tea with her, grew radiant. But they had been up all night. They had to sleep.

"I should go," he said finally.

She looked away. "I'm sorry," she said, after a little while. "After all you've done it's a lot to ask."

"What?"

"Would you mind, Michael?" She looked at him directly, her eyes raw. For an instant he saw the face of an old woman—her face, thirty years away—and wondered what she saw as she looked at him.

"Would I mind about what?" Though he knew what she was asking.

"I don't want to be alone in this house. We have a guest room."

He nodded, slowly, but his relief was overpowering.

"Of course," he said.

"I know I'll have to face it eventually," she said. "I know I'm being silly."

"You're not being silly. I didn't want to go home anyway."

"You didn't?"

"I don't know anyone here."

She smiled a wan smile then, and in a little while they both got up and she showed him to his room. It was only a short way, and he put his arms around her, briefly, as they stood in the doorway, before she turned to go.

He needed a shower but was far too tired to bother. The room, he saw, was as clean and anonymous as the rest of the house, the bed made tightly. It reminded him of a hotel. He wondered if anyone had ever slept there.

He undressed quickly, pausing only to drop the blinds across the windows. All he wanted, in that moment, was to sleep; it was sudden, passionate. He fumbled with his clothes, the laces of his shoes, his shirt, then drew back the sheets and slid beneath them. The muscles of his legs and back throbbed, his knees and shoulders ached, but for the first time in years he didn't feel alone.

He woke to someone shaking him. It was gentle at first, but then rougher, and finally, as if through many layers of cloth, he heard a woman's voice calling his name.

He bolted upright then, and she jumped back. It was Nora, and the light was on. He saw her clearly, but it was still a few more moments before the events of the recent past came flooding back, and he knew where he was.

"What's the matter?" she asked.

"What?" he said, blinking his eyes, trying to shake his head clear. He drew the sheets up, covering himself.

"You were screaming."

"I was?"

"You were making this terrible sound."

"I'm sorry," he said, shaking his head again.

"I would have let you sleep, but—"

"No, no, I'm glad you woke me up. What time is it?"

"Almost nine."

"At night?"

"Yes. You've been sleeping all day."

"When did you get up?"

"I've been awake for hours," she said. "Were you having a nightmare?"

"I don't remember."

"Well, that sound you were making. . . ." She trailed off, looking away. He had frightened her badly, he saw.

"I didn't mean to upset you." He didn't know what else to say.

"Are you all right, Michael?"

"What do you mean?"

"I think that was the most frightening thing I've ever heard. I can't even describe it."

"I was screaming?"

"I don't know what you were doing. It was something between a scream and a moan. I've never heard anything like it."

Her face, her voice—he had done something, it was clear, and though he had no memory of it at all it chilled him. The aftermath, still in her eyes.

He let out a deep breath. He wondered how many other times, in recent days, he had done the same thing. Without knowing, because there was no one to hear him.

"Well," she said, more calm, "you're awake now."

He tried to offer her a smile and she smiled back, briefly. They were alone in the room. He was nearly naked beneath the thin sheet.

"I was going to wake you up anyway in a few minutes. I've made some dinner," she said. "You must be hungry."

To his surprise, he was—he was starving, ravenous. He couldn't remember the last time he had eaten.

"I'll be in the kitchen," she said, and left the room.

When he followed a few minutes later, dressed in the same clothes, he smelled the food as soon as he stepped into the hall. The kitchen curtains across the windows were drawn, and the small table was set with good china and silver. Nora was peering into the oven, where something bubbled and hissed, and then she stepped back, closing the oven door, and he felt a gust of hot, rich air brush against him. She turned as he entered.

"Would you mind closing the door?" she said.

Nora had bathed and dressed. She wore jeans and an old wool sweater. Her hair was pulled back behind her head, and the age he had seen in her face, the thirty years of future, was gone. She's lovely, he thought.

"This looks incredible," he said, but the commonness of his words grated. He felt vulgar, somehow, when what he wanted to say was *This is beautiful. You are beautiful.*

"I needed something to do," she said. "I didn't want to think."

"What are you making? It smells wonderful."

"Roast chicken. Bread, too. It should be ready in a few minutes."

The kitchen was warm, redolent.

"Do you want some wine?"

"Please," he said, pulling out the chair from the table at an angle and sitting down. She reached for the bottle on the counter and poured two glasses. The wine was a deep red, and she poured it carefully, allowing no drops to spill.

"Aren't you going to sit down?" he said. She glanced at the clock on the stove.

"Only if you let me know when two minutes are up," she replied, pulling out the opposite chair. Her back was to the clock. "Here," she said, and handed him the glass of wine.

The glass was delicate, and he knew as soon as he touched it that it must be old.

"Was this your grandmother's also?"

"I don't know why I wanted to use these tonight," she said, looking down at the bone china, the silver and glasses. "But I felt I should. It's probably silly."

"No, it's not," he said. "I think it's kind. It's respectful."

"This is the first dinner he will never have," she said, "and I wanted it to be a good one."

She laughed suddenly, the kind of laugh that can effortlessly turn to tears, but then she stopped herself.

"I'm sorry," she said. "This is so difficult."

He nodded.

"I'm glad you're here, Michael," she said. "I'm glad I didn't have to eat this meal by myself."

"I'm glad I'm here also."

"Well," she said, lifting her glass, as if to make a toast. But then she paused. "I'm sorry," she said, shaking her head as if in wonderment. "It's a habit. Now I don't know what to say."

"You don't have to say anything."

"Then I won't," she said. "Let's just touch glasses."

There was a small ringing sound, and they each took a sip.

"I'm no expert," he said, "but I like this."

"My father liked good wine." She paused. "That's what I mean. That's why this is so hard."

"I'm sorry," he said, and she smiled and shook her head again.

"Your two minutes are almost up," he said, after a while.

Salad came first. She tossed it quickly, at the table, and served each of them. Oil and vinegar, the faint bitterness of the lettuce, and then hot bread.

"Save room," she said, because he was taking mouthfuls of warm bread and mouthfuls of salad as if he were a starving man.

"I will," he answered, between bites, which he washed down with wine.

"Of course," she said, "you're not supposed to drink red wine with chicken."

"I don't care."

"Well," she said, "I never liked white wine. So I have red wine with chicken and fish." She blushed, he saw, as soon as she spoke.

"I can't believe I said that," she said.

The sharp edge of his hunger was gone now, dulled, and he put down his fork for a minute.

"You don't always have to say serious things."

"But I should be thinking about serious things. I should be making an effort."

"You are making an effort."

"How?"

"This meal is serious. It's beautiful. I'm grateful to be part of it." He was surprised by the intensity in his own voice. "I can't think of any better thing you could have done for your father."

"He wouldn't have understood it."

"Then it would have been his loss."

She started to cry a little then, and he waited, patiently, until she stopped, dabbing her eyes with the heavy linen napkin in her lap.

"Let's have some chicken," she said finally.

The skin of the chicken was a crisp golden brown, the meat full of juice and garlic. He was not one to whom food meant much. There had been many times in his life when the need to eat weighed on him joylessly, had forced him out into the streets to cheap takeouts, fluorescent lights, and waxed-paper cups of soda.

But now he could not remember ever being so aware of his hunger. It was not so great, he knew; there had been many times in the past where he had gone far longer without food. But his awareness of it was great. He felt as if he were standing at attention—the crispness of the skin, the whiteness of the meat against the scarlet cranberries, the depth of the bread and gravy—all of it shone in his mouth. Another sip of wine, each of them quiet now.

It took only a few minutes for them to eat their fill. The best meals, he thought, were always that way—hours of preparation going up like newspaper in a fire. He cleaned his plate carefully, with nearly the last of the bread.

"That was great," he said, after a while. His voice sounded rough again, crude to his ear. He was starting to feel strange again. Something was whispering.

"Thank you," she replied.

She had also eaten. He'd expected her to peck at her food, but her plate was clean.

"I didn't think I'd be so hungry," she said, as if on cue. "But I was starving. Funny, isn't it."

"Why is it funny?" Concentrate.

"That you never know how you'll react. To anything. You can never predict how you'll feel."

"Oh, I don't know. Sometimes you can."

"I mean with big things."

"I know what you mean," he said, though he didn't exactly.

"In a lot of ways I think I hated him," she said softly. "And now that just makes it worse."

They were quiet for a moment.

"Would you like some coffee?" she asked.

"I would," he said. "Thank you."

From a distance, he watched as she put three spoonfuls of the black powder in each filter, then hung them above the cups. The kettle came to a boil so quickly it seemed as if no time had passed. He watched her, and she seemed like a statue, even as she poured boiling water into the powder. He heard it crackle where it fell. He shook his head quickly before it could come on again, the shift, the change, the traveling, the vertiginous distances, all in the time it took a wisp of steam to rise and vanish.

"Excuse me for a moment."

"Where are you going?"

"The bathroom," he said. "I'll be right back."

He ran the water cold and plunged his hands into it, bringing them up against his face. His cheeks in the mirror were flushed, his eyes were bright, and when he stepped up close and opened his mouth, it was there.

Sometime later, how much longer he could not say, he heard knocking. It was tentative, at first, but then grew louder. She was calling to him so he opened the bathroom door.

"You've been in here for almost a half an hour," she said.

"I have?" He shook his head, but it wouldn't clear, and he felt a wave of conscious terror flow through him, as if he might run wildly through the house and out into the darkness outside.

"Is anything wrong?"

He rubbed his face hard, feeling the sand of his black stubble on his palms.

"I'm just tired," he managed. "I'm sorry."

She took a step back into the hall. She looked wary.

"Can I show you something?" he asked.

"Show me what?" she said, after a pause.

"My throat has been bothering me."

She looked very confused.

"You have a sore throat?"

"Yes," he said, for lack of a better explanation. "I'll show you in the mirror." He turned away and stepped up again to the glass. He could see her in it, tentatively taking a watchful step toward him.

"I want you to tell me what you see," he said, and opened his mouth.

It was clear as day now, it couldn't be missed. What once had been a suggestion, a whisper, was now a tiny thread, uncoiling from behind his left tonsil, halfway to his uvula. With Jonas, he thought, dimly, there had been many threads, many paths to follow, but here, for some reason, there was only one. I just need to follow it, he thought, like string through a cave, and for a moment the thought calmed him, as if nothing could be simpler.

She was approaching now; he could feel her near his back and then the warmth of her breath, on his left ear.

"It's in the back of my throat," he said, before opening his mouth again. "I want you to tell me what you see."

She stood on her tiptoes, and he felt her hand, lightly on his shoulder, for balance. Her face, ghostly and close, was just over his shoulder.

"I see a white line," she said.

"Are you sure?"

"Of course I'm sure. It's a tiny white line, like a thread."

He stepped back, closing his mouth. Her words rushed through him, filling him with a sudden inexplicable gratitude.

"Thank you," he said.

"Why are you thanking me? What is it?"

"I thought I might have something caught in my throat, that's all. But I couldn't see it that well."

"You thought you were imagining it?"

"I wasn't sure."

"Well," she said, puzzled and troubled, "you're not. It's there."

He nodded, trying to calm himself. The sound of his breathing filled the small space. He turned toward her, knowing what she must see. What must he look like to her?

"What do you think it is?"

"I must have scratched my throat on something," he said, and forced himself to the sink. He splashed some water on his face and, after a little while, began to feel somewhat better.

She watched him, her eyes narrowed. She looked troubled and uncertain and deeply tired.

"Are you sure you're all right, Michael?"

He nodded as best he could. "I was sick last week, and I don't think I'm completely over it. I'm sorry, it just came over me."

She put her hand on his shoulder. "Maybe you should go back to bed," she said. "I think we both should."

She moved close to him and let him put his arms around her, rested her head briefly on his shoulder. Then she began to cry again, and this, more than anything else, allowed him to collect himself. He stroked her hair for a while, and then she wiped her nose on her sleeve and made a sound halfway between tears and laughter.

MUCH LATER THAT NIGHT, HE LAY WIDE AWAKE AND LISTENING. CRACKS of light came through the blinds from the street, and the earlier traffic was gone. Nora had gone to bed hours ago, and for the moment he knew that she was asleep on the other side of the house. He had come close to telling her, but now, lying alone and afraid, he was glad he had not. He had not indulged himself in weakness, he had not laid yet another burden at her feet. But she had seen it, she had seen it plainly, and this fact made the choice before him clear.

It was no effort at all to leave the warmth of the bed. His eyes had been adjusting to the dark for hours, and though the room was full of shadows he quickly found his clothes and slipped into them. Quietly, he crossed the few feet from the bed, stepped out into the hall, and closed the door behind him. The hall was brighter; light entered from the far kitchen windows, and he eased himself toward them. She must have stayed up, because all the dishes had been put away.

The back door opened to the yard, and he was careful to leave it unlocked behind him. The sky was overcast, he saw, with few stars. Continuing around the side of the house to the street, the grass felt slick beneath his feet, and his ankles ached. But he could see well, he thought—very well. The ghostly dark houses, the gray glimmer of the road, the black of the grass.

He slipped into his car where he had left it by the curb, started the engine quickly, and pulled away, letting three houses pass before he turned on the headlights. The street leaped up before him. It was important, he thought, to remember what he was doing. Just go in, change clothes, pack a bag, and find the envelope beneath the letter slot. Just that.

He pulled into his driveway, shut off the engine and the lights, and got out of the car. His house looked strange in the darkness, as if he were coming home after a long time away.

Inside, he stood in the light of the hall, looking down. It was there—a thin envelope, with a cellophane window and the name of the lab—among the bills like a personal letter. Only a few more moments, he thought, as he turned away for the stairs, only a few more, and then I have to open it.

Never had his bedroom seemed so empty. The patterns of the wallpaper, the bedspread, even the unwashed sheets—these were his things, his skin on the cotton, his cells on the toothbrush in the bathroom, yet it felt as if he were entering the life of another person entirely, one who was away, who was traveling, who had left this behind.

No one, he thought, should see themselves so well. He clung to the thought, in all its self-pity; he clung to it long enough to step into his walk-in closet and toss a few handfuls of clothes into his overnight bag. Then into the bathroom, quickly, for his toothbrush and razor. He felt the stubble on his cheeks and then he was moving again, down the stairs, to where the mail lay scattered like a hand of cards on the brown oak floor.

Then he bent down, picked up the letter, slid it into his pocket, and left the house. His car was warm when he got to it, but he turned on the heater anyway and drove slowly back to Nora's house. He sat there awhile, at the curb, with the dome light on. Anyone awake on the street could see him.

When it was clear that his breathing would not slow down, he opened the letter. He did it crudely, his finger through one corner, then down the full length, like gutting a fish.

He had to squint at the rows of small numbers. Liver functions, kidney functions, electrolytes—normal, normal, with his finger beside them.

His platelet count was twenty-eight thousand, less than a quarter of what it should have been. The number leaped out at him, with the computer's small star for guidance—a little north star, he thought, which was Polaris, high above the arm of the Big Dipper—just follow the line and it will lead you by happenstance along the long axis of the earth, which wobbles only slightly, once every twenty or thirty thousand years.

And now his breathing did slow, of its own accord—he felt it, somewhere in the distance beneath him. Verified by repeat analysis. Next to the star, but there they were, his platelets, falling away, just as they had done for Jonas, clear on the page.

He left the guest room early the next morning, before Nora was awake, leaving a quick false note of explanation—he was taking care of a few things at home and would call her later—on the kitchen table. Now he sat for a long time in the hospital parking lot, watching the growing stream of people coming and going through the wide doors. As he sat there he had the odd sensation that he would be able to remember each of their faces for days, some expressionless, some smiling, others looking unconcerned, still others afraid. They could, he supposed, have been anywhere, doing anything, but they were here and so, now, was he.

For a while, it seemed almost impossible. Who do I talk to, the elderly volunteer at the information desk? The emergency room, where they would roll their eyes and ask if he had called his primary doctor? He had managed to bring himself here, and yet the distance between him and the rest of the world had never seemed so great or so difficult to cross. He should have called, he supposed. He knew them slightly, from the two lectures he'd given at the medical school, when he still cared about making an impression.

In truth, the place was well down the ladder as far as academic medical centers went—lower, certainly, than where he had trained. This fact had been a little source of pleasure to him in the past, when he had driven by and looked at the neon sign over the building:

UNIVERSITY HOSPITAL. But now, as he sat motionless in his car, the sign loomed above him and he saw it for what it was—the place where his fate would be decided.

There was a bruise on his elbow. Casual, just a knock he could not remember, the doorjamb, maybe, or the nightstand. Painless, almost unnoticed. He rolled up the sleeve of his shirt once more, to look at it again. It was as unchanged as a silver dollar, blue-black, a jet of ink on the white surface of his skin. He was not one to bruise easily, so he knew what it meant. If he had been at home, in privacy, he would have undressed and examined himself. Not that it mattered. If there was one, there were others.

He felt the beginnings of nausea. A few more moments passed, his nausea grew, and he felt as if the clear windows of the car were closing in on him, and just like that he opened the door and stood up, with his palm on the roof for balance. A few more seconds passed, he felt rushing in his ears, and warmth, and then he bent forward, resting his damp forehead on the roof of the car. People walked by.

"Are you all right?" A woman's voice, behind him. He managed to turn, holding on to the open door.

She was a thin black woman, wearing a red bandanna like a cap. She had no hair, he saw. A plain white blouse, dark slacks, flat gray shoes. A yellowish cast to the whites of her eyes, which were fixed on him. A pleasant face, he thought, looking at him with some concern. She looked oddly familiar to him, but he could not place her.

"I'm a little dizzy," he said.

"Would you like me to call someone?"

She was staring at him, and as she did he felt the nausea begin to recede.

"No," he said. "I'm fine. Thanks."

"Are you sure?"

He smiled weakly at her. "Yes. I'll be fine."

Her eyes didn't leave his face. "You don't look so good," she said. "Where are you going?"

"I was looking for the emergency room." The signs were everywhere, with arrows, he couldn't help but see them. But the words left his mouth on their own.

"It's over there," she said, pointing.

"Thanks," he said. He was standing more easily now. But the woman seemed to hesitate.

"Here," she said. "Come with me." She reached out, taking his arm in her small brown hand.

"I'm all right. Really."

"Don't argue. Just come along now."

She was leading him off, and he had taken an involuntary step with her before remembering to close the door. He debated locking it, but already he was two steps gone, and there was nothing in there anyway.

"Do you work here?" he asked, walking with her. Her hand was softer now on his arm, and in any case she was a small woman who could not have held him if he fell. Nonetheless, he enjoyed the feel of her hand on his arm, just for an instant.

"I used to," she said. "You look pale. Are you having any chest pain?"

"No," he said.

"Short of breath?"

He was looking at her bandanna.

"Are you a nurse?"

"I was," she said. "I guess I still am."

"No," he said. "I'm not short of breath."

"Well, you were looking pretty diaphoretic there. I thought you were going to pass out on me."

They were almost at the door now.

"That means sweaty," she said.

"I know."

She looked up at him. "You do?"

"I'm a physician," he said.

She laughed pleasantly. "Well, what do you make of that? A sick doctor and a sick nurse going to the hospital."

The bandanna, the yellow of her eyes. "You're here as a patient?"

"My appointment's in an hour." They were at the door to the ER now, and she opened it. "After you," she said.

He stepped through, and they were in the waiting room. It was early; only a few others were there. A clerk sat behind a glass partition. She was an older woman, thin as a sparrow, with straight white hair and thick overlarge glasses.

"Can I help you?" she asked disinterestedly.

"I'm here to be seen," he said.

"Name?"

"Michael Grant."

"Date of birth?" He gave it.

"Social Security number?" He gave this as well. A new wave of nausea came over him.

"Insurance?"

He nodded and spoke. She was far away.

"What's the reason you're here?" The first of the questions. Both women were looking at him.

"Nausea," he said finally.

"Have a seat, sir, the nurse will be with you in a moment." She gestured to one of the plastic chairs bolted to the floor all around him.

The woman's hand was on his arm once more, leading him to the chair, and he sat down heavily.

"I think I'm going to be sick," he said, taking several deep shuddering breaths.

"Just try to relax," she said. "They know you're here."

He nodded, as the wave began to subside once more. "I think I should have a basin," he said.

"I'll be right back," she replied, and went to the window.

It was all down to the moment—her kindness, a kind strange woman walking to the glass window and knocking, the overwhelming nausea that blotted out everything, and the dim awareness of his soaking shirt, and now she was coming back with a pink plastic bucket in her hand, and the door was opening behind her, and a male nurse in dark blue scrubs was following her. Michael held the bucket between his knees, bending over it. He gasped for a few more moments, then looked up. She was still standing there, the male nurse beside her. The nurse held a blood-pressure cuff in his hand, and he was asking questions. The blood pressure cuff tightened on his arm, the thermometer entered his ear. Let them do it, he thought. Stop thinking.

His nausea came in deep waves, with a small period of silence in between. He knew he would give in soon, no matter the reluctance. Each time it was closer, each interval clearer and more brief. It was hard labor, he thought; it was making him throw his heart into it, and there was nothing he could do, nothing he could think of anymore. It didn't hesitate at all.

He was by himself now, with curtains around him, shivering on the gurney with his bare legs against the metal bars, nearly naked beneath the thin gown, hunched over the pink plastic basin on his knees.

He felt the vomit rising in his chest, out of the hard knot that had become his belly, and then it was all over him, in his throat, in his nose, burning and stinking, he was making that sound, and the fluid was pouring out of him, striking the basin. His eyes were closed. It came again, the sudden weight of the basin, splashing, and now there were cooling dots all over his legs and his lips and fingers trembled and sang. He retched again and opened his eyes.

The basin was full of warm blood.

He stared at it for just a moment before the nausea came again, the briefest moment—the pink basin, the deep red pool in the overhead light. At least a unit, he thought, with more to follow. And now he could taste it too, through the sting of acid in his nose—the unmistakable taste of blood, clotting on his teeth, coating his tongue, oily and slick and new.

"What's going on in there?"

The curtain parted; it was the nurse in the blue scrubs. Michael looked up. He saw the nurse as if through a haze, through heat on a summer road. Something was running down his chin.

"Oh, boy," the man said, and turned, calling loudly over his shoulder into the space beyond. "We've got a GI bleeder here. I need some help."

The world began to fade a bit then, to contract and expand, and he lay back heavily on the gurney, his legs hanging to the floor. He held the basin, though, he held it tightly, even as the fluid slopped warmly onto his stomach and chest.

The nurse was busy and fast at the cupboard in the cubicle, his hands glinting with needles and clear plastic.

"Do you drink alcohol?" he said, as he turned.

Michael felt another kind of wave now, a wave of deep exhaustion, as if he were somehow entering the warm stain on his chest. He did not answer, and then the man was on his knees beside him and his left arm began to burn. It felt pure, he clung to it—the sear in his forearm, the man's hands deft on the needle, sliding it in, lifting the bag of saline high to the rack above, rolling his fingers across the wheel that released a cascade of little balls into the clear tubing.

"I need some help in here," the man shouted again, as he moved around the foot of the gurney to the other side, and this time it took him longer; there were three hot coals, one after another, until the line was in.

"What's going on?"

It was a small woman, wearing a white coat, with close-cropped very blond hair and a long pale neck. Michael half saw her, standing by the curtains, and realized vaguely that she must be a resident because she was so young, but it was all he could manage now to hold the ache in his arms clear in his mind like a single point. He could think of nothing else—he wanted to think of nothing else—only the ache in his arms and his breathing. He was flat on his back and it was going to come again.

"What's his pressure?" Her voice was hard and clipped.

"Eighty-five systolic," the nurse said, readying another needle. "I was going to come and get you."

"Get him to the resuss room," she said. "Now."

"I just thought he was vagal," the nurse said, his voice rising. "He looked OK in triage."

But she was gone.

The nurse was hanging IV bags from hooks attached to the gurney, and now the gurney was moving, he was gliding out into the light of the hall, the object of many eyes, and doors were opening.

It didn't seem strange, any of it. The room was large and blinding, with machines and lights and strangers around him.

"Are his fluids wide?" It was the long-necked woman who looked like a girl. They were sticking things to his chest, they were taking off his gown. The blood pressure cuff stiffened against his arm. He was naked now, lights were everywhere, and the stains on his chest were the color of rust.

"Of course, Carrie. Relax." This from an older woman with wide heavy thighs and a stethoscope around her neck.

The balls were tumbling from the IV, pouring into his arms, and he felt them enter; he felt the cold rising up toward his shoulders.

"Type and cross for six units," Carrie said tersely. "Let's get some O-negative down here. I want a CBC, LFTs, Sma-ten, twelve-lead, coags, portable chest. Call GI. I want an NG and a Foley."

The wide woman with the stethoscope around her neck sighed. "Carrie, are you sure you want a Foley?"

"When you go to medical school," the long-necked girl replied, "you can decide."

The woman sighed again and shrugged her shoulders approaching the bed.

A Foley catheter, through his penis up into the bladder.

"I'm Melissa," she said, looking down at him. "We're going to be doing a lot of things to you. Just let it happen, OK? You're going to be fine."

He stared at her: gray-hair, a lined face. Others had been here before him.

"No Foley," he managed. She smiled. Her teeth were off-yellow.

"Hear that, Carrie? The patient is refusing the Foley."

Carrie's lips tightened. She was looking hard at the nurse, and then she too approached the bed.

"I'm Dr. Wilson," she said. "I need to ask you some questions. Can you hear me?"

He nodded weakly. The taste of blood was strong in his mouth.

"When did this start?"

"Just now." It was an effort to speak.

"Have you noticed any black or bloody stools?"

He was shaking his head. He licked his black caked lips.

"Do you have any other medical problems, like AIDS or hepatitis? Can you hear me?"

"No," he said. "I need to tell you . . ."

She wasn't listening. She was looking down at his chart, which she held now in her thin white hand.

"Are you allergic to any medications?"

"No." It was coming again.

"And you just came in for nausea?"

He nodded, and just then it bubbled out of him again, making him turn his head aside, letting it flow and splatter down the railing of the gurney to the floor. The long-necked woman jumped back, but nonetheless a few scarlet specks caught her on the sleeve, startling on the white cotton.

"Great," she said, looking at her stained sleeve, even as she took off her coat.

"I'm a physician," he said, as loudly as he could.

This got her attention. "You're a physician?"

He was lying on his side. "Yes," he said.

Something crossed her face then, quickly, an uncertain narrowing of the eyes. "Oh," she said.

He could see it happening; he could see her placing him somewhere else in her mind, in another category altogether. She glanced again at his chart.

"Do you drink alcohol, Dr. Grant?"

"That's not it," he said, trying to sit up a little, so that he might cover himself, though the effort made his eyes go dark. "It's my platelets. They're low."

"Why are your platelets low?"

"I don't know."

She looked him in the eye again, briefly, before turning away. He realized that she was putting on a protective gown, a face mask, a surgical hat, and gloves, until she was recognizable no longer.

"I need an NG," she said loudly, through the mask. "Everyone needs to stop standing around."

"Calm down, Carrie. I'm doing it right now." It was the nurse, Melissa, again, and now she had a long clear plastic tube in her hand, smearing the exposed tip with Vaseline even as she spoke.

"Can you sit up?"

"I don't think so."

"Did you hear me, Dr. Grant?"

"His pressure's sixty." Another voice, someone else.

"Get him in Trendelenburg," Carrie said, her voice rising. "Hang the O-negative right now."

He felt his head dropping back, so oddly, and his legs rising, as they stood him on his head, and his mouth began to fill completely, as if from a slow tap. He felt himself falling into it, as one falls into impossible weariness, and almost without comprehension, he saw the deep red bags of blood going up like flags in the air above his arms.

It wasn't silence, exactly. There were voices, he knew, and other sounds, bells and alarms. And a figure, which he knew was his own, lying at an odd angle, legs in the air, head down, the lower face and chest smeared dark red, the rest of the body white and smooth, the brown genitals wrinkled and exposed. Others bent over him, the heavy woman and the long-necked girl, who crouched over the head with the glint of metal in her gloved hand. The face was obscured by the long-necked girl, who was doing something to the mouth, prying it open with the silver blade in her left hand, reaching in also with her right. There was a repeated sucking sound, like a straw at the bottom of a glass, as she worked her right hand back and forth, and even as he saw it from a distance he felt air on the surface of his tongue. His throat was beginning to swell. He could feel his jaw lifting and something deep in the back of his throat, the blade entering, something following the blade, and he could not breathe, there was blood everywhere, rising into his nose, spilling out of his nostrils down the sides of his cheeks like tears. He heard gagging, he saw the arms of the figure reaching up toward the covered face.

The girl was breathing hard.

"I'm going to have to paralyze him," she said. "He's fighting me."

"I'm calling anesthesia, Carrie," Melissa said.

"OK, call them. Give him one hundred fifty milligrams of succinylcholine." Her voice rising like a puff of smoke.

Someone was crying out, gurgling, as if underwater.

"Give him the sucs," Carrie said.

"Sat is eighty." A man's voice, distilled.

"Shit," Carrie said. "We can't bag him like this."

"One-fifty sucs is in," Melissa said, pressing the plunger smoothly by the left arm.

"Get me another Yankauer," Carrie said. She was trembling. "I need more suction."

A telephone rang. Someone answered it.

"Anesthesia's on their way," a voice said.

The paralysis hit him all at once. It was a deep, impossible power, arms going loose to the sheet, his mouth opening, weakness everywhere, and a blackness now, unable to move, to do anything but watch and listen, darkening—and she was above him, her cap full of red drops, a smear on her gown, her beaded plastic mask, and the blade in her hand was coming back, entering him again. He felt it in his mouth, horribly intimate and strange, an immense pressure, and then a choking, tearing pain deep in his throat. He could feel her breath, which came in gasps, she was so close to him with her trembling hands; he could feel her desperation even then.

But then she stepped back, sliding the red-stained blade out of him, and there was a clear tube inside him now, rising out of his mouth like a root. They were attaching something to it—a blue bag—which Melissa began squeezing in her plump hands, as if she were kneading bread.

Then his chest, with a sudden life of its own, rising and falling, his eyes beginning to lighten, just like that.

"Twenty-three at the teeth," Carrie said, still trembling. Her voice, just above him. The tube, twenty-three centimeters down.

"He hasn't had any sedation," Melissa said. "Can I give him something?"

"What's his pressure?"

"Up to ninety systolic."

"Give him some Versed. And get GI on the phone."

The woman was moving again, fiddling with syringes. A few moments passed, and then all the many voices drifted away.

As a child in the summer, he had often gone swimming at the nearby lake—the usual jumping and splashing, his chest worn raw on the white Styrofoam board, his exposed shoulders aching and red from the sun—but there were other moments also, when he'd simply floated on his back, eyes closed, lips a few millimeters above the surface, drifting in the shallows. His breathing slowed, and after a while, even thought seemed to stop. Green water, the long yellow shadows through the trees at the bank, the slap of lake waves on the rocks—all these things had drifted away, until it was only his breathing, the heat of the sun on his forehead, and the cool currents from the bottom. Then something would happen. His lips would dip below the surface, and he'd come up sputtering with his toes full of black mud, back where everything was bright.

But now he woke by degrees, as if rising. He began to remember things: the flash of needles through a haze; the feel of hands on his body, turning him; a warm wet sponge between his buttocks. Odors, also—feces, moist hair, and sweat—a sting in his penis, the hard crackling bed beneath him, the thin sheet. All this, drifting through him and past him. Somewhere there were voices. A woman laughed.

The room was dark. Over his head, a weak glow of lights. The tube felt like a hook in his throat. He couldn't make a sound, but he could move now, barely, and he lifted an arm, reaching up to his mouth, until it stopped, suddenly. He was tied to the bed. In the far reaches, down by his feet, something was moving.

"Well," a man's voice said. "Look who's awake."

He couldn't speak. There was someone standing over him now, a form in the dark.

"Can you hear me?"

He nodded.

"Good. I'm Richard. I'm your nurse this evening."

He nodded again. He had the overwhelming desire to pull the tube out of his mouth. He felt his hands strain against the straps.

"Calm down," Richard said. "Relax. I can't take the tube out now. You've got to wait till morning."

But he was choking, retching, and suddenly there were bells in the room. The ventilator beside him hissed and flashed.

"What's going on?" Another voice, someone else, in from the lights of the hall.

"He's bucking the vent. I told Carrie not to wean him off the Versed tonight."

"I had him yesterday. I snowed him."

"She said she wanted him completely awake."

"So what? They can do it in the morning."

Richard seemed to be considering this.

"You're right," he said, stepping away from the bed. Michael could not see him. He wanted to cry out.

"Back to sleep you go," the man said, a few moments later, and then something passed through him as casually as the wave of a hand.

So it came again, the slow wheel of dreams and voices, on and on, and the regular hiss and sigh of the ventilator, his languor on his back in the shallows, his lips at the surface, his throat in embers, his eyes half closed to the ceiling, with its exact pattern of cracks and flaws.

He lay in half sleep, waiting for morning. He lay as if cast from silver, on the edge of absence, with time going by, bathed in irregular voices from the hall, the steady rise and fall of the ventilator beside him like surf.

When he was aware again, sometime much later, it was full morning, and someone was speaking to him.

"Can you hear me? Open your eyes."

It was the long-necked girl. There were others, also, though how many he could not say. His throat was a razor again, he was aware of his hands, which pulsed, and his feet also, cold under the cheap sheet. It took him awhile to focus on her face.

"Do you want the tube out?" she asked, bending over him. "We're going to take it out if you cooperate." She spoke loudly, as if he were deaf.

He nodded.

"Now take a deep breath, as deep as you can."

He gasped.

"You need to do better than that. One more time."

He prepared himself and then, though even the smallest motion of his head scalded him, took a deep, shuddering breath, as if he were sucking through a straw.

"How was it?" Carrie said, over her shoulder.

"Forty millimeters of water," a voice answered, which seemed to please her.

She turned back to him, her fingers busy with the tube in his mouth.

He smelled soap on her hands, and then something settled in his throat. A cascade of coughs.

"OK, this is it. I just deflated the balloon. When I tell you, exhale. Do you understand me?"

He nodded again.

"One, two, three, *now,*" she said, and pulled the hook right out of him, trailing its strands of bloody green mucus across his lips. He felt as if flesh had come with it, and there was a sudden stench, and foul taste in his mouth. She dropped the tube directly onto his chest, an expression of distaste on her face.

"OK, sit up, sit up," she said, and there were hands on him now, on his arms, and a whirring sound as the bed lifted his shoulders into the air.

He was sitting, each breath ragged and full of needles. He coughed again, retching, spitting green phlegm onto the stained sheet. They were attaching something to his face now, a mask, full of mist, thick enough to drink.

"Keep coughing," Carrie said. The tube slid down to his lap, leaving a wet streak on his chest. The sheet followed. He felt so naked.

There was a moment of silence as they all watched him.

"Good," she said, after a while. "He's not stridorous."

They watched him some more.

"Are you breathing all right?"

He nodded.

Carrie turned away toward the door. "Give him ten of Decadron," she said. "Keep him on the cool mist until noon."

He felt empty, so weak he could barely keep his head upright. He lay there, and after a while they left.

The mask hissed and steamed, and it was all he wanted to think about. Gradually, the pain in his throat began to recede. His lips and nose were tingling, as if he had stepped outside on a winter's night, though the rest of him felt feverish. The desire to cough and keep coughing—this is what occupied him. It was the only thing he was able to resist, and only if he lay completely still, anticipating each new breath.

His body felt like someone else's entirely, inert, heavy, falling into its own weight. Even the most casual of gestures required a summoning of will—to reach up and feel the surface of the mask, like a tortoise shell, or the coarse hair on his face around it.

His thoughts came with icy slowness. Only the immediate was possible, the way the light from the window passed through his closed eyelids, the vague ache of the needle in his arm, the greater pain of his throat. He was aware of this, somehow, aware that he was not thinking well or clearly. For the longest time, it seemed sufficient just to lie and breathe. The sheet beneath him crackled when he moved.

At some point he must have been dozing, because he awoke with a start, and it was enough to bring the nurse in from the hall.

"Are you all right?"

He didn't answer.

"It's me, Richard," the man said. "You're doing fine. You just fell asleep, that's all."

Richard seemed to be wagging his finger.

"You're quite a sight," he said. "You look like someone rescued off a desert island."

He'd nod off and wake with a start, as if he were a passenger in a car. Each time it was a little better, and toward the end Richard no longer turned from his stool in the hall. Noon must have come, because suddenly there was Richard again, shaking his shoulder to awaken him.

"Time to take off the mask," he said, and turned a knob on the wall. The mist went quiet and his face tingled in the air, though it was awhile before the sensations of the mask and the band around his head, holding it in place, left him entirely. It was only a little oxygen now, a clear tube sweeping from the wall beneath his nose, hissing, and gradually his cheeks dried. He could turn his head; he could look out the window. From where he lay, there was no view, only the gray concrete of an adjacent building and, above it, the soft blue of the sky, a few clouds. The hours continued to pass, and for the first time he was aware of the clock on the wall in the corner of the room. He watched the minute hand intently. It lived right on the edge of the visible world, just slow, or just fast, enough. It would stop, and then, as the gears meshed, it would shift almost imperceptibly forward again. He'd never watched a clock so intently with so little purpose. There was nothing he was waiting for, but he watched it anyway, listening to voices out in the hall and the rough gunmetal doors opening and closing to the rest of the hospital. For a while, he was almost content.

"Well," Richard said at four o'clock, "your lady friend is here again."

He looked back at the man without comprehension.

"Come on, you have a visitor. Don't you want to see her?"

He didn't answer.

"Don't just lie there, say something." Richard seemed amused, smiling at him.

"I don't know what to say," he said. The sound of his own voice—it came out of nowhere, a croaking whisper.

"Well, well," Richard said. "He can talk after all."

There was a pause.

"Don't worry about how you look," Richard said, as if he suddenly understood. "She's been here a lot. You look better now, believe me."

Richard stepped out into the hall and beckoned.

She walked into the room tentatively, clutching her purse in both hands. She wore a deep blue blouse and gray slacks, with her hair pulled back as if she had just come from an office. The sun fell on her from the windows, and for an instant it seemed as if he could see each black hair, each single thread of gray—they leaped out at him—and then she was through the door, out of the glare, approaching the bed.

"Michael?"

He looked up at her and managed his first weak smile. He nodded, then lifted his hand, heavily, and she took it. She smelled of the outside world. He had no idea who she was.

"Oh, my God," she said, and began to cry.

He watched her tears—how they sprang from the corners of her eyes, how one or two fell away, in shining particles, like motes of dust. They seemed like magical things, beautiful, and he watched them leave her face. They were like passengers, he thought, departing, and they filled him with an odd warmth.

"Don't cry," he said.

"They thought you were going to die."

He nodded. It was the truth—he knew it as something he had brushed against, casually—but now here he was, on the other side.

She took her hand from his to wipe her eyes, and then she smiled at him. "How are you feeling?"

"I'm tired," he said. "I smell."

She wrinkled up her nose and laughed. "Yes, Michael, you do. You need a bath."

"I'm sorry. . . ."

But she waved her hand, dismissing it, then turned away for a moment and pulled a chair from the corner up close to the bed and sat down. The bed was high, and he was looking down at her.

"My face," he said.

"What about it?"

"I have a beard. I don't remember having a beard."

"I wouldn't exactly call it a beard. It's more like scruff."

"Hair grows after you die," he said. Just then it had occurred to him. She looked at him quizzically.

"What?"

"If you're buried clean-shaven they exhume you with a beard."

"What are you talking about?"

"Nothing. I'm sorry. . . ."

"Do you think you're dead, Michael?"

"No."

"Of course you have a beard. You've been here for eleven days."

He looked at her again, closely. She was telling him something. It was important, that much was clear, and she was returning his gaze directly.

He closed his eyes for a moment, just a little while.

"You did know that, didn't you?"

He shook his head, bewildered.

"Have they told you anything?"

Her voice, the feel of the sun on his exposed left shoulder, the hiss of oxygen beneath his nose—everything deepened his confusion.

"No," he said, after a while. "I don't think they have."

He must have dozed off then, if only for a little while, because she was sitting a little farther away from him now, as if she'd eased the chair back, and she was looking down at her lap. He shifted, and she raised her head again.

"I didn't mean to be rude," he said.

"Don't apologize, Michael. It's all right."

They were silent for a while.

He felt peaceful with her presence, the smell of shampoo in her hair. He wanted silence, to lie here with her beside him, and she must have sensed it also, because she was quiet, and minutes passed. Finally, a tentative knock, against the open glass door, and he opened his eyes. It was Richard.

"You should probably go," Richard said. "He's pretty worn out."

She nodded and stood, stepped up to the bed, and bent down and kissed him on the cheek.

"I'll see you tomorrow, Michael," she said. "I'm so glad. . . ." She paused and held the side of her fist against her mouth. It was a familiar gesture, somehow.

So he smiled at her, and nodded, and kept smiling. She would go soon. He'd close his eyes, and feel the echo of her presence with him.

Sometime later—that day or the next—the long-necked girl finally came to see him. It was late morning. The weight remained in his limbs, but already he could feel it receding. His throat, also, was better, less of a presence, and the liquid part of the room, the exquisite clarity of details, had settled as well, until it was merely a hospital bed, regular, proportioned, like the others around it. The day's work, continuing.

He was only one among many. It was comforting to think for a few moments about the other lives around him, some going away and some, like him, coming back. It must be visiting hours again, because people were walking by, dressed in street clothes.

And he was coming back. The rest of his body was emerging from the background, past the pain in his throat. His aching hips, his heels, sore from their days against the bedsheet, and his hands, which he could not warm—these things, and others, made their presence known.

Carrie walked in without knocking and stood by the side of his bed.

"I understand you want to see me?" She looked very tired and very young, and she brushed a loose strand of hair out of her eyes as she spoke.

"I did?"

"Your friend asked me. Nora, isn't it? She said you wanted to talk to me."

"Oh," he said.

His memory came back in that moment. The alignment, the correct switch, the light waiting patiently to be lit—Nora's name, perhaps, or something else, sent it flooding through him in a single overwhelming instant.

Where was it, exactly, that he had been?

"Do you know where you are now?" she asked.

He was fighting back tears. "I'm in the ICU. I've been here for a while."

"Twelve days," she said.

"I was bleeding."

She gave a little half laugh. "You bled continuously for about a day. We could barely keep up."

"I was intubated."

"Your lungs weren't working well. That sometimes happens when people bleed a lot. Their lungs get damaged and fill up with fluid so they can't breathe."

"I know."

"Oh," she said, pausing. "Yes, of course." She continued. "To be honest, none of us thought you were going to make it."

He thought about that, or tried to think about it, but it was too near. "Do you think I'm going to make it now?" he managed.

She nodded. "Your platelets are rising, your ulcers are healing, and your lungs are much better."

"My ulcers?" he asked. Question and answer. He was looking at the wall behind her, though her mouth was moving again.

"You had bleeding ulcers. Small ones, but there were a lot of them. We've scoped you three times. I've told you this before."

"You have?" he asked, but even as he spoke he remembered being lifted onto a table and hands holding him.

She nodded. "You have ulcers and gastritis. Fairly severe. It explains the bleeding."

"Lots of patients in the ICU get stress ulcers. Gastritis also."

"That's true. But they weren't stress ulcers. GI says they look chronic."

"Oh," he said, thinking, Leave it alone. She continued.

"So that's what happened. You had bleeding ulcers. The rest was due to shock and all the blood we gave you."

"I had no pain," he said.

"Ulcers are often painless," she replied. "You know that."

"Did they see anything else on the scope?"

"What do you mean?"

"Did they see any lesions? Did they see anything in my throat?"

"No," she said. "They didn't."

"Did they biopsy the ulcers?"

"Of course. There was nothing unusual about them. Just inflammatory changes."

She was looking at him carefully, her eyes narrowing. He could see the blond down on her cheeks. Her certainty and confidence. Her youth and her discipline. This is how the world is, she seemed to say, this is what happens, and this is what we do when it does. Now she was speaking again—something about medications and avoiding alcohol—but he looked away, because suddenly he wanted to watch the pigeon, which had just landed on the windowsill.

The pigeon's head turned exactly, stopped, turned again. It reminded him of drops of water, a drop, a pause, another drop. He was only a few feet away, close enough to see its black glass eyes and the iridescent blue-green arc of tiny feathers, like fish scales, above them. It was only a pigeon, but it seemed wonderful to him, beautiful, and then, just as it had appeared, it flew off, like the gray shake of a handkerchief.

"Pay attention, Dr. Grant," she said, irritated. "This is important. Do you know how close we came to never having this conversation?"

"Yes," he said, turning his head toward her. "I know it much better than you do."

This seemed to deflate her suddenly, and she looked down at her feet for a moment.

"I think," she said, "that we can send you home in a few more days. As soon as you can walk and take solid foods."

The world was there, in all its finery, and somehow, for no reason at all that he could see, it was allowing him back.

"You don't know what this is," he said.

"What do you mean?"

He nearly continued then, he nearly placed it in her hands. It was there, like an offering—tell me, free yourself, become flesh alone. It was all over him in a moment, the silence, the field of grass, the headstone flowers drying in black iron sockets. Just like that she was somewhere else entirely.

"I'm tired," he said, as if declining an invitation. She looked at him for a moment, then nodded.

"I'll let you sleep then. We can talk later."

He could feel her questions, but they were faint and would leave easily, like a spark, a crackle from lit tinder, gone by the time she reached the door.

"Thank you," he said finally. "Thank you for saving me."

She paused, turning around, then nodded in a curt self-conscious way and looked down at her feet. But she flushed slightly, with pleasure.

"I was just doing my job," she said, as her pager went off.

Early that afternoon they moved him to another ward. For the moment he was the room's only occupant and was given the bed by the window. The window opened to a highway, with a field in the distance.

"I'm Mary," his new nurse said. She was in her fifties, with graying hair in a bun and a puffy face. Heavy, with webs of red capillaries on her cheeks. He nodded and smiled.

"We're going to get you up," she said, "and then we're going to put you in the chair. Would you like that?"

The oxygen hissed in his nostrils. He shrugged.

"Oh, come on," she said, as if he were a child. "We need to make you better."

It took two of them, one on either side, to lift him to his feet.

"Good," she said, as he stood there, knees locked, swaying. "Come on, Michael. Let's go to the door and back."

So he was Michael now, he thought. She knew who he was, what he did for a living, but he was Michael now, because he could barely stand. It didn't anger him as once it might have done, but he noticed it clearly. His weakness, in their arms, taking a few new steps toward the door.

The muscles in his thighs threatened to give way, but he was able to walk nonetheless, and after a few paces they only touched his elbows, one on either side. He felt tall, as if he towered above everything. His hips ached with each step.

"You're doing very well," Mary said.

"Thank you." Was that what a Michael would say? Thank you. Look at me, I'm a good walker. You see? One foot in front of the other. You're not carrying me at all.

Afterward, before they left, they covered him with a blanket and sat him in a reclining chair by the window. The effort of walking had exhausted him, and he was content to sit there, watching cars pass on the highway. There would be more of this, he thought, months perhaps, before his body could occupy space without effort or self-knowledge, and until that day every moment would remind him of this fact.

Nora came into the room a few minutes later. She was dressed as before, in office clothes. Her hair was pulled back, and she wore a red scarf that leaped from the gray charcoal of her coat. She smiled at him.

"You look almost human," she said.

"Nora. . . ."

She sat down on the side of the bed beside the chair. "I just thought I'd check on you," she said.

"I'm getting better," he said.

She looked as if she was going to cry again.

"I didn't mean for this to happen," he said, and she laughed, suddenly.

"And all this time," she replied, "I thought you'd done it on purpose."

He looked down and smiled. His knees were two points beneath the blanket.

"So, Michael," she said. "Have they figured this out? Do they know what happened to you?"

"They think I have bleeding ulcers."

"And what do you think?"

"I don't know."

She looked down at her hands. "I told them you were acting strange," she said.

"What did you say?"

"I told them about that sound you were making in your sleep. And that you were under a lot of stress and I thought you were depressed."

He nodded. "The sound," he said.

"They asked me whether you had any psychiatric problems."

"Yes," he said. "They would. What did you say?"

"I said I didn't know."

He looked out at the field. "I'm sorry about your father," he said.

"Do you have psychiatric problems, Michael?"

He turned his head toward her. "What do you think?"

She met his eye. But it wasn't the look of an interrogator. There was no suspicion there that he could see. She was merely looking at him closely, even tenderly. There were tiny wrinkles in the corners of her eyes.

"I don't think so," she said. "I just think you've been having a hard time."

"I don't know what's happening to me, Nora. I don't know what's going on. I don't know what this is. . . ."

He tried to stop. He covered his eyes, he felt his shoulders hunching, and suddenly it was all around him, the terror of the past weeks, sweeping the room away. Her hand was on his shoulder.

"You're getting better, Michael. You're going to get well."

But he did, finally, start to cry. He sobbed openly, and she sat there, taking it all in, watching him, watching his tears, his hands twisting of their own accord.

After a while, he stopped. Warm air began flowing out of a duct above his head.

"It's all right," she said, reaching forward, stroking his shoulder.

His rheumy eyes, his physical weakness, the smell of his body and hair—there was nothing to do but lean back, let the dark recede, and let her presence quiet and comfort him. They sat together for a long time in companionable silence, and then, finally, she spoke.

"I've got to go, Michael. I'll see you tomorrow."

He nodded, but he couldn't bring himself to look at her. He felt her hand pass briefly across his hair as she got up to leave.

Some time passed. He looked out at the cornfield beyond the highway, and the sky above it, full of drifting clouds. In the distance, some low buildings: barns, another road. This small city, small enough that the countryside intruded still, in eddies, here and there between neighborhoods. This place—the small city, with its surrounding farmland, and the low pines stretching away to the power cut—how much of his life had it already taken? Only a few months, he thought, counting back as best he could, and yet his whole life seemed out there before him, on the black line of the roadway or in the gaps between the young green corn.

He felt as if he were looking into the past. No matter the immediacy of the air just beyond the window, or the sounds that came through it, it looked like the past, where he had lived as a young man, keen-eyed, full of knowledge, full of faith in the laws of invisible things.

It was not so different from looking out on a clear evening, where distance is history, where the stars go back, one after another, until they're out of sight.

The next morning it was Susan, after he'd taken his place in the chair again. She looked both delighted and distraught, clutching a handful of flowers and a brown paper bag.

"You scared me half to death," she said.

He smiled, thinking, It's so good to see her.

"I didn't mean to."

"Well, you did. And right after Ronald. . . ." Her words trailed off; she was wiping tears away, sitting down on the bed by his chair.

"I know."

"I didn't know what to do. I had to close the practice. Nora helped me."

It made sense, of course, but it hadn't even occurred to him.

"I hope that was the right thing to do."

"Of course."

"I referred them. I wanted to wait to talk to you, but you were so sick. . . ."

"It's OK, Susan. You did the right thing."

"I came to see you before," she said. "Do you remember?"

He shook his head. "No," he said.

Her face quivered. She wiped her eyes on her sleeve. "We'll open the office again when you get well."

"Yes," he said. "We will. Don't worry."

"I knew you were sicker than you were letting on. I knew there was something wrong. I should have done something."

"You did do something."

"Oh, you know what I mean. It was clear you weren't right. But then Dr. Gass died, and I was so shocked. Harold said he'd never seen me so upset."

Harold, he remembered, was her husband, a dour, silent man who made model airplanes in their garage. He'd met him once, at the office. It was surprising, he thought, that he remembered Harold at all, but he did; he could picture the man's face perfectly.

"I worked for Dr. Gass for twenty-four years," she said. "That's a long time. We went through a lot together."

"I know you did, Susan."

She continued. "He wasn't an easy person. I never felt that I really knew him. But after a while it almost didn't matter. Do you know what I mean?"

"I'm not sure."

"Well, I don't know how to say it. I guess what I mean is that you fall into a routine. You get familiar with someone's habits, that sort of thing. After a while they almost become part of you, even if you don't know them all that well personally. Does that make sense?"

"I guess so."

"I mean, we never socialized or anything. We never had dinner together or anything like that."

"He was a private person."

"Yes, he was. Very private. Anyway, Michael, I should be talking about you. I'm so happy you're better. I'm sorry if I'm talking too much."

"You're not talking too much," he said.

"Yes, I am. I always do. I should let you rest."

"I've had plenty of rest. All I get is rest."

"Do you want a cookie?"

"What?"

"A chocolate-chip cookie. I made some for you. My kids love them. They're always after me."

"I haven't eaten much yet."

"Oh, come on. They won't hurt you."

She fumbled around in her paper bag and withdrew two. She took a bite out of one and offered him the other.

He smiled. The expression on her face was somehow placid, tender, and grief-stricken all at once.

"Thank you, Susan," he said, feeling a warm wave of affection for her sweep over him. He nibbled the cookie in his hand and felt a rush of saliva in his mouth, the beginnings of hunger.

"It's delicious," he said.

"Of course it is."

She smiled at him then, fondly, maternally, which filled him with profound gratitude. Suddenly her presence was an absolute blessing, without mystery or darkness. It was simple kindness, simple human warmth, without subtext, unabashed and open. "So," she said, after a bit. "Are your ulcers better?"

He took another, larger bite. "I think so," he said.

"It was too much stress for you," she said. "Getting divorced, and moving to a new place, and then the terrible thing that happened to Ronald. That's what I think."

He shrugged and tried to smile.

"But you really shouldn't be so hard on yourself," she said. "Bad times are a part of life. Everyone has them, and then things get better."

"Thank you, Susan," he said.

She patted his hand, and they were quiet for a while.

"How are your kids doing?" he asked, after a few moments had passed.

He found, to his astonishment, that he could remember their names and even a few details about them. In no time she was off and running, and he realized as he listened that at any other time in his life he would have been bored to tears by the information that followed: school, grandchildren, a son's new job—all of it tedious. But now he felt as if he were drinking from a well. Time passed, and after a while they'd eaten everything in the bag.

After she left, he felt the gradually increasing need to urinate. He should call the nurse, he thought, and ask for a urinal. But for the first time the indignity of it struck him. The bathroom was perhaps fifteen feet away.

He stood with difficulty, swaying for a moment, holding on to the back of the chair. Then he took a deep breath and set out across the room. Though it only took him a minute or two, he felt as if he were walking along a knife's ridge, with clouds and towns below him on either side—step after step, his hands out in front of him as if feeling their way in the dark. Five feet, four, a last lurch, and he reached the bathroom door, resting against it for a few seconds.

Once inside the bathroom, it was easier. There were railings, for the wheelchair-bound, and he leaned on them as he emptied his bladder into the toilet. He realized that he was proud of this moment—proud that he was able to urinate and walk without assistance. For a little while, as he stood there, he did not feel afraid.

He washed his hands carefully at the sink, and then, without further thought, he stepped up close to the mirror, opened his mouth, and exposed himself as completely and as thoroughly as he could. He looked into his throat for a long time, until he was certain. But there was no sign at all.

At first Michael didn't see him. He stood in the hall, just outside the open door, and he must have been gathering his courage. The recent past, so raw and comfortless—but he did it anyway. After a moment of hesitation, Reverend Williams knocked and entered the room. He was dressed for visiting—a dark suit, a thin red tie, an immaculate white shirt.

Michael sat up abruptly in bed. This man, walking toward him across the cemetery grass those months ago, the handshake, the prayers, and what followed—it all came back to him in stunning, exquisite clarity.

"I didn't mean to startle you," Reverend Williams said.

Michael took a deep breath. It seemed unreal, hallucinatory, but now, with the sound of the pastor's voice, the moment passed.

"It's OK," he said.

"May I sit down?"

Michael managed a weak nod.

"Thank you." Reverend Williams took off his jacket and folded it carefully over his arm, before sitting in the chair by the window. "If I don't take it off," he said, "it gets wrinkled down the back."

Reverend Williams seemed thinner. His face was wintry and drawn, but it was the same face, with wide brown eyes and wrinkles beside them, the same sparkle of gray in his coiled black hair, and the same slow, studied pace in his gestures, as if each one were a kind of reflection.

"I'm surprised to see you," Michael said, after a bit.

The Reverend nodded. "A member of my congregation is here. I've known her for many years." He paused, looking down at the floor. "I only learned you were here yesterday."

Michael was silent. There was a great deal to be said, it was clear, but it was difficult to speak all the same.

"How did you find out?" he asked, after a moment.

"I called your office and was told it was closed. I made some inquiries."

Both were silent again.

"Thank you for coming to see me."

"I was ministering to her," Williams said, "but all along I was thinking about you."

"It was good of you."

The other man sighed. "I don't know," he said.

Michael looked away, in the direction of the door. Figures passed in the hall.

"What do they think caused your illness?"

"They said I had bleeding ulcers. It's quite common."

"And what do you think?"

Michael put his hand up to his eyes. All this distance has outdone me, he thought; it has crept up on me; it has offered nothing but deception, and ghosts, and a million pale reflections. His visitor watched him in silence.

"I think I had what Jonas had," he said finally. "I had white lines in my throat. I saw lights. I had visions."

For the first time the Reverend met Michael's eye directly. "Are you certain?"

"Yes."

"But you're alive."

"I got to the hospital in time."

The Reverend stood up suddenly and began to pace, back and forth, at the foot of the bed. "Did they find it?" he asked.

"They didn't find anything. Only ulcers."

"Why wouldn't they have found it?"

"I don't know," Michael said.

"So it might still be there."

"I don't think it is."

"Why not?"

"I don't feel it anymore."

The Reverend paced. "You're a scientific man, Dr. Grant. You believe in evidence." It was a statement, spoken flatly.

"I suppose so," he said.

"Is there any evidence?"

"Not for me. But I kept some of Jonas's blood. And the results of the biopsy. And his feet."

"His feet?"

He did not know, Michael realized, but it was too late to take back the words. "I'm sorry," Michael said. "His feet survived the fire."

Reverend Williams closed his eyes and opened them again, and Michael could see him will himself past it, no matter that it was the kind of detail one returned to, hours later, in solitude.

"Did you tell your doctors about any of this?"

"No," he said. "I didn't. Not yet."

"Why?"

Michael shook his head. Only part of him was clear.

"I'm not even sure," he said at last. "I don't think I could convince them now." *What was true? That I'm here in this bed, so weak I can barely stand?* "But I was just like Jonas," he said. "I was just like him."

"My son," the Reverend began, but then paused, as if he did not know what to say, and a long moment passed. "When I was very young," he continued finally, "God came to me. I cannot describe it for you. Those were difficult times. I was a black man. There was nothing for me. Do you understand?"

Michael nodded.

"The details are unimportant. But He came to me, and His presence gave me everything."

There was a change in the man now, as if he were looking out or looking through. Michael saw it clearly—a kind of balance, a kind of urgent waiting. A little pocket sermon, for him, in private, where all he could do was listen.

"For many years, and even now, I feel Him most near me when I speak."

"When you preach?"

"Yes. I can't describe it for you. But I feel it come over me, and sometimes I don't even remember what I've said."

He paused.

"I believe that those moments—" He stopped once more, as if at a loss for words. "What I'm saying is difficult. What I'm saying is, those were the moments when I was most myself. When I could not watch myself."

"Are you questioning your faith?"

The Reverend shook his head impatiently. "No, no. You misunderstand me. What I mean is that I could not resist myself as God's messenger."

Michael struggled to make sense of the words.

"I believe," the Reverend continued, "that this is what took my son away from me."

"I don't understand, Reverend. I'm sorry, but I don't."

Reverend Williams nodded, as if he expected the answer. "I wanted to believe that Jonas was being punished. I wanted him to come back to me. I wanted him to repent."

Michael waited.

"The gospel of Saint Luke describes men like me." He looked off, out through the window, and began to recite from memory.

"*Beware of the scribes, which desire to walk in long robes, and love greetings in the markets, and the highest seats in the synagogues, and the chief rooms at feasts; which devour widows' houses, and for a show make long prayers: the same shall receive greater damnation.*"

"You thought," Michael said, after a moment, "that Jonas was getting what he deserved?"

Reverend Williams sat back down in the chair. "Yes," he said. "But what he deserved was forgiveness."

Time passed, the Reverend closed his eyes again. In a moment, Michael thought, he would get up to go, in a moment he would stand, and put on his jacket, and be gone.

"Do you believe me?" Michael asked. "Do you think I had it also?"

There was a long silence. The Reverend did not answer directly. "You have not considered this fully," he said.

Michael felt suddenly tired again, a running exhaustion. When will this be done?

"My little girl," the Reverend continued. "My granddaughter. I want your help with her."

"What do you mean?"

"She needs to be exhumed," the Reverend said, "and I don't know how to arrange it."

The moment, when it finally came two days later, was nearly too much for him. He felt so afraid, so immensely public. He was in the lobby of the hospital, waiting for Nora to pull the car around. They were sending him home.

It was a state hospital, but nonetheless some efforts had been made here: a few overstuffed chairs, some low tables, an information desk in the center, offices nearby. It would have been possible to confuse this place for the lobby of an insurance company, or perhaps even a bank, and were it not for the handful of people waiting around him—this one in a wheelchair, that one with an elaborate orthotic brace on his leg—one would not guess. An old woman in a lab coat sat at the information desk. She was, he knew, a volunteer, a retired person who chose this to occupy her days.

It was difficult to look around the room, difficult to watch people coming and going, passing through the doors, out into the fresh air. All he wanted to do was sit there, with the palms of his hands pinned between his thighs. For the first time he was dressed in his own clothes, because Nora had gone with his key and gotten them. The others had been soiled, thrown away—even his shoes. But here he was. They were letting him go, and he had to face whatever it was that the world held in store for him next.

He realized that he had come to accept his room and his bed and his window upstairs. It had not been necessary to think, but now, as he sat and waited, he began to feel the ache, the blinking wonder of survival in the face of a power that cared nothing whatever for his life. He did not feel spared, he felt cast aside. Life or death, one way or the other—neither path had any significance at all to the fine weather outside, or the man scratching his leg through his orthotic brace, or the elderly sweet-faced volunteer who sat patiently waiting for questions. Suddenly, though, it mattered most desperately to him, and no matter how he tried to calm himself it was no good at all. He felt as if he were coming apart, as if he had been blown above rooftops, and all he was doing was sitting in a chair. *Only a few more minutes. She'll come with the car. Get a grip on yourself, calm down.*

The weather had been good for some time: sunny days, one after another. Scattered showers were expected later in the week, but for now there was nothing but blue sky and a few white clouds. She took his arm, because even though his unsteadiness was less visible it was there. They walked through the doors into the daylight, and he had to pause twice to rest before he made it to the car. It was just a short distance, but it was enough to make him stop and pant and watch the black beads in the asphalt at his feet.

"Close the door, Michael," she said, reaching across to buckle his seat belt.

"Oh," he said, as his arm reached out.

She started the engine, and he heard it in great detail: the click and whir of the starter, the sheets of steel spinning across films of oil, the whispering life that followed.

They began to pull away from the building.

"This is your father's car," he said.

She glanced at him briefly before turning her eyes back to the road. "Yes."

She wore slate-gray slacks and tiny green earrings, which matched the color of her blouse. A stranger, looking in the windows, would think her a poised, professional woman at the beginning of middle life, driving a fine car, dressing well.

"I got a job," she said. "I needed something to keep me occupied."

"What is it?" he asked vaguely.

"Nothing much. It's a nonprofit, actually. It's someplace to go. But that's why I'm dressed like this."

"You look nice," he said.

She turned to him and smiled. "Thank you."

The car floated along. The windows were full of green fields and neat houses in rows. He could see the office buildings in the distant center of town. There were more of them now, more each year, more banking, more money, a larger lunchtime flurry of suits. The outskirts also were growing, entering the surrounding fields.

"My father's estate is already settled," she said. "I thought it would take longer."

He turned to look at her. He felt better in the car. The fear in the lobby had lessened.

"And?"

She shook her head, slowly, back and forth. "He left everything to me. His affairs were perfectly in order."

"That's not surprising," he said. A few hundred yards passed.

"No," she said. "It was just like him. He considered every possibility."

"You should be thankful for that, at least."

She looked at him again. "Thankful? I suppose I should be. But he wasn't very old, Michael. He wasn't even sixty-five."

"Things can happen. He knew that."

She nodded. "Yes," she said, "but it's chilling anyway. It's chilling how clear he was about everything. And he never once talked to me."

She laughed, briefly.

"It turns out that most of my problems are over. I'll have a modest income for the rest of my life. I only have to work if I want to."

He thought about this for a while. It was a relief, to find something else to think about. He was quiet, looking out the window. They were getting closer to the neighborhoods.

"What are you going to do?"

She seemed to be thinking. She turned left at the light.

"I'm going to sell the house," she said. "And I'm going to get rid of this car. But after that I have absolutely no idea."

He let his head fall back against the leather rest. A few moments passed.

"I'm sorry, Michael," she said. "I've been talking about myself."

"That's all right."

"No," she said. "It isn't. It isn't at all."

"It's a relief to talk about something else right now."

She looked at him again and nodded and then was silent for a while.

"Nora," he asked finally, "where are you taking me?"

"What do you mean?"

"Are you taking me back to my house?"

"Oh," she said. "Well, it seems to me that you should have someone with you, at least for a few days. So I thought you could stay in the guest room until you felt strong enough. Is that all right?"

A wave of relief and weariness came over him as she spoke. Perhaps he should protest, but he couldn't. It would have been a lie in any case.

"Thank you," he said, rubbing his temples.

She reached out, touching his shoulder with brief but unmistakable tenderness.

"I won't let you be alone, Michael," she said. "Don't worry."

Light fell on the road, on the green streaks of grass on the shoulders, on the oncoming cars. They were silent for the rest of the way.

His days soon settled into a routine. One followed the next, at a slow and steady pace, in the silence of the large house when Nora was at work. At first, walking even a few feet tired him, but as time passed he grew stronger. She left early, long before he was awake, and there would be coffee waiting in the pot by the time he got up, the kitchen full of midmorning sun. He would drink it out back, on the patio. The yard was large, a half acre of grass and flower beds: quiet also, at this time of day, when the neighbors were at work. Everyone, it seemed, was carrying on around him, continuing just as they had always done and would continue to do. He felt, on those mornings, like an invisible presence, a man drinking coffee when he should be elsewhere, working. There should be life around him, a place to go, a family even, but for no clear reason, there wasn't. There was just the wide world of strangers doing whatever it was they did, ignorant of his presence, glimpsed briefly in the early evenings, getting in and out of their cars. Sometimes, when the windows of their houses were open, he heard voices.

The notion that he was his own ghost came gently. For the moment, he indulged himself with it—when he finished his coffee, as he stood and went back inside. How quickly rituals develop: coffee on the patio, then back to the kitchen, washing the cup with the liquid soap, putting it carefully on the blond wooden rack by the sink to dry. Then he would walk through the house to the front door, where the paper lay waiting on the stoop in its clear plastic bag. He was grateful for the paper, because it gave him another hour and sometimes, if he was careful and read it all, nearly two.

He might have let himself go, and probably, had he been at home, he would have. But here in Nora's house he was careful to shower and shave and dress neatly every morning. He washed his dishes, made his bed, and picked up his clothes in the guest room. Soon, in a few more days, he would begin to go out again. He would go to the store, he would collect his mail, he would call Susan and begin all the discussions that were necessary. There were letters to be written, phone calls to be made. But for now, it was enough to rinse the dish soap off the coffee cup, and feel it squeak against his fingers, and set it out to dry.

As the sun passed overhead, it lit different rooms. First the kitchen, east facing, which darkened toward noon. Then Gass's study, which had a skylight. Finally, the living room in front. So each afternoon, when Nora came home, he had to squint against the glare, unable to see her clearly against the open door.

His body had nothing but reassurance to offer. It was getting stronger, it was consuming things—the sandwiches Nora left for him, the dinners she made in the evenings after work. The needle of the bathroom scale inched upward, and the bones of his face visibly withdrew.

Inevitably, with nothing to do during the day, he began wandering through the various rooms of the house. He opened drawers, looked inside them, and closed them again, careful to leave their contents undisturbed. He wasn't looking for anything in particular. But he couldn't read books, not really, his eyes fluttered across the page, but the words refused to draw him in. So he peered in closets and looked in desks, even in Nora's room. He felt ashamed as he did this, thumbing through the lives of others; it was, he supposed, what ghosts did. But he did it anyway, because the alternative was to pace, and feel the world passing over him and around him as if he were a stone in the current. So I am the one, he thought, who makes noises in the quiet when no one is at home. Ronald and Clara and I.

He thought of returning to his house, but he couldn't. Nora did come back, every evening, and she would cook dinner, and he would do the dishes, and they'd sit and talk for a while, sometimes outside, sometimes not. It was firefly season.

LATE ONE EVENING, AFTER DINNER, HE ASKED IF SHE HAD BURIED HER father. It was not an idle question, though he phrased it like one, because he wanted to know if Gass was still in the house. He wanted to know whether he would find his ashes in a sack somewhere, in a closet or under a bed, so that he might prepare himself.

They were sitting outside on the patio. It was dark, but the light through the kitchen window enabled them to see each other and their coffee on the white iron table. The few mosquitoes were not enough to keep them inside.

"Yes," she said. "I did it as soon as I got the ashes from the funeral home."

"Was there a service?"

She smiled. "Oh, no. He was very clear about that. No service of any kind."

"Why are you smiling?"

"Because it's the same old thing. Services are for the living, anyway."

"Did you want one?"

"I'm not sure. It probably would have been too depressing."

"More depressing than not having one?"

"I think so. My father didn't really have friends. So people would have come only out of politeness. That's what I mean."

"But you did bury him."

"Yes. Next to my mother."

He must have looked relieved.

"Why does that matter to you?"

"I don't know," he said. "I guess I just wanted to know if he was still in the house. When you're at work."

"Michael," she said, "are you afraid to be in the house by yourself during the day?"

He looked down. "Sometimes," he said, "I feel strange."

"To be alone? Or to be here?"

"Sometimes I feel as if I'm not here at all. I feel that life is going on around me, that everyone is well except me. That everything is just going past me like I'm not even here. Like I'm a ghost."

"You're not a ghost. You're getting better. Even in these last couple of days."

"Yes," he said. "I know. Physically."

"You went through something terrible. Give yourself time."

"It's not that I expect to feel well. That's not what I mean."

"What *do* you mean?"

He paused, thinking. "I'm not the same," he said.

"You seem the same to me."

"No," he said.

"Well," she said, "of course. You almost died."

"I haven't told you anything," he said.

She looked at him intently. "What do you mean?"

"Remember when we went out to dinner? Before any of this?"

"Of course."

"I didn't tell you about my patient."

"The one in the fire?"

"Yes," Michael said. "The one in the fire. The one who was bleeding."

"I remember."

"His illness was a mystery," he said. "I didn't know what it was. But I think he gave it to me."

"I thought you had bleeding ulcers," she replied.

He shook his head. "Before he started bleeding he had white lines in his mouth. And in his eye. I didn't hospitalize him in time."

"But you didn't have any of that," she said.

It was suddenly terribly important to him that she believe him. He found himself sitting on the edge of his chair and leaning toward her, wearing, he was sure, a look of desperation on his face.

"I did," he said. "I had all of that. And I showed it to you."

"When did you show it to me?"

"The night after your father died. In the bathroom. The white line in my throat."

Something crossed her face quickly—fear or suspicion, perhaps—but it was gone in an instant.

"The night you made that sound," she said, "in your sleep."

"Yes. Do you remember it?" His voice was rising, he knew, but he couldn't help himself.

"I do remember," she said carefully. "You weren't yourself. But it didn't look like much. It wasn't any bigger than a hair."

"I was terrified," he said.

She looked troubled and confused, suddenly uneasy, and he realized what she must see—a wildness on his face, his hands gripping the edges of the table.

"I didn't make that sound," he continued. "It made that sound. I think it happened many times and no one heard it."

"I don't know, Michael," she said, after a while.

"I'm not making it up, Nora. My patient had the same symptoms. He saw lights. He was confused. He got lost. Everything that happened to me happened to him."

"But who was he?"

"His name was Jonas Williams."

"And you don't know what he had?"

He shook his head. "I've never seen anything like it," he said. "I have no idea what it was."

She was examining him now, carefully.

"I know it's unlikely," Michael said. "I know how it sounds."

"How did you get it from him?"

"I drew his blood and spilled some of it on my hands. It must have been that."

"Did you tell anyone about this?"

He nodded. "I told your father. He even came to my house to see me."

"What did he think?"

It was difficult to say what he had to say, because he saw himself clearly, as if from a distance, sitting at her table, beseeching her.

"He said I was letting my imagination get the best of me," he said. "He didn't see anything in my throat."

There was a long pause.

"Why don't you think he saw it?" she asked, looking at him directly.

"It came and went," Michael said. "Sometimes I could see it and other times I couldn't. But I always knew it was there."

"Why would that be?"

"I don't know," he said. "It doesn't make any sense."

She watched him.

"But you saw it," he continued. "You did."

"I saw something," she answered, "but it was small, Michael. It was hardly anything at all."

It was turning out badly, he realized. There were questions in her eyes, as if it had occurred to her that he might not be entirely in his right mind.

"Excuse me for a moment," she said, standing abruptly.

"Where are you going?"

"To check something in the study," she said.

He could do nothing but sit and wait, and when she came back a few minutes later she looked more troubled than before.

"I just checked my father's books," she said. "We never sent anyone by the name of Jonas Williams a bill. There is no record of him in the accounts."

"I was seeing him for free," he said. "I never billed him. But he should be in Susan's appointment book. Do you have it?"

"I think so," she said.

"I have evidence," he said, as calmly as he could. "I can show it to you."

"I think you need to."

"I don't have it here," he said. "And I need to tell you the story from the beginning." He looked her in the eye. "Nora," he said. "Please."

For a long moment she seemed undecided and concerned, watching him. He put his head down in his hands.

"All right, Michael," she said. "But if there is no Jonas Williams in the book, I think maybe we should go back to the hospital."

So he sat there and hoped, and after what seemed like a long time she came back into the kitchen, put her hand on his shoulder and nodded, and sat down beside him.

"They're going to exhume her tomorrow," he said finally, by way of beginning. "The Reverend asked me to be there."

Michael stood on the grass. The backhoe was small, as yellow as saffron, trundling across the grass on wide black wheels, pulling a little trailer.

The driver was young, twenty at most, and thin, with stringy brown hair and a baseball cap worn backward on his head. He had empty blue eyes and rough red fingers.

"This the one?" he shouted, when he reached them.

Reverend Williams nodded. The engine was loud in the air, but then the boy turned it off and everything was quiet.

It was ten in the morning, hot already. His car was still in the lot where it had been towed those weeks ago, and Nora was at work, so Michael had taken a cab to the cemetery. He had dressed for the occasion: a light summer suit, a tie, his hair combed black and neat. As they stood together in the shade, he was glad that he had done this, that he had dressed well. It felt necessary to be here, to be part of this moment, standing quietly with the Reverend. It was a kind of dreaminess, a sensation that he was part of what was happening, part of this ritual and the simple odd beauty of the morning. He was still weak and had not been out much. He felt at once calm and fragile. But the boy, in work boots caked with yesterday's mud, was clearly unmoved. He was off now, on the grass, with the shovel in his hand and an incurious glance in their direction.

The blade of the shovel made a distinct sound, like a dry sponge torn in brief quick strokes. The boy was good at this, and quick. Already he was halfway around, already the perfect rectangle was taking shape on the green surface. They watched him from the shade of the pines. The Reverend's lips were moving, but though they stood next to each other Michael heard nothing.

The boy ignored them as he worked. He was on his knees now, lifting the edge of the sod, and for an instant a gap was visible, beneath the green edge and the earth below. He began to roll it up carefully, like a rug, from one end of the rectangle to the other, and then, with an audible grunt of effort, he heaved the loose weight of it out on top of the flat black headstone in the grass. For an instant, Michael thought of skin grafts.

The boy rose, stretched. The light brown earth, the perfect rectangle, stood out in relief against the green. He turned, swung up into the seat of the backhoe, and started the engine.

It was loud again. They watched him from the shade, the backing and positioning, the wide yellow feet that lifted the rear wheels of the machine until there was a sliver of daylight beneath them. The hoe uncoiled with the hiss of a lever.

The boy was careful. He placed each new gallon of earth on top of the last. He worked from right to left, the hoe going in, the pitch of the engine rising as it worked against the resistance there, then falling as the stream of earth poured from the upended bucket. The mound to the left rose and the hole to the right fell, quickly and steadily, the boy's hands easy on the levers. First one, then the other, back and forth and back again.

Soon, from where they stood in the shade, they couldn't see how deep the hole was. They began to edge closer, out into the sun on the grass, but the boy waved them off, and so they went back to the shade. After a while, the hoe became delicate. The deep oarlike pulling gave way to a kind of gentleness, and soon the hoe never came out of the ground at all. It stiffened and relaxed and stiffened again, but slowly and carefully, so they knew. Then the hoe lifted into the air, folded back on itself, and twisted aside, and suddenly there was silence, and the odor of exhaust, and a blue haze drifting off toward the trees.

They reached the lip just before the boy jumped in. And there it was, perfectly excised, with only a thin curtain of earth covering its surface. It was black, little larger than a suitcase, and in a few minutes it would begin to shine as the trailer shook it clean on the way back to the parking lot where the hearse was waiting.

Standing there on the grass, in the sweet warm air, with Reverend Williams praying silently beside him, Michael felt another part of him return. The unearthed coffin, the wind moving in the trees, the flat sheets of the sun on the cut grass, and the deep red brick of the distant chapel—it was all teeming around him, and filling him, and going by.

Reverend Williams turned to him. "I asked them to send the report to you," he said. "I'm leaving it in your hands."

When Michael called Sam James's office the next day, expecting nothing, a secretary answered the phone.

"Is Dr. James there?" he asked, keeping his voice level.

"He's out of the office today," she said. "May I ask who's calling?"

"Dr. Grant. Do you know if he did the postmortem on the Williams child?"

"Oh, yes," she said immediately. "Dr. Grant. He was trying to call you. He did it right away. We sent you the report by priority mail yesterday afternoon."

"Do you know what he found?"

"I'm sorry," she said, "I'm not supposed to give that information out over the phone. He's very strict about it."

Nora was looking at him as he hung up.

"I need to go home," he said. "I've imposed on you."

"No," she replied. "You haven't."

"They've probably turned off the power by now."

"It's on, Michael. They gave me your keys when you were in the hospital. I paid your bills."

She blushed a little then, just enough for him to see. She was open to him in that moment, and he saw it clearly, and before he knew what he was doing, he reached out across the table and touched her hand.

"Thank you," he said. "How much did it come to?"

"Oh, I don't know. It wasn't much," she said. "It wasn't like I had anything else to do." She smiled a small smile. "The truth is I like having you here. The house isn't so empty."

There was a long silence. He sat down at the kitchen table, and after a moment she did so as well.

"Do you believe me?" he asked, his voice blunt and sudden and far harsher than he had intended.

She bit her lip and watched him. "I don't know," she said. "I keep thinking of the sound you made. I can't get it out of my mind."

He didn't answer.

"I want to," she continued carefully, "and I know you believe it. But I'm not sure. You've been through a lot."

"Will you let me show you?" he asked, keeping his voice as even as he could. "Will you do that for me?"

She took a sip of water from a glass on the table and nodded.

Something occurred to him then for the first time, and it was shameful, he knew, that he had not thought of it long ago. It should have been the first thing in his mind, these past days, but it hadn't been. Now, because of her openness in this moment, her kindness, whatever it was, the thought came swimming up.

"Nora," he said. "Promise me something."

"What?"

"If strange things start happening to you—if you start seeing things, if you see lights, if you get lost in familiar places—tell me right away."

She looked at him steadily. "I'm not going to get sick."

"I'm serious. If you experience anything like that, you need to tell me. Even if you're not sure about it."

"I'm not a doctor," she said, after a moment's thought. "But it seems to me that if this were really contagious, many other people would have gotten it. And that hasn't happened."

"It is contagious. It must be. I just don't know how contagious. And different people may respond differently to it."

"What do you mean?"

"Some people have tuberculosis and never even know it. Others die. It depends on the host."

"I don't think anyone else is going to get this, Michael," she replied. "I don't even know if it's real."

"You saw it. You saw the line in my throat."

"I did see it. But that doesn't mean it's what caused you to get so sick."

"It's an infectious disease," he said, his voice rising again. "It has to be. There's nothing else that explains it."

"Then why hasn't anyone else gotten it?"

"Someone may have, we don't know. Just because a new disease appears doesn't mean there's going to be an epidemic. Most of the time there's only a cluster of cases and that's it. There are lots of examples. These things are impossible to predict."

"And no one knows about it but you?"

"That's right," he said. "No one but the Reverend and me."

She looked away and was quiet for a while. "Are you angry with me for doubting you?" she asked finally.

He shook his head. "No. I'm not."

"It's all right. It will be all right," she said.

In the end, she drove him home. He steeled himself, and as he closed the door of his house behind him he heard her car pull away.

His place looked as if it had just been cleaned, with no sign of what had passed. Nora, he saw, had done more than pay his bills. It would have looked exactly the same, he thought, had he not returned at all. This was his absence—the medical books on the shelf, the chairs, the table, all the objects he had acquired with so little thought, simply because they were necessary. He stood in the living room, looking around. They meant so little to him that he knew he could not live here again. It was not a place to return to. He saw that very clearly. There were no photographs, no visible past. It was a furnished room.

And so he continued, climbing the stairs to the upper floor. His study, his desk. His bedroom. The blinking red light of the answering machine, which no doubt held Sam James's voice. Much clean white paint. His shoes, squeaking on the wood. His clothes, hanging in the closet. His socks, untouched in the drawer, in a neat line.

He stared at his socks, and they reminded him suddenly of cats. Years ago, in medical school, he had stepped into an elevator in the basic science building. A lab technician in a white coat stood next to a stainless steel cart. On the cart, lined up in rows, lay a dozen house cats. They were on their way down to the animal physiology lab in the basement. For an instant Michael had thought the cats were dead. But as he stared at them he realized they were breathing. They had been anesthetized and then laid out in neat rows, like a buffet. For some reason, as he stared into his open drawer of socks all these years later, he thought of those cats, little sleeping animals, white and brown and gray.

Through the bedroom window, he could see his neighbor's house. There was a flowering tree in the man's yard, with many red petals. The house was a soft yellow, the grass a deep clipped green, as if no one walked there. And this, he thought, was what it would have been—this orderly absence, a soulless house, a few closets, a few cabinets of papers. Clothes for the Salvation Army.

He was breathless from the stairs. But he had to climb them, to look, to feel what was around him, and as he descended the stairs again he felt boiled down to a clear hard ache, even as he cast his eyes around the house and dismissed it, consciously, like a man who turns his back and is done.

The envelope lay on the floor in the hall by the mail slot in the door. He picked it up and opened it.

The body received is that of an eight-month-old female in the advanced stages of decomposition. Partial mummification is present.

It was important, he thought, to look closely.

Coagulative necrosis is present and extensive throughout the cranial, thoracic, and abdominal cavities. The extent of decomposition renders pathologic examination of the individual organs impossible.

Walking upstairs to the room, harried, late for the office, leafing through the chart at the desk. The early morning of another day, nothing more, the little girl sleeping so quietly in her cot, the sound of other children crying in the rooms beyond.

There were photographs. Polaroids, a half dozen or so, and at first he turned them facedown. He imagined the stench of the room, Sam James in his mask and gloves and rubber gown, feeling this with his hands, how soft it was, how little the knife was needed. The scale, the ledger, the stainless steel counters, the table where she lay.

Decorative beads are present in the hair.

The photographs were numbered. He took a breath and looked at the first of them.

He had expected nakedness: threads of flesh, cracked gelatinous eyes. But she wore a white-and-blue-striped dress, high white socks, tiny black shoes. The dress was stained with fluids, the socks also, but the beads and the braids and the patent leather shoes looked as if they had just been made. It was a terrible image. The dead he had seen had all been new, still warm when he left them. But this was what followed, when even the faintest claim to life was lost.

In the next picture, the clothes were gone. He wondered whether Sam James had undressed her or simply cut them off.

The narrative continued, neatly typed, step by step, careful and clear. This and this. This also. A pause for the flashbulb, a notation. The entry of hands, of gloved fingers. The room must have reeked; it must have been overpowering. They must have rubbed their upper lips with liniment. He wondered how long it had taken. An hour? Two? It was impossible to tell.

Dental eruption is present.

He could see it also, on photograph number three, which was of the mouth: two new teeth on the mandible, a deeper row of others. She was teething. He thought of fossils, of shark teeth in the desert.

At the request of the referring physician, special attention was given to the eyes.

The residue spooned out, carefully, the dried black thread of the optic nerve—and finally there it was, so thin and delicate a thing it could easily have been missed and lost, but Sam James had been careful, with his tweezers and balls of cotton, pulling away, daubing, pulling away, until he was at the back, where the retina should have been.

He had cleaned it with great care and lifted it high for the photograph. He had not let it crumble to dust. It was a wafer of bone, an exact cast of the left retina, a seashell, a little full moon, or something else entirely.

They were in the Reverend's living room.

"She had it also," Michael said, as gently as he could.

"Are you certain?"

"You were right."

The Reverend's expression did not change.

"How did you know?" Michael asked. "I didn't think of it at all."

"It came to me," he said.

"What do you mean?"

The Reverend closed his eyes and leaned back in his chair, the first visible sign. "When you got sick," he said, "I knew."

"I have a photograph to show you," Michael said. "It's not that bad."

"It doesn't matter if it is."

Michael was glad he had not brought the rest. "It was in her eye," he said, handing it to him.

The Reverend held it up to the light, looking: the wafer, held high in the pathologist's tweezers.

"What is it?"

"It's bone. It was in her eye. It was in Jonas also. And in me, I think."

"Bone in the eye," Reverend Williams said, turning the photograph over and placing it on the coffee table, facedown, like someone dealing a card. Time passed. It was late afternoon, and the house was stifling.

"When I first saw Jonas," Michael said, "he had just come back from somewhere else. Where was he?"

"He was up at Rosemary's cabin. He went there after he left his family."

"Rosemary's cabin?"

"Her people were from a town up in the mountains. There's an old cabin up there that's been in her family for years. That's where Jonas went."

"He went by himself?"

The Reverend nodded. "We used to go up there in the summer when the children were young. There was a swimming hole nearby. I haven't been back since she died."

"Do you own it?"

"Yes. It's not much. The girls use it sometimes. But it's hard for me. Rosemary is buried there."

"She's buried at the cabin?"

"No, she's in the town cemetery with her family. It's where I'll be too, someday." He shook his head. "Jonas loved it up there. He loved that swimming hole."

"How long did he stay?"

"Months. He could stay there for nothing."

"Did he ever take his daughter with him?"

"Once, for a little while. But then he said he couldn't take care of her."

"And the mother let him?"

"I think she hoped he would come back."

"But he didn't."

The Reverend shook his head. "No," he said. "He didn't."

"How did you change her mind about the autopsy? She must have agreed to it."

"I asked her. I asked her to do it for me. And I told her about Jonas." He paused. "It was hard on her," he said. Just that—but the woman had lost everything, and Michael thought about her, walking away from her daughter's grave in her best dress toward the parking lot. What was it she had said? That she was leaving it in the Lord's hands? He was quiet. Too many questions, he thought, however necessary they were. How could I have been so blind?

"Jonas did do wrong," the Reverend said. "He did. He abandoned his family and his faith." He stopped again, as if he were struggling to be as clear as he possibly could. "My son humiliated me," he continued. "My congregation must have asked themselves, How is it that our pastor's own son turned his back on the Lord? How can he comfort us, and claim the word of God when his own son rejects him and abandons him?"

"How did he abandon you?" Michael asked.

"He went away. He did not tell me where, and I heard nothing from him. He spurned me and left me. Then he returned, and I had a chance to show him I loved him and wanted the best for him, but I didn't take it. I should have welcomed him with open arms, but I did not. And when my granddaughter died I didn't think he cared. He didn't even come to her funeral. He told me he forgot."

"But you sent him to me, Reverend. You did that."

"I sent him to you because you were his daughter's doctor. I thought highly of you. But I wanted him to feel her loss. I wanted him to feel what he had done to me. I did not know it was something that could kill him."

"Why did you think highly of me?"

"You came to the cemetery. I could see that her death upset you. And you were honest with me. I believed that you did your best for her."

The words were hard to bear, and Michael nearly told him then. But he stopped himself, because the Reverend was wide open, as vulnerable as Michael had ever seen him, and what possible good would it do him to hear the truth now? He trusted me, Michael thought, and it was the first of his mistakes.

"If Jonas forgot to go to the funeral," Michael said finally, "I'm sure it was because he was sick. It wasn't his fault."

"I realized that too late," the Reverend replied. "And I didn't exhume her in time."

"What do you mean?"

"They had the same illness," he said. "But she was an innocent child. She could have done nothing to earn what happened to her."

He paused.

"I was wrong," he continued. "I never knew what Jonas suffered. And I believed the worst of him because I didn't understand him."

"It wasn't your fault either, Reverend. You had her exhumed. You saw the connection and I didn't."

How difficult it must have been, Michael thought. So much had been poised in the balance.

"Too little," the Reverend replied, "and too late."

"Reverend," Michael said, "you're a good man. I know you are."

Reverend Williams did not answer.

"Is there anything I can do for you?" Michael asked. "Anything at all?"

"Yes," the Reverend said. "You can find out what it was. There are others to think of."

"Then I need to go up there," he said. "To the cabin."

"Why?"

"Because that's where they may have gotten it."

A moment passed.

"I'll give you the key," the Reverend said.

"Will you come with me?"

"I have responsibilities here."

Michael looked out into the room, at the photographs hanging on the wall, and the red chair, and the fireplace, and then, finally, he stood. Reverend Williams began to stand as well.

"That's all right, Reverend, don't get up."

"I've got to give you directions," the Reverend said. "And the key. And I want to give you something else."

"What do you want to give me?"

"It's in the other room," he said. He stood up, with effort; he looked exhausted. "I won't be long."

He returned with an envelope in his hand.

Nearly an hour passed before Reverend Williams felt steady enough to rise again from his chair. Words come easily, he thought, when someone is listening. But the doctor was gone, and he was alone.

It was early in the evening. He considered going to bed or trying to eat. Instead, he found himself lifting his jacket from the hook in the hall, taking his keys from his pocket, and stepping outside into the darkness. He turned carefully, in the light of the stoop, and locked the door behind him.

It was a habit of his, a form of exercise—a brisk walk through the neighborhood in the evening, when he could collect his thoughts. He would walk, letting the streets carry him along for a while, waving to his neighbors, sometimes stopping to talk.

But now he walked with purpose. The streetlights were on, and as he passed them his shadow rose up in front of him, monstrous for a while, vast, then fading as the pool of light receded behind him. He began walking faster, watching the rise and fall of his shadow. His heart began to pound. Long minutes passed. He clung to the streetlights and they led him on, one luminous bead after another. Soon he had left his neighborhood entirely, and the few people sitting on their porches were strangers. Some part of him knew they were watching him carefully, with suspicion in their eyes: a large man, walking down their sidewalks, looking neither left nor right. He was breathing hard, sweating, refusing to let himself rest. His shadow lumbered on.

It was six miles to the church. He knew the distance exactly, though in the past he had always driven his car there. He did not know how long it took him—one hour, two—but despite the pain in his knees and his aching back it seemed like nothing at all, and when he reached the street he felt as though he had just left his own home.

He went in through the side door, remembering, somehow, to punch the buttons on the pad that turned off the alarm. The interior of the church was silent, with only the vague rows of pews and the dim light from the high windows. The stage at the far end of the room, the lectern where he had stood for twenty-seven years of Sundays, could not be seen at all.

The stairs to the basement were completely dark, so he turned on the light, descended them, and opened the door. As always, he closed it again behind him, and then he stood for a while, allowing his eyes to widen and the single yellow band below the door to flow into the darkness around him, until he could just make out the wall where the dials for the lights lay.

He let his breathing settle a bit, deliberately, and took careful steps, with his hands in front of him, until the wall came to his outstretched fingers. He fumbled along the wall to the switches and turned on the lights. The room sprang to life, and he blinked in the glare for a moment before dimming them.

There was a chair next to the lectern in the center of the room, and he lowered himself into it because he did not know how long he could stand. He was beginning to shiver, as the sweat dried on his chest and belly. He felt as if each breath were filled with the cold of the glass, but still he looked out into it and tried to begin, nothing but a wick, as he thought of it, nothing but a filament in a bulb, and then, finally, he gave in to it and let it overcome him.

For so long I have offered You, for so long I have given them to You, and told them You are the balm and the solace, that You are Easter in the world of Fridays, and yet You give me only Fridays, You have given me a life of Fridays, You have taken the world from me and denied me Your presence; You have given me the death and suffering of those I love most on earth; You have made me fall on my knees in penance; You give me wilderness, yet You ask me again to stand before them, this week and the next and the next; and when is it that You will come forward, when is it that You will show Yourself as one who comforts, as one who answers for the bitterness of this world with grace?

For a moment, until he regained himself, he felt as if he were not there at all, as if the silence of the building above him and the sound of his own breath were only the chaos of dreams, without order to guide him.

He stood, then, and moved back to the switches, turning them on as high as they would go, until the room was a dance studio again. His own reflection, as he stood by the door, was as clear as day. He looked at himself for a moment but then turned away and opened the door and went up the stairs. The light below him flooded up into the church, so he could see its full expanse—the neat wooden pews, the hymnals in their pockets, the red line of carpet running up the aisle toward the pulpit.

He sat in the last row of pews. He sat for a long time, head down, resting his arms on his knees. I need to call my girls, he thought. I need to ask them to come home, if only for a little while.

Absently, he saw that someone had carved their initials in the back of the pew. He would not have noticed it had he been sitting upright, but bending forward it was clear: the letters RK, cut deep in the wood just under the overhanging lip. He realized that it was not the work of a few minutes. It must have taken weeks, he thought, at least several Sundays of steady effort.

For a moment he wondered who RK was. But then he imagined himself standing in the pulpit, looking out into the congregation, and it came to him.

RK must be Robert Katrell, Mrs. Katrell's youngest grandson. A tall and quiet boy, just old enough to drive, he brought his grandmother here each Sunday and sat beside her, bowing his head with rest. Many times Reverend Williams had seen him slowly crossing the parking lot before the service with his tiny hunched grandmother clinging to his arm in the same pink dress and hat she always wore. She would shuffle along, beaming, pausing every few feet to greet people, and Robert would stand patiently beside her. Then, after the service, he would help her carefully into her old battered car and drive her home.

Mrs. Katrell was one of his most enthusiastic parishioners; she had in fact been coming to the First Baptist Church longer than he had. For years Mrs. Katrell had let it be known that while, in her opinion, he had improved over time, he was still no match for his predecessor in terms of either oratory or fire, and he had long understood that only the most apocalyptic of his sermons met with her considered approval. The more he invoked damnation and the torments of hell forever, the more she liked it, and even now he could see her rapturous, uplifted face, there in the back of the crowd, asking for thunder.

For twenty-seven years this had been his life. He had been present for it all, the growing children, the graves and hospitals and graduations, the marriages and baptisms and funerals. He had seen their happiness and their grief, their kindness and cruelty, their love for one another, their thirst for blessings, and after a while, as he sat there in the pew, he began to feel the presence of his congregation around him: Rachel, thin and dour and alone, without a kind word for anyone; Winston, the janitor, whose enthusiasm for singing was matched only by his inability to carry any sort of tune. For years the Johnson sisters had been trying to remove Winston from the choir, and it was only through Reverend Williams's intervention that Winston's loud bass had remained, damaging hymn after hymn.

He let them flow over him, one after another, their faces rising up and falling away, their flutter of coughs each Sunday as he mounted the three steps to the pulpit and turned toward them with his sermon in his hand, waiting until they were quiet.

Soon he would have to go, soon he would have to ready himself for the long walk home. But for the moment he let his fingers follow the deep grooves of the letters. Just that—his fingers on the initials, over and over, and the image again of Mrs. Katrell, coming unsteadily up the stairs through the wide front doors, with expectation in her eyes.

They were in the hall. Over her shoulder Michael could see the blank space where the photograph of her parents had been. Her sudden diffidence, as she answered his knock, the flush on her face, knowing it was him, seeing him walk past the windows to the door. The envelope was in his pocket.

The house seemed larger than ever. He had the sense of space suddenly, all around him, as he followed her down the hall, his shoes loud on the hardwood floor.

She made him tea. The kettle must have just been used, because it began to sing almost immediately, and again he watched as she poured water onto the teabag in the cup and brought it to him with a lemon wedge and a bowl of sugar.

"There's no milk," she said, as she sat down. "Sorry."

The tea was hot; he blew a little hollow in the surface.

"What is it, Michael?" she asked.

He knew it was more than a question, so he slipped the autopsy report out of his jacket and handed it to her.

"Don't look at all the pictures," he said. "Just the top one. But it should answer your questions."

She took the envelope from his hand and sat down at the table opposite him. He watched her as she read, how her face tightened and darkened. Minutes passed, and she did not take his advice, turning the photographs over, one after the other, looking straight at them. He blew on the tea.

After a while she looked up at him, and he could see her mind at work, weighing and choosing, back and forth and back again.

"This is the photograph that's important," he said quietly, reaching out and shuffling quickly through them until he found it. "It's bone. It was in her eye."

She brought her hands up to her lips. She said nothing, but his relief was enormous and it was only then that he realized how much of his own mind he had questioned—but the image was there; it was not imagined or conjured from elsewhere.

"But what is it?" she said.

"I don't know."

"There must be someone who does."

"Maybe," he said, "but I don't know who that person is."

"You have to call someone," she said, looking down at the photograph in her hand.

He didn't respond directly. "Do you have an atlas?" he asked.

"An atlas? You mean a map?"

"Yes. Of this part of the country."

"I think my father had one somewhere. Why?"

"Can you find it?"

"I think so," she said.

"Can you do it now?"

"OK," she said, puzzled, standing up from the table.

For a few moments he was alone in the kitchen. He sat there waiting for her, drinking tea from the cup. *What else? What have I forgotten?*

She returned a few minutes later with a green book in her hands.

"It's old," she said. "It's probably out-of-date."

The atlas looked as if it had not been opened in years. The barest hint of must rose from the pages, like the pews of churches.

Inside the cover, a name stamped in black: Ronald Gass, M.D. Neat and exact, for decades unseen.

"He did that with all his books," she said.

He thought of Gass at his desk, painstakingly pressing the stamp into the ink pad. The idea of order, but random anyway, a habit or a belief or a Sunday-morning task when there was nothing else to do.

The book was heavy, thick enough for all the continents. It was not the kind of book anyone took anywhere. It was not, he thought, made for traveling. It had another purpose altogether. The idea of traveling, perhaps, or the idea of somewhere else.

The paper was good, and the greens and blues were bright, as were the red and black lines of the roads. Some must be gone, he imagined, or have different numbers now. But the cities and the sea and the curved gray lines of elevation—all these were the same, as if they had just been drawn.

He turned the pages carefully. The gloss was on them still, after all these years, the hills and estuaries, the names, the distances between them. Three hundred miles west. A day's drive. If you kept going, and left early, you would be there by afternoon. The town was there, small but clear, in the mountains. He touched it with his finger.

Nora stood, walked around the table, and put her hand on his shoulder. She did it casually, as if without thought, and leaned against him, peering down.

"What are you looking for?"

"This town," he said, and touched it again before closing the book.

She looked at him. "Why?"

"Because it may be there."

"I don't understand."

"I know," he said. "So let me tell you."

That night he lay unable to sleep, thinking of her on the other side of the house, over and over again, until finally he gave in to it. He threw off the covers and stood up and made his way out into the darkness.

He crossed into the living room, over the expanse of the carpet, past the dim shapes of tables and chairs. At each step he nearly turned back to the safety of his own bed. His uncertainty was everywhere—how unlike him this was, how vulnerable he felt—yet one foot followed the other, leading him to the far side of the house and then down the hall to her room.

Her door was closed. He stood there a long time, struggling with himself, and again he nearly turned back. He took a step away from the door, down the hall—and then, suddenly, he realized that he could not face what waited for him there: a solitary room, the sleeplessness of crisp sheets, and all his failures, until morning.

He turned the knob, then, and eased open the door, as quietly as he could. He could see her clearly in the streetlight cast through the window. Her bed was by the far wall, her hair black on the pillow. She lay unmoving, like the sleeping figure she should have been, and he could hear the sound of her breath. He looked at her, and then, suddenly, she shifted, and he realized that she was awake.

"Michael?" she said, as she sat up.

"I'm sorry," he replied. "I shouldn't be here."

Before he could stop her she turned on the bedside light. He blinked in the sudden brightness, standing in his boxers and T-shirt, as defenseless as he had ever felt in his life. His face burning, he began to murmur another apology. But she stopped him.

"Michael," she said again, softly, as she stood up and walked toward him and took his hand.

It was only a few seconds, but it seemed as if they stood there for a long time, and then, finally, she turned without a word and led him back to the bed, pausing to switch off the light.

She lay down on the bed and moved aside to give him room, and then he was beside her, with his arm around her, and her breath in the hollow of his neck, and her hair falling across his face.

"Nora . . ." he said.

"Ssshh."

"I couldn't sleep," he said.

"It's all right, Michael."

He wanted to speak but there was nothing he could think of to say, nothing to offer but his arm around her shoulders. They were quiet for a while.

"Do you mind if we get under the covers?" she asked finally. He didn't answer but sat up to pull back the bedclothes and take off his shirt, and she stood, briefly, before slipping in beside him.

It was not a dream, exactly, that followed, but neither was it the conscious world. It was somewhere or something else—a suspension, a place between shadows—their breathing, the silence between them, the immense warmth of her body through her thin gown, on and on, the absence of sleep. They lay closely together and then, finally, her hand began to move in circles on his chest and he could feel her breath quickening against his cheek. He had to force himself to speak.

"Nora," he whispered.

It was nearly dark, but as he turned toward her he could see her anyway: the faint wrinkles around her eyes, the shine of gray in her hair, her quiet, questioning face.

"We can't," he said softly.

She closed her eyes and her hand went still.

"I want to," he continued, "but I'm afraid."

"Why?" she asked, turning her head away.

"Because I might give it to you," he said. "It may still be in me."

She sighed and did not reply, and her desire for him magnified his own—the ache of her body against his, his involuntary hand on her thigh, and the will he required to keep it still.

"I think you're beautiful," he said. "I thought it the first time I saw you."

She smiled, then, and turned in to him.

"It's all right, Michael," she said again, and he felt a deep lassitude come over him, though his arm beneath her began to tingle and soon he would have to move it. Her weight against his shoulder, her breath against him—he allowed himself, as time passed, to rest there, to drift away without thought, as one falls asleep in the sun.

MICHAEL WOKE UP FIRST. SHE LAY CLOSE BESIDE HIM, AND HE WAS careful not to move. He was intensely aware of her breathing. It was early in the morning.

He was too warm, so he eased the sheets down his chest and turned to look at her.

She slept on her side, with her back pressed against him. He couldn't see her face, only her hair, long and dark and undone, and the curve of her shoulder, and her arm, cast out into space beside her.

She must have felt him move, because she began to wake up. She did so gradually, in a slow cascade. Her hand began to move, she murmured once, and then she rolled over on her back and opened her eyes. She took a quick breath, and then her body stiffened in a wave before relaxing again.

"You're awake," she said, turning to look at him.

He smiled.

"What time is it?"

"A little after seven," he said, glancing at the bedside clock.

"I need to brush my teeth," she said.

She slid from beneath the covers and stood up in the light from the window. Her body was clear through the nightgown as she stretched, comfortably, lifting her arms above her head.

"I'll be right back," she said, and he watched her as she walked across the room, her hair midway down her back. In that moment she looked lovely to him, and still young, and somehow untouched by the darkness of life.

He heard the sound of running water, the flush of a toilet. He lay back on the pillows, thinking of nothing but this: the sunlight falling through the windows, her lingering warmth in the bed beside him.

"Thank you, Michael," she said, when she was back beside him.

"For what?"

"For coming here last night."

"I wanted to," he said. "I've wanted to for a long time."

He looked down at his body, and it surprised him again. He felt achingly thin, and the points of his hips were visible even beneath the sheet covering his groin. Already there were times when he could forget his weakness, his reduction, but now he looked like a stick figure beside her.

"I'm sorry I'm so thin," he said. "I'm sorry I look like this."

"Don't worry," she said. "I'll fatten you up."

She settled her head in the hollow of his shoulder and they were silent for a while.

"I feel good," she said, "right now, for a few more minutes. But then I have to get up, and it will be there again."

"What will be there?"

"My life," she said. "And what little I've made of it."

"I haven't made much of mine either."

"You're a doctor. You're respected by people, at least."

"I'm not a very good one, Nora, I'm just average. I don't have anything else. And I spent my whole life working for it."

"What else would you have done?"

"I don't know. I don't have any idea. I just picked a path and followed it. I never even liked it that much."

"Then why did you do it?"

"Because it was clear. I knew exactly what I had to do. I didn't have to think about anything."

"But now you do."

"Yes," he said. "Now I do."

She stroked his thigh. "Let's make breakfast," she said.

A few minutes later, after a quick shower, he found her in the kitchen. She nodded toward the refrigerator.

"Why don't you get out some eggs and milk," she said. "Mix them up in a bowl."

He did it clumsily, cracking the eggs on the lip of the bowl, leaving specks of shell in the yolks. She smiled.

"I'm good at making coffee," he said, as he beat the eggs and the milk to a creamy yellow froth.

She was slicing strawberries. She asked him to set the table. He laid out place mats and silver and glasses, and soon the room filled with the smell of bacon.

"Do you mind turning on the radio?" she asked, nodding to it on the table. "I like it sometimes."

It was a classical station. Suddenly it felt like Sunday morning, with Nora piling French toast high on their plates, and arranging the strawberries, and pouring tall glasses of orange juice for both of them.

She stood at the counter with her back turned, and he stepped up behind her and put his arms around her. She paused and leaned back against him.

"This is so nice," he said. "It's so peaceful."

"I know," she replied. "Let's not talk about anything serious right now."

"I hope," he murmured, "that sometime we'll be together in that way."

"In that way?" she said, turning to face him. He was blushing; he felt it in his cheeks.

"Yes," he said.

"Good," she said, reaching up and brushing his hair with her fingers, looking directly into his eyes.

"Come on," she said lightly. "Let's eat."

LATER, HE WASHED THE DISHES.

"Will you come with me?" he asked suddenly, without thinking.

She paused, holding a glass and a dish towel. "Where are you going?"

"The Reverend's town," he said. "The town on the map."

She nodded. "If you can wait until this weekend," she said, "I will."

They left early, with a guidebook he'd bought the evening before in a convenience store. She'd washed her father's car and it waited in the driveway, a radiant blue, full of black leather and buttons.

"I am going to get rid of this car," she said, opening the trunk for the bags, "but we might as well drive it now."

She looked rested, in her white cotton blouse, her hair pulled back; she'd slept well beside him, though he had tossed and turned, all night full of dreams. The coffee should start to work soon, he thought, and the morning air. He wore sunglasses. The greens and whites around him seemed distilled in the lenses, and the blue side of the car became deeper.

She glanced at her watch. "Come on," she said. "We don't have much time."

"Time for what?"

"You'll see," she said, opening his door, and he shrugged and got in. She ran to lock the house and then was back, adjusting the electric seat and the mirror to suit her.

"I don't mind driving," he said.

"You can drive later."

He turned his head away briefly, wondering why they had to leave right now, a few minutes before nine in the morning.

It took him awhile to realize where she was going. Other cars were out on the roads, families with children, going to ball games, going to public pools. A day off for nearly everyone, but nonetheless there were tractors in the fields.

The parking lot was perhaps a quarter full, and there were a few people standing by the chapel with flowers in their hands. A service, he supposed, but at the other end, far enough away. She checked her watch again.

"I hope they haven't come already," she said, and got out.

He followed her across the grass. For a moment he thought about them—those patients of his, all of them young—how they had come to him, week after week, and how they were sucked into the ground. How little he had helped them, and how cold he had been. But he had been careful, and he'd been clear, and he'd done what he could, and just then his sin of heartlessness didn't seem so great. He might have taken them in his arms, he might have wept for them, but they would be here anyway, and he would still walk past, because in the end there wasn't anything else to do. They hadn't cared so much about his coldness, he thought, or whatever absence he carried, not really, because they simply didn't have the time to waste. All they could see was the steady approach of this field, and everything else was the periphery. How terribly excited and afraid they were.

She stopped where he knew she would, and stood looking down, and he joined her. He hadn't seen Ronald Gass's grave before, but there it was, tucked next to his wife, under the stone.

"Good," she said. "They haven't come."

He looked at her, questioning.

"Let's go over to the shade," she said. "I don't want to ruin it by telling you."

He followed dutifully and sat down beside her. In the distance by the chapel, a few well-dressed children ran and yelled until a woman hushed them.

They were quiet. The sun fell through the tree above their heads for a while. He enjoyed their silence, and the sheets of green grass at their feet.

"Look," she said suddenly, touching his arm. "There he is."

A man walked toward them, studying the ground as he went. He wore a brown uniform and carried a white plastic bag in his left hand. He also held a clipboard and consulted it several times. He'd pause at each line of graves, read them quickly, and move on.

"What's he doing?" Michael asked.

"You'll see," she said. She watched the man intently.

It didn't take him long. He looked down at his feet, stopped, and glanced at the clipboard again. He was only a short distance from them, and he looked their way, briefly, before setting the clipboard and the bag down on the grass. Carefully, as if not to prick himself, he withdrew two bundles of roses from the bag, wrapped in white paper. He unwrapped the roses, put the paper back in the bag, and laid the roses down across each grave. Then, in a gesture that seemed oddly tender to Michael, he stood up again, took a step back, looked carefully, and made a small adjustment to the bouquet on the right, Clara's. He nodded to himself, gathered up the wrappings, and with another glance in their direction began to walk back toward the parking lot.

"Who is he?"

"He's my father's will," Nora answered. "He's my father, grieving for himself."

"But he looks like a delivery man."

"He is a delivery man. My father arranged it all. The first day of every month, he and my mother each get a dozen roses automatically put on their graves."

"Do you know him?"

"I've never seen him before in my life."

Michael shook his head. "Strange," he said.

"I wanted to see it actually happen."

"It almost seems like a joke," he said. "Like an ironic gesture."

She nodded. "I think it was. And I really shouldn't blame my father for it."

"Why not?"

"It was my mother's idea. She asked him to do it."

"She did?"

Nora nodded again. "I think it was her way of getting the last word."

"The last word over what?"

"Over him, I think. Over their failures. I'm not even sure."

He thought about it, as they walked back toward the car.

"Why don't you drive," she said, and handed him the keys.

She was quiet as they passed through the edge of town, looking out the window, but as they pulled onto the highway she spoke again.

"I'm glad I saw that," she said. "I think I really needed to see that."

He'd driven the car before, but slowly, the day he'd taken Gass home from the office. Now, on the open road, its power became apparent to him, as the speed increased effortlessly, and the shoulders became a green wash on either side. He pressed the accelerator further, and the engine hummed, and the yellow center line stretched out before them.

"You're going fast," she said. "You'll get a ticket."

"Do you care?"

"No," she said, starting to laugh. "I don't care at all." And she rolled down her window with the press of a button.

The air, the roar of the fields, and the roadside poured in and whipped her hair into strands. She laughed again.

He had never driven so fast. It was exhilarating, as they closed on the slower traffic and he drifted around it with the barest movement of his wrist, into the oncoming lane for a few seconds, then back. Part of him recognized how reckless it was, and how dangerous, but the rest of him reveled in the speed, the exaltation of the open window, and the flash and stutter of the fences. Miles passed. The small city, where he'd begun again, where he'd spent these last few months, his house, his profession, what life he'd made and would make—all of it receded and after a while was gone, out of sight in the flat country behind them. Gradually the fields gave way to scrub pines, and the color of the earth began to change. He could see it redden where a few miles east it had been black.

There were no police. He'd long expected their lights in the mirror like thunder, but they never came. There is nothing to stop me, he thought; there is no one waiting. It seemed clear, premonitory, somehow irrefutable, and so, after a while, he slowed down again, as if his point had been made.

"Are you done?" she asked, smiling, turning toward him. I was somewhere else, he thought, but then she touched his hand and just as suddenly he was back.

The hours passed. They sat together, quietly, comfortably, sometimes speaking. They stopped for gas; they got out and stretched.

Soon they were in the hills. They left the highway, the road began to twist and coil, and the pines in turn withdrew. It was maples and oaks and larches, many green leaves now, and the air cooled noticeably. He flipped off the air conditioner and rolled his window down.

The numbers on the odometer rolled forward, the sun fell lower in the trees, and many times they heard the sound of streams pouring through culverts beneath the road, though they rarely saw them.

She dozed for a while, and as they rounded the curves he saw her body shift slightly, left and right, and her head roll from side to side. Her eyelids fluttered, her hands lay loosely in her lap, and her lips parted, a glint of saliva between them. I could drive for hours, he thought. I could keep going, with the wind pouring against my cheek, and the crackle of water in the undergrowth, and the road as if it had just been painted black. There were times when the trees converged about them and the interior visibly darkened, then filled with light again. Once, out of the corner of his eye, he saw the white flag of a deer leaping from the end of a meadow, but it was gone before he could wake her.

It's beautiful country, he thought.

She made a small sudden sound, then opened her eyes and yawned deeply.

"Where are we?"

He glanced at the clock on the dash and again at the odometer.

"About an hour away," he said. "Maybe less."

"Good," she said, and closed her eyes.

The town was in a valley. He knew it was beneath them somewhere, through the trees, when they crested the hill. It took a few minutes before the road descended, but then the town appeared, bright in the afternoon sun. There were a few cattle in the fields, and barns, some gone gray, falling down, abandoned for decades, with trees growing from them, others new and full of work.

Ahead of them, a flock of birds rose together over the road, turning in a single dark mass, back and forth for a few seconds, before disappearing over a line of trees. Sparrows, he thought, or starlings.

"It's pretty," she said, looking around.

"Look in the guidebook," he said. "See if they have any recommendations."

She began to read. "It's old," she said. "It was founded before the Civil War."

"A lot of these towns were, I think."

"Robert E. Lee had a summerhouse here."

He smiled.

"But the town didn't grow to the size it is today until the introduction of the railroad in 1926."

"Are there any places to stay?"

"I'm getting to that. This is interesting. There was a sanatorium here."

"Tuberculosis," he said. "They used to send them to the mountains."

He thought of them, those men and women in the 1920s, thin, desperate, leaving their loved ones. He thought of them getting on trains from the northern cities, and he thought of them waiting endlessly, in deck chairs on lawns and terraces, wrapped in blankets, reading or writing letters or simply looking out at the hills.

"There's a bed-and-breakfast," she said, "and a motel. I vote for the bed-and-breakfast."

"Where's the cemetery?"

"Let me see," she said, following her finger down the page. "It's not marked. But there's a church," she added. "Maybe that's where it is."

They had their own little cottage just behind the main house. One room, decorated with the past in mind. A wide wrought-iron bed, a soft cotton quilt, a mirror with a dark wood frame. Dried flowers in a wicker bowl on the dresser, and old photographs on the walls: the town a hundred years before. An open window, through which the breeze passed, and a flower bed just outside.

"It gets chilly in the evenings here," the old man at the desk had said, "so make sure you put on enough covers. There are extra blankets in the chest."

They'd thanked him.

"You folks here for one night or two?"

"We're not sure," Nora said, looking at Michael.

"Well, you don't have to make up your mind until tomorrow."

From the small porch behind the cottage, the town stretched out below them down the hill. They sat on wrought-iron chairs, with a small round table between them, and drank the sweet iced tea the old man had brought them after they'd carried in their bags. Leaves moved overhead.

"This is a wonderful place," Nora said, squeezing another lemon wedge into her glass. "What do you think it was?"

"I don't know. Maybe a plantation house."

"It seems too small for that," she said, stretching.

Michael drank the last of his tea, letting the ice fall against his teeth.

"I think I'm going to take a nap," she said.

They dozed for a while on the bed. It was languorous and cool, with the breeze through the window, and the smell of flowers, and finally, in the distance, the sound of a train flowing up the valley.

It was the train that woke him. He looked at his watch. Maybe an hour, he thought, of full daylight left. He eased himself up off the bed, carefully, but she woke anyway.

"Where are you going?" she asked sleepily.

"I want to see the cabin."

She sat up. Her hair was rumpled, and she yawned.

"Why don't you wait until tomorrow?" she said. "It's getting late."

He put on his shoes anyway, and felt for the key, and slipped the envelope carefully out of his open bag and put it in his pocket.

"Do you want me to come with you?" she said then, watching him from the bed.

"No," he replied. "I don't think you should."

"Why not?"

"Because I don't know what's up there."

"Do you really expect to find something, Michael?" she asked.

"Probably not," he replied. She watched him as he laced up his shoes, and his determination must have been clear on his face.

"What time do you think you'll be back?" she said finally.

"I don't know," he said. "It depends on what I find."

He followed the Reverend's map—the streets, more or less, the church, the line of the tracks, and the sidings, in a clear, exact hand. The map ended after only a few miles, at a chain-link fence. A sign—JOHNSON FREIGHT AND SHIPPING—hung from the gate. Beyond the gate was a small rail yard with a few low metal buildings. The tracks stretched away on either side, and a heavily wooded hill stood in the distance behind the yard. He sat alone in the expensive car, looking at the map, and after a while a man came out of the nearest building and walked toward him.

"You lost?" he called through the fence.

He was in his fifties, black, heavy, with a pleasant, mildly inquisitive smile on his face. A large man, starting to show his age.

"I'm looking for a cabin. The Williams place."

"The Williams place?"

"Yes. The one with the swimming hole. Or a pond."

The man looked puzzled.

Michael got out of the car and approached the fence. "Do you know where it is?" he asked.

"I know where it is," the man replied. "But nobody lives there. It's been empty for years."

"I need to go up there," Michael said.

"You mind telling me why? I keep an eye on it," the man said.

Michael looked down. The fence, the man just behind it, wondering who he was and what he was doing and where he had come from—so many questions phrased as one.

"Reverend Williams asked me to," he said. "I'm a friend of his. I have a key."

The man's face changed then, his suspicion visibly receding. "Oh," he said politely. "In that case, why don't I show you?"

The path up the hill began a short distance from the yard. It was warm still, though the sun was low on the horizon. The man was sweating heavily. Michael felt his own shirt begin to cling to him, and his rising weakness reminded him again of how easily he tired. It was an effort to follow.

"Thank you for doing this," Michael said, breathing hard.

"Nothing else to do this time of day."

"Are you the watchman for the rail yard?"

"I guess you could say that," he said. "I own it, so I watch it."

"I'm sorry," Michael said, but the man only smiled and led him farther.

After a few minutes the path began to level off, though through the trees they could see the hillside continue above them. Nearby, the sound of a stream.

The cabin stood in a small clearing about half a mile into the woods. There were oaks in the clearing, far larger than the surrounding woods—first growth, Michael thought, looking at the old weathered planks, the red tin roof, the dust visible on the windowpanes. An outhouse and a wide porch, deep in shadow. It was small—three or four rooms, a brick chimney. A few patches of sun fell on the high, unmown grass.

"This is it," the man said. "You want to go inside?"

"It looks old," Michael said, and the man nodded.

"It was a sharecropper's place," he said, "just after the Civil War. Lots of them around here."

"It's beautiful."

"Well," the man said, "that depends how you look at it."

But it was beautiful. The cabin had been there so long it seemed to have grown into the surroundings, as much a part of the meadow as the trees overhead or the luxuriant thickets at the edge of the woods. The red roof, the dark wooden door, the thick gray trunks of the oaks rising out of the high grass—it was lovely.

"Do you know the Williams family?" Michael asked.

"I knew Rosemary a long time ago," the man replied. "But I haven't seen the Reverend in years. Their son was up here a couple months back, though."

"Did you see him?"

"Once or twice. He kept to himself."

Michael was silent, thinking. "Has anyone around here been sick?" he asked awkwardly. "Has anyone been ill?"

"My neighbor has cancer," he said, after a moment of thought. "But he's an old man."

"That's not what I mean. Has anyone had fevers? Or problems seeing? Anything like that?"

"I don't think so. Why do you ask?"

Michael took a breath. "I was just wondering," he said.

The man looked troubled now, and confused, shifting from foot to foot.

"If any of your neighbors had an illness with unusual symptoms," Michael continued, "would you hear about it?"

"This is a small town," the man said. "I know pretty much everyone. I couldn't help but hear about it."

Michael nodded. It would have been so simple, he thought, but somehow the answer did not surprise him. Weeks had passed since Jonas's death. A breeze moved in the boughs above them.

"Where's the pond?" Michael asked suddenly.

"The pond? You don't want to go inside?"

"Not yet."

"There was a pond pretty close by," the man said, looking carefully at him, "but they filled it in a while ago. Must be ten years at least."

"Why did they fill it in?"

"Mosquitoes. They're terrible around here. Don't know if it helped, though."

"Do you think," Michael said, "that you could find it? Do you know where it was?"

The man was looking at Michael uncertainly. "There used to be a path," he said, "but it's probably all grown up."

On the far side of the clearing they had to pick their way through the thickets. In a few minutes Michael had lost all sense of direction; it was all tangled undergrowth, and the smell of pines, and the dense leaves of saplings. But the man was purposeful, plunging straight ahead, and he followed.

"Somewhere around here," the man said, looking up. The trees began to change, becoming young and thin, with fewer pines, though the ground underfoot was the same. "This is it," he said finally.

"Are you sure?"

"The trees here are shorter," he said, "and they're in a circle."

Michael saw it clearly then. It was as if they were standing in what had once been a field, years ago, until someone let it back into the forest. The thin trees, twenty feet shorter than the rest, all in a rough circle; it would be decades, he thought, before the last sign was gone.

The sun moved down a little through the trees, and they stood for a while. Michael looked around him, at the young maples and oaks, the ferns at their feet.

"Good place for deer," the man said, glancing uneasily at his watch. "Do you think you can find your way back?"

They weren't far from the cabin, but again it felt as if they were deep in the forest, without landmarks to guide them.

"I'll be fine," Michael said. "Thank you so much."

The man slapped his neck and looked relieved.

"I'll leave you alone then," he said.

Michael reached out and shook his hand, and thanked him again. For minutes afterward he could hear him, crashing down through the brush, full of unanswered questions, but then the sound trailed off, and he was left with his breathing, and the insects, and the silence.

The mosquitoes came by the thousands, it seemed, pouring out of the trees. He knew they were feeding, he knew they were on his neck, and in his hair, and on his hands, but he didn't really feel them. He let them come, full of the blood of animals, and it didn't seem like much, somehow. He stood staring at the circle in the woods.

For days now he'd seen himself standing here, looking into water, but it was only a circle of trees within a field of trees, and the pond was long since gone into the ground. He went forward anyway, pushing through the brambles and the high grass and the saplings, until he was where the center might be.

After a while, he took the envelope containing Jonas's ashes carefully from his pocket and opened it. He stood for a moment, wondering if he should speak. But the services of his childhood were so long ago that nothing came to him, and so after a moment he simply shook the envelope, and the thimblefuls of ash fell out into the air and fluttered. A few gray flecks clung to the high blades of grass, but the rest—the small amount that the Reverend had given him—was gone.

He stood for a while longer in the center of the circle, in the heavy undergrowth, breathing, listening to the whine of mosquitoes, but there was nothing else there, nothing to be seen, so finally he turned back and followed the trampled undergrowth through the trees until he could see the light of open ground.

The red tin roof of the cabin glowed in the late afternoon sun as he stepped out into the clearing. Perhaps ten yards separated the cabin from the edge of the woods, and from where he stood he could see a vegetable garden in the space between the cabin and the trees.

The garden was large, invisible from the rest of the clearing, and as he walked around the side of the cabin he saw that it had been neglected: weeds grew, a handful of rotting tomatoes lay half eaten on the ground. There were sunflowers, and corn in rows, grown to the height of a man. Carrots and potatoes, green bushes rising out of the ground. A bird feeder on a pole stood where it would be visible from the windows of the back room, and a wire-mesh fence, three feet high, encircled it all.

It was clear that a good deal of work had gone on here—a tangle of shovels stood propped against the cabin wall, and a new trowel lay sparkling on the wooden step by the back door beside a half-empty bag of fertilizer. The top of the bag was rolled down and held in place with clothespins, but in the weeks that had passed rain had fallen, and the bag was wet. He thought of Jonas, shirtless in the heat of the day, on his knees like his father, working the trowel in and out.

Just beyond the wire mesh fence, a chain lay in the strip of grass between the garden and the edge of the woods. Unlike the trowel, it was rusted and dark, and at first, glancing down, Michael thought it was a branch or an old hose.

The chain wove in and out of the thick grass, visible only in places. It took effort to pull it up, and he wasn't sure, at first, exactly why he did so.

The traps were small, only a few inches across. There were six of them attached to the chain, and they stretched all the way around the back of the garden. All were tripped, their jaws lay clenched tightly together, and he followed the chain to each of them. To his relief, the traps were empty, but several held tufts of brown fur, and many of the teeth were stained. Whatever bait Jonas had used was long since gone.

It took a good deal of force to open the jaws. He spread one of them carefully, over his knee, until there was a click and the trap lay poised and open. He set it down, and found a twig, and touched the plate that had risen up between the teeth.

The trap struck the twig with enough force to lift itself entirely off the ground. A hiss, barely audible, and then a crack, clipping the twig nearly in two, as the power of it flashed up into his hand. He wondered if the rabbits had died instantly, or whether they had lived for a while. He wondered if Jonas had eaten them.

The traps looked old, fifty years at least, and likely more. Hundreds of animals must have passed through them, and they were good still. The springs were oiled, the teeth sharpened.

Jonas must have tripped them before he left, or else, Michael was certain, they would not have been empty. It was likely one of the last things he had done. A casual mercy, nearly an afterthought, before lifting his bag and walking the half mile back to the world.

The Reverend's key fit the lock in the front door under the wide eaves of the porch, but the door itself was warped and he had to use his shoulder against it. It squealed as it opened, and Michael found himself standing in a dark and narrow hall. The air was thick and close.

He fumbled along the wall, but there were no switches to be found. There was no power, he realized, but the light from the open door behind him was enough for him to see that rooms opened on each side.

The first room was brighter than the hall. It had windows, which looked out over the front porch and the clearing beyond it. The interior was in shadow, but he could make out a table in the middle of the room.

A large white candle, as thick as his wrist, stood in a dish in the center of the table. A box of kitchen matches lay beside it. The matches were damp, and he struck several of them before one flared up. But the candle caught, sending its yellow light out into the room.

The room was barely furnished—a wooden table, four plain wooden chairs, a black iron woodstove near one wall, an old couch—but there was nothing else, no sign of a recent occupant, and so, carrying the candle, he stepped through the doorway to the next room.

It was a kitchen, with a gas stove and a sink with a single pump handle hanging over it. A well, he thought, not even hot water. A plate and a cup lay in the sink, as if they had just been washed.

Idly, he put down the candle on the counter, and reached for the pump. It took a few seconds until he felt it, somewhere deep in the pipe, and then a gush of clear water burst into the sink. He kept pumping, put his cupped palm down into the water, and brought it up to his lips. The water was cold, faintly alien, with a pleasant touch of bitterness, like an odd spice or a high minor note. Iron, he thought, or other metals, or something else in the ground.

The next room had not been used. Sheets lay draped over the chairs, and there were cardboard boxes stacked against the wall. For a moment he considered opening them, but when he looked closely he saw that they had been labeled—books, blankets—as if they had been there for years.

The last room was full of life. It was a bedroom, bright enough that the candle was unnecessary, the largest room in the cabin, with windows on two sides that opened to the vegetable garden in the back. A double bed sat in one corner, neatly made, and a carpet covered the floor. Several large plants, dry and dead, stood in pots in the corners. Under one window was a large desk, with a high-backed wooden chair. There was a bureau and an open empty closet with wire hangers.

Drawings of birds hung on the walls: a portrait of a robin, another of a common sparrow, a third—he knew their names from the ornate script beneath them—a yellow finch. They were reprints from another century, intensely detailed but slightly off, as if each were drawn weeks later, from specimens rather than from living things.

A child's crib stood next to the bed. It was made of wood and looked old, but its light blue coat of paint was recent. The crib stood on newspapers laid down neatly on the floor, which puzzled him, and he paused to examine it.

On one side of the crib, dozens of tiny red roses had been stenciled to the bars. But when he knelt to look closely, he saw that the other side of the crib was unmarked, and that the newspaper beneath it held many dry drops of blue and red paint.

Jonas must have spent days, Michael thought, sanding and painting, aligning the stencil again and again. But the crib had not been finished. A few child's toys—a doll, a small stuffed bear—lay waiting on the sheet. They looked new, as if they had never been used.

He looked at the crib for a long time. It was a work of tenderness, he thought, of hopes and plans, but here it was anyway, half done and full of stillness.

Finally, he turned away to the desk. The window above it faced west, and the sun cast bars of shadow from the high-backed chair out onto the carpet. Lit up on the desk, a book, a pencil, and a note pad lay covered in a veil of dust.

Without thinking, he sat down in the chair. Sunlight reflected off the varnished surface, so strong he had to squint, and points of dust rose and tumbled around him as he put down the burning candle. He shielded his eyes.

The book was a field guide to birds. The pages were dog-eared, with notes in the margins, and much of the text was underlined. There were color photographs: nuthatches, woodpeckers, owls, and hummingbirds. The book was only a few years old, and it held the name *J. Williams* neatly on the flyleaf.

The writing on the note pad was small, with dates and times. The words were cryptic, but in places there was a palpable enthusiasm. *Purple martin! 11 A.M.* Later that same day, a scarlet tanager.

The note pad was nearly full. Occasionally there were comments; a grocery list was in one margin. But for the most part it was only birds. The common ones were noted, but those that Michael imagined were unusual were underlined heavily, so one could tell at a glance, looking down the page.

He kept flipping through the note pad, staring at the neat, clear hand, so painstaking and exact. The sun fell deeper behind the trees and the glare at the desk lessened, until he could look through the window without difficulty.

The bird feeder stood on a pole at eye level, a few feet outside the window. In the weeks that had passed, the seed in the feeder had been consumed, and there was a visible ring of husks in the grass at the base of the pole.

He was watching from shadows, from empty spaces, with absence behind him, and for the briefest moment, as he looked out at the green leaves and sunflowers and high rows of corn, he felt as if the room was not any part of this world. It was somewhere or something else, and he thought of Jonas, calm and hopeful, the pencil and the book expectant at his fingertips, the sun flooding the room. A sanctuary, or a meditation, the streaks of red and blue and yellow, there for a moment, seen clearly, then gone in a flash of wings.

It was nearly dark when Michael stepped outside again, and locked the door carefully behind him. The cicadas were roaring, and a handful of fireflies opened and closed at the edge of the clearing. There was just enough light to find the path, and make his way down the hillside through the half mile of trees.

"I was worried," Nora said anxiously, in the doorway. She had seen the lights of the car. "You were gone for so long."

"I'm sorry." He had no idea what time it was.

"I was sure you were lost. I was about to call someone."

He didn't respond but, instead, entered the room and sat down on the edge of the bed. She closed the door, turned to face him, and he saw that she was both angry and afraid.

"I'm sorry, Nora," he said sincerely. "I didn't mean to worry you."

She shook her head, but then, after a while, her expression softened.

"I didn't want to leave you here," he said.

She sat down next to him on the bed and put her hand gently on his arm.

Two paper plates lay on the dresser. There were bread, apples, hard yellow cheese, and a bottle of wine, along with a stack of paper cups.

"Where did you get that?" he asked, gesturing.

"I walked to the store. It's just down the road."

"I should have driven you," he said, but she shrugged.

"It was nice out. I didn't feel like going to a restaurant, did you?"

"No," he replied. "I don't."

"Did you find anything?" she asked, after another moment passed.

"I'm not sure."

"What do you mean?"

He rubbed his eyes. "I don't know how to say it. It was very strange."

She looked at him intently.

"I found the cabin," he said. "There's no power or hot water. It's way up in the woods."

"Was anyone there?"

He shook his head.

"No. But I talked to a neighbor. He was quite sure that no one in town has been sick."

Nora nodded her head, as if it were the answer she was expecting.

"Jonas was trapping rabbits," Michael said. "There were a lot of mosquitoes. There were a lot of birds. There was a well. He was growing vegetables."

He paused.

"I think he liked living there," he said. "I think he liked it a lot."

"Why do you say that?"

He wasn't sure exactly why it came to him so strongly. But he was convinced it was the truth, that Jonas had loved the place and never would have left on his own. How brutal the world was, he thought, that it would come for him there.

"Because I liked it a lot," he said.

She looked at him, puzzled.

"It's beautiful," he said. "It's one of the most beautiful places I've ever seen. I never expected that." He paused again. "He was up there for months. I don't think he came down at all. It must have been where he got it."

"Then how do you explain," Nora said, "why there are no other cases? It doesn't make sense. A lot of people live here."

"I can't explain any of it, Nora," he replied.

He knew that she was full of questions: Would it reveal itself again? Would it return for him or for anyone else? But he closed his eyes, and she must have seen that he had no answers for her, because she said nothing further.

He leaned back in the chair, thinking of the cabin deep in the woods, the little girl in her crib, and Jonas at the window, young and strong and full of life. I poured him into the ground, he thought, and even now there is a dusting of him inside the envelope in my pocket.

"All I can do is try," he said finally. "It might be the rabbits. It might be something in the well. It might be the birds or the mosquitoes. It could be anywhere and it could be anything."

She stood then, without speaking, and opened the bottle of wine and handed him the paper cup. She filled his cup, then her own, and sat down closely beside him. But as they drank, he did not feel that he had come back empty-handed. On the contrary. He had felt it resist him, like a flash at the feeder, gone by the time he turned his head. Was the beak yellow or white? Was the tail split? Was there a red stripe on the wing? Did it make a high-pitched cry?

THAT NIGHT WAS SLEEPING WEATHER, WARM BENEATH THE BLANKETS but cold in the room, and bright with dreams. Her breathing beside him, the road, the rattle of sunlight through rows of trees, the stenciled flowers on the crib—over and over, and he would wake up with a start before drifting off again. Earlier, she had clung to him, but now she slept deeply, no matter that he tossed and turned and once, he was certain, cried out.

The hiss and sigh of the ventilator, the doors opening and closing outside in the hall. Richard's hands, turning him in the bed, the odor of his body at the surface, waking up or coming back—

It's gone, he told himself. It's passed through me.

Beads are present in the hair.

His breathing, hers, the early sounds of woodlands. The line of traps, empty in the grass. The teeming feeder, the rush of wings, back and forth and back again. *Purple martin! 11 A.M.*

By five he had slipped from the warmth of the bed, dressed in silence, and stepped outside to the small porch. The air was cold—in the forties, he thought—so he crept back inside, and opened the chest at the foot of the bed for a blanket. The hinges creaked suddenly and he paused, but her breathing didn't change.

So he wrapped himself up. The sky seemed clear, as best as he could tell, but there were few visible stars. After a while he realized that the sky was lightening and the shadows around him were taking the shapes of known things. The black of the sky gradually went gray, and one by one the faintest stars went out.

He began to see the mountains. They were vague at first but revealed themselves as the minutes passed, covered in mist.

He started to shiver beneath the blanket. He stood up, then, and went back to the warmth of the room. His shoes, a light jacket, the keys to the car. No pen, though, for a note, and so he debated waking her. Just now he could see the top of her head on the pillows. He hesitated for a moment, but she looked as if she would sleep for hours.

The cemetery was behind an old church at the far edge of town. The church stood at the end of a long winding street, obscured by trees planted on both sides of the road, and it took him a while to find it. The sun was coming up when he finally pulled into the parking lot, but there was no one else there, and he felt his solitude acutely. He got out of the car, and stood in the cool morning air, looking at the church—the old red brick, the shuttered windows, the green, freshly painted door, with flower beds beside it. A plaque on the wall told him that it had been built in 1834 by slaves, and that all of the bricks had been baked on the site.

The cemetery behind the church was traditional, with neat rows of erect headstones stretching back across several acres of grass to the edge of the woods. It was much larger than he expected, and could not be seen from the road. There were hundreds of graves. The whole history of the town was before him—the remembered and the forgotten alike.

There was a great deal of dew on the grass. It soaked his shoes and stained the cuffs of his pants. At first he was methodical, starting with the nearest headstones, walking down the line. Name after name, date after date. The old, the young, the middle-aged, the biblical last centuries—Ebenezer, Ezra, Joshua, Noah, and Ruth—giving way, as the rows passed, to the modern Katherines, to the Roberts and Richards and Helens.

After a few minutes, he realized that the graves were arranged chronologically, as if the town had simply cut deeper into the woods as time passed. It was like walking across the rings of an ancient tree. Some years held more graves, others less. Good times and bad, years of drought, years of fine weather.

The twenties and thirties were many rows deep. It must be the sanatorium, he thought, because here they were, those who had no place else to go, whose families did not want them back or were too poor to bring them home. They had waited also. Some were so young. And you could see, he realized, exactly when the cures began to work, because the yearly rows of graves grew thin again.

He found her, as he knew he would, in the beginnings of the nineties, halfway down the line, a simple headstone, like so many of the others. But the name leaped out at him across the grass.

ROSEMARY WILLIAMS. 1942–1991

He felt an intense stillness. He felt the water on his shoes, and the growing brightness of the air about him. He heard the birdcalls coming from the trees, even as he noticed the small shadow her headstone cast toward his feet.

Beloved Wife

There was another plot beside her, empty and waiting, just as he had known there would be.

Someday soon, Reverend Williams would rise and dress and knot his tie and get into his old car again. How weary he must feel, and how determined. Michael wondered what he would say, what possible lesson or story he would tell, as he stood in front of his congregation and looked out into their faces. There must be something they could offer him, there must be something they could find to lead him, if only for another week, or another day, or an hour. Give them your sorrow, he thought, give them your mistakes and your regret, and let them carry you. Give them the chance to be merciful, and maybe they will take it.

For a little while he continued to think about these things, of Reverend Williams, and of himself, and all the work that was required—the animals to gather, the birds, the water from the well, the samples of the child, the vial of Jonas's blood in the freezer, his own body. And briefly he thought of those he would notify, the Carries, the Anns, and Ronalds of the world, peering through their electron microscopes, examining their assays and specimens—the flesh of birds, of animals and children, the bloody entrails of mosquitoes—hoping to see it clearly, hoping to claim it as their own, when all along it was just another whisper in the corner, another match struck in the underworld.

But then he stopped thinking and knelt for a moment, and when he finally stood his knee was soaked through.

He kept walking, studying the names on the graves. The years rose, one after another, and soon he was nearly in the present. The few graves at the edge of the cemetery were fresh, and the new sod lay over the coffins exactly. It would be months, he thought, before the grass absorbed the lines and they were as smooth and untroubled as the rest.

Only a few yards separated the last of the graves from the first of the trees. Enough for the immediate future, but soon the town would have to cut into the woods once more. He paused in the space between the cemetery and the woods, but nothing was there, and so, finally, he turned back and walked through the graves to where the car waited in the parking lot.

He took his time driving toward town. It was early still; he saw no other cars, and just then he thought of Nora, still sleeping in their bed. All he wanted in that moment was to be back beside her, and the restlessness that had woken him began to fall away into the trees on either side of the street, and the passage of houses set back on long driveways—white and yellow and gray, half-seen from the road. The sky overhead was full blue, and soon the town would come to life again.

As he rounded a bend, there was a flash of white at the side of the road. At first he thought he'd startled a deer, but as he turned to look he realized that it was a person running along a path through the trees. He slowed down, looking into the woods, until he came to a break in the undergrowth.

He saw her clearly for only a few seconds. She was perhaps twelve, still a girl, but tall and gangly, wearing shorts and running shoes, her black arms standing out against the white T-shirt that had caught his eye. She must have heard his car, because she glanced through the gap in the trees, and looked directly at him for the briefest of moments. Her deep brown eyes, the beads in her short braided hair—but then she turned her head, and was gone again.

For a few minutes he followed the bobbing white shirt through the dense green leaves. She ran easily and well, and once, in another gap, he saw the words CROSS-COUNTRY printed on the back of her shirt. She's growing up, he thought. She's almost a woman now.

He realized what he was doing. He shook his head, quickly, to clear it, and then he accelerated down the street away from her. She was only a girl on the track team, he told himself, out training. But the image of her running figure stayed with him all the way through town. People were waking up, shades were being raised, sprinklers already were at work on the field at the high school. He continued past the bank, and the post office, then down the long street by the park, and on to the turn, and up the driveway past the main house to the cottage.

The curtains were drawn when he entered the room. He took his time, and let his eyes adjust, then undressed quietly in the darkness. Nora slept through it all, and as he eased himself into the bed, and felt her warmth against him, he thought of the girl, still running, mile after mile, the trees opening and closing around her.

ACKNOWLEDGMENTS

My deepest thanks are due to all those who read various drafts of this book, and whose suggestions were so helpful and sustaining to me. To my family, Helena Brandes, Frank Huyler, Marina Huyler, Scott Huyler, Tracy Hardister, Holbrook Robinson, Kira Robinson, and Jane Brochin, and to my friends Chris Bannon, Scott Graham, Scott Meskin, Lisa Hempstead, Beth Hadas, Brian Phelps, Tim Steigenga, Johanna Sharp, Brad Brooks, Rod Barker, Julie Reichert, and most especially to Janet Bailey, I owe you the debt of gratitude. To Paul Auster and Siri Hustvedt, your kindness and encouragement meant, and continue to mean, a great deal.

Particular thanks, also, to David Sklar, and the Department of Emergency Medicine at the University of New Mexico, for so generously supporting my efforts and believing that the humanities have a place in the medical world.

Finally, I'd like to thank my agents, Don Lamm and Christy Fletcher, and, last but certainly not least, my wonderful editor, Jennifer Barth.

ABOUT THE AUTHOR

Frank Huyler is an emergency physician in Albuquerque, New Mexico. His poetry has appeared in *The Atlantic Monthly, The Georgia Review,* and *Poetry,* among others; his book about his experiences as an ER doctor, *The Blood of Strangers,* is available from Picador.